WIT'S END

WIT'S END

James R. Scafidel

St. Lukes Press
Memphis

St. Lukes Press

Distributed by Peachtree Publishers, Ltd.
494 Armour Circle, N.E.
Atlanta, Georgia 30324

Library of Congress Cataloging-in-Publication Data

Scafidel, James R.
Wit's End / James R. Scafidel.
p. cm.
ISBN 0-918518-76-8
I. Title.
PS3569.C245W5 1989
813' .54--dc19

For information address:
St. Lukes Press
4210 B.F. Goodrich Boulevard
Memphis, Tennessee 38118

OTHER WORKS BY JAMES R. SCAFIDEL

As James Raymond, Pseud.
Lewis and Clark: Northwest Glory, Dell 1981

As Jonathan Scofield, Pseud.
Far Shores of Danger, Dell 1982

As Lyn Phillips, Pseud.
The Game, Tor Publishing Company 1983
Tomb of the Shroud, Dell 1983
If the Flesh Be Willing, Capital Publishing 1984

As Amanda Jean Jarrett, Pseud.
The Passion and the Fury, Dell 1983

As Lee Davis Willoughby, Pseud.
The Sooners, Dell 1982
The Assassins, Dell 1984
The Frontier Detectives, Dell 1984

AUTHOR'S NOTE

Since this book is a work of fiction, any connection between the characters in *Wit's End* and actual persons living or dead is accidental and coincidental.

The one exception to this is Judy Moon, an actual individual, a former TV anchorwoman who is now known by her married name.

I don't know Judy Moon. I met her once, when she interviewed me on the evening news. I enjoyed being on her show then. I hope she doesn't mind being in my novel now.

James R. Scafidel

WIT'S END

When the Delta flight attendant notified me through the toilet door that we were beginning our descent into Jackson, I raised my elbows off my knees and asked her if she'd mind holding off on the descent until I was finished with my current plans.

"We can't do that, sir," she said. "We're behind schedule."

"So am I," I said.

"But you can't stay in there," she insisted. "We can't allow passengers to descend into the airport on a commode."

"Not even in Mississippi?"

"No, sir. It's against regulations!"

Sulking in my metal tent, I held my ground and observed that it looked to me as though nothing was sacred anymore.

But the lower our big bird sank in the sky, the firmer of purpose this girl's voice became. Finally, she was downright demanding about it. I've got to give her credit. She took her job seriously. "Sir," she said, "I'm afraid if you don't come out of there, I'm going to have to call the captain!"

What an idea. Was that what pilots did nowadays to earn their wings? Years of rigorous training in order to talk an obstinate forty-four-year-old sportswriter out of the can?

"All right, I'm coming," I told her. I rose to my feet, banged a knee and an elbow on some unresisting plastic, and somehow managed to pull my trousers on without tying up all my assets in the zipper. I counted myself lucky at that. All I had to work with in there was crawlspace, room for me and my dilemma and nothing else.

When I came out of the facility, I encountered an anxious young lady in blue with a compact body and a round, pale face that was hastily made up with a mixture of orange and burgundy cosmetics. Underneath all this Play-Doh was natural beauty, but I couldn't help thinking her face looked like a Wheat Thin smeared with port wine cheese.

"I'm sorry, sir," she apologized sincerely.

I smiled at her and returned to my aisle seat where I leaned back and closed my eyes and tried to assure myself this particular trip would be vastly different from my other trips home. I couldn't see that it promised much though. In honor of the Marshall High football team, which was about to win its one hundredth consecutive game under Wilson Reed, my old class was to meet for an informal reunion on the campus. Now that I considered it, I was sorry I was not going to be allowed to return striding a commode, for that was what naturally came to mind when I thought of Marshall High.

I mean the famous school toilets of Mr. Floyd, of course, our self-made principal, a man constantly, irreparably embarrassed by everything in life, who placed a solid "Er-uh" in every sentence he ever uttered, like a rock in the rapids or an island in the stream. He also blushed, stammered, and vigorously rattled the change in his pockets at every public appearance. Since he always had a good supply of coins, I was afraid he was going to injure something in there. For all I know, he might have, for he never married.

One day in assembly, Mr. Floyd called a meeting exclusively for the guys in order to stop us from crapping on the commode seats. Of course, he could never actually say crap, or shit, or even defecate, the way ordinary college graduates would. All he said was that he wished we would refrain from depositing our waste matter upon the seats of the stools, inasmuch as the toilets were the sole property of the state of Mississippi.

"What waste matter is that, Mr. Floyd?" asked my best friend, Bubba Henderson.

"Er-uh," he stammered and called for a brand new demonstration toilet to be wheeled into assembly on metal coasters. After circling it like a Mexican around a hat, he pointed at it as if he were a farmer posing for a *Gazette* picture with a giant mole he'd just dug up out of his yard. Then, as stern and red-faced as a Reservation Indian, he gingerly traced the rim of the seat with his index finger. "Er-uh, what I'm talking about is this area here," he said. "I want this area as clean as a whistle from now on." To emphasize the point, he blew an embarrassed whistle through his teeth and rattled his change. Rapt in Mr. Floyd's demonstration until well after his cheek color had faded, we erupted at the conclusion into such applause that he was forced to leave the premises in a new flush of red.

Two weeks later, after the Milltown boys ignored his plea and went right ahead with their degraded antics, Mr. Floyd was forced to remove all the seats from the stools in order to save face. That decision made life pretty testy for the male contingent. Thereafter, if your sister hogged the john at home and you didn't get to use the facilities in the morning, you wound up placing your bare behind upon the porcelain itself in the men's room on the north side of the building and taking your chances. As a result of these trying conditions, many members of Classes '60 to '66 were forced to trudge through their courses grumpy and out of sorts.

I was relieved when the wheels of the plane struck pavement, delirious to be on the ground, any ground, for I am always uneasy in a state of flight. I believe if God had meant for sportswriters to fly, he would have given us, instead of wit and wisdom, something useful like feathers and beaks. In all the thousands of miles I've flown for the *New York Times,* I have never gotten used to the idea of sitting aloft with a mile of empty air beneath my rear end. It never fails to throw me a curve.

As the smokers and nonsmokers filed indiscriminately past my seat, I tried to imagine who I'd be seeing at the reception which Betty Lynn would be throwing at the gym. Betty Lynn, you see, adored receptions. She'd go out and arrange for the lodge or the gym if more than four showed up for bridge. My old buddy, Bubba, would be there, once a visionary Perry Mason, now the owner of Stanley Haymon Ford Co., on Elm Street. So would Tommy Ray Felton, who was arrested in 1956 for copping the overdue fines from the public library in order to buy his aging grandmother a large-print edition of the King James Bible. Fortunately for Tommy Ray, the judge let him off with a lengthy lecture and a few quotes from Exhibit A. I would be looking for Margie Bowen, too, a toothsome girl who could tell a Big Chief from a Trojan by feel alone by the time she was in her teens. And Freddie Thornberry, who got his words so mixed up, he spent two years in the second grade trying to figure out the *dramatis personae* of the Dick and Jane books. For a long time, Freddie believed his country 'twas a tree, because that was what it was called in a song. He also thought Ellsworth Bunker was a place where soldiers hid from the Germans. Of course, Betty Lynn would be present, too, coolly concealing a carefully nurtured crop of redwood-colored pubic hair which she used to allow selected ones of us to ogle behind the Ag building for twenty-five cents.

And of course, Nancy, my ex-wife. I was a bit antsy about how that would go. A lot of years had passed since Nan and I were down on the floor biting each other's heels. I could hope that now we would be civil and grown-up with each other. For all I know, she might be. But a man can't ever really be either of those things with a woman who once turned him inside-out. Guilty, yes. She had raised our two teenagers with nothing from me except money. Anxious, I suppose. But civil and grown-up? I couldn't count on it.

I knew I had reached the sunny South when I saw Uncle Harley in one of the dark blue fiberglass chairs at the gate, humped like a squirrel over a pecan, desperately trying to put together a decent cigarette. Uncle Harley was a school bus mechanic, a kind of poor man's Richard II, warped into a question mark by bending his frame over GMC hoods for years. He was wearing faded Lee overalls and dirty black leatherette boots, and was rolling his own out of Prince Albert tobacco. Uncle Harley's technique was horrible. He spread the tobacco too thinly on the paper and licked the roll like an eager St. Bernard; the result looked like the butts you see in a bus station urinal. Under these conditions, lighting up was hardly a snap. Just try to ignite saliva. Watching him prepare a smoke was fairly disgusting, I thought, after a breakfast/snack of dry-roast peanuts and with the bitter taste of coffee on a 727.

He arched his gray, twisted eyebrows when I came up. Uncle Harley was okay, but not even an aging widow with diminishing hopes would have accused him of being a handsome devil. He had thin white hair, a nose which looked as if a plate of safety glass was pressing against it, and motley teeth, alternately the color of Kandy Korn and Sun Maid raisins. His distinguishing feature was his forehead which my mother claims is "beetled." Mom is a lovely Wagnerian woman who thinks of herself as a malcontent teacher at the junior college in Summit. "Actually, I'm an anthropologist," she insists, and likens herself to Margaret Mead in her prime. "I'm merely teaching sociology to pass the time." She's been passing the time for about thirty years now.

A while back, Mom concluded that Uncle Harley's jutting brow was a distinct indication that the man was a throwback. She believed he was a specimen equal to any you'd see on a *National Geographic* special. She pined for the day when her discovery would be revealed to the outside world, and she could hear someone with an Alexander Scourby-type voice describe Uncle Harley's instincts and native habitat on television. She wanted that situation to occur soon, while she was still in her heyday.

My mother tends to measure intelligence and, therefore, human value by the relative amount of bone matter in the brow and by cranial capacity. In the sixties, she flung herself tooth and tongs into the civil rights forays at the PTA on the liberal side. On an unholy tear once, she cornered every living soul at the community center and regaled them each on the compelling subject of the cranial index. Another time she took her calipers to a meeting in order to measure the brains of the high school faculty. "Now let's just see who's smart and who isn't!" she declared and whipped them out of that suitcase she calls a purse. The other ladies acted as if she were some out-of-town obstetrician with forceps, and ran for the hills. The president of the PTA lingered at the door long enough to inform Mom where she might put her precious calipers and left her alone to ponder her unorthodox ways.

"Morning, Uncle Harley," I said and stole a look at his fabled brow.

He waited until he got his cigarette to burning—a very long time—before he spoke. "You're late," he finally muttered and blew out the flame at the end of the roll.

"Didn't Mom and Dad come?" I said, looking around. I swear, every human being in that airport looked better than my uncle. But I didn't care. He was the only human being there I knew.

"Nope," he answered. "Neither one."

Even though I had never been around Uncle Harley much, I knew his ways well enough. One of them was to disdain the proper use of names. That is to say, he preferred pronouns—the vaguer the reference, the better he liked it. My brothers were "them other boys," my sister was "that girl," my parents were "him and her." Everyone else was "the others."

"You by yourself?" I asked him.

He nodded his head. He was already nearly done with the cigarette, a Harley roll never having more than a couple of drags in it. If he pushed it too far, the damp, smoldering paper would surely scorch his lips. After one last suck on the stump, he rose unsteadily to his feet. "Getting old!" he grunted and stumbled out of the Delta gate into the tunnel.

Before I could catch up to him, he was in the midst of a coughing fit. In a moment of horror, I imagined him skittering on the concourse floor, choking to death on wet paper and wet tobacco, gasping at passers-by for artificial respiration, with each Good Samaritan shaking his head and saying, "Not me, brother!" I suppose I would have given him mouth-to-mouth in order to save his life, but I'm not sure either of us would have been the same afterwards.

I knew what the guys back at the *Times* would say about this. My stocky friend Russo would have tsk-tsked a couple of times and found a way of getting a *putz* or a *schlang* into the conversation somehow. He was Italian and knew Yiddish about as well as I know Arabic, but pricks he was familiar with. Mitchell Davis, a tall, good-looking native of Brooklyn, would have been seriously befuddled by the apparent cultural disparities in the case.

"Jesus, Ted!" he would have exclaimed. "Something like this happens every time you go South! Why don't you just take a cab, for Christ's sake!"

"Because nobody takes a cab from the airport in

Mississippi," I'd tell him. "Somebody has to pick you up."

"Why?"

"Because if you ride home in a cab, you're admitting you have no friends."

I could see Mitchell shaking his young blond locks in confusion, and Russo interjecting a word or two about schmucks and turning his wide back to the whole affair.

Finally recovered form the jaws of death, Uncle Harley dropped the offending butt into the cat litter ash tray against the wall and spit on it to put an end to the matter.

"Did they tell you I'm in the oil business now?" he asked me.

"Did who tell me, Uncle Harley?" I asked him, always trying to trick him into a noun.

But he wouldn't bite. "Him and her," he said.

"Oh," I said. "No, they didn't."

He curled his thin lip in an obvious gesture of disappointment. "I reckon they didn't tell you I'm working on a way of getting oil out of the ground without turning a bit either," he said sullenly.

"I don't remember anybody mentioning it."

"Well, I am," he said. "Through the use of ordinary sea water. Plain, everyday sea water."

"Is that right?"

He was hauling the makings of a new roll out of his overalls, "Don't worry," he said. "I haven't told another soul. Ain't giving this theory away, by God."

With images of Mr. Floyd and his commode and Nancy in her peignoir and Betty Lynn with her red hair dancing in my brain, I wasn't exactly in the mood for another one of Uncle Harley's theories, so I didn't ask for elaboration. Of course, to be fair to my resourceful uncle, he did entertain a lot of intriguing ideas (such as his theory that the Chinese water torture was a technique which the Communists stole from the Methodists). But I wouldn't call most of them bell ringers.

There was his theory of dust, for example.

After Uncle Harley built a two-bedroom house on Black Springs Road out of scrap depot lumber, his wife, my father's half-sister Reba, announced she'd as soon move into a gourd with a bunch of blue martins as spend the rest of her life pushing good dirt after bad out of a house in the country.

This was Aunt Reba's one and only word on this particular project. She was a quiet woman who hated to talk because it hurt her tonsils, and because she thought most things in life were so obvious they didn't need talking about.

And that included dirt.

Even so, I heard her say once she figured by the time a girl from Oklahoma reached puberty, she'd probably lapped up enough dust from the air around her to fill her own grave. So it's likely she didn't figure it made sense to leave the Southwest for the South, just to swap one kind of dirt for another.

What Aunt Reba wanted, of course, was to live where the land was covered not so much with dew and honey as with a lot of pavement, such as in Boston. All the time she was an adolescent in the Dust Bowl, she dreamed about getting married and starting a family on asphalt and concrete. Only, since she never bothered to tell Uncle Harley any of this, he went and built another house.

To settle the dust problem, he built into this one what he proudly called flow-through ventilation—in other words, without any doors to block the movement of air from one room to another. Nothing but drapes, all over the place. It looked like a gypsy palm reader's place, with all those curtains hanging everywhere. I suspect he stole the idea from Madame Su's sitting room in her little house on Highway 51, which was practically doorless itself. Even though Madame Su's design was owing to the necessity of her having to beat an occasional retreat from town, Uncle Harley had vision enough to see the possibilities for himself.

When Aunt Reba began to complain a few years later of a surfeit of filth in the vestibules of the house, Uncle Harley put his rounded shoulders to the wheel and came up with a new theory—that if a house was built close to the road, the dust would very likely float harmlessly over it. In accordance with that idea, he erected a third house along the lines of the other two, this time six-and-a-half feet from the roadbed itself. In the spring of 1958, he unveiled his masterpiece, which was graced with features even Frank Lloyd Wright had never come up with. For instance, he placed all the water pipes above the foundation slab, leaving them exposed throughout the house, so that a body could get to them in record time in case one of them happened to spring a leak. I remember sleeping there once, and waking up in a cold sweat to a harangue of clanging noises around me. When my bleary eyes took in all those elbowed pipes in the semi-darkness, I panicked and fled for the drapes. I hopped over those lines and sleeves and connections like a freshman majorette, thinking I was either in hell or a submarine.

In this house, Uncle Harley, along with his wife and their six lovely children, spent the next few years, more or less covered with dirt.

"Er-uh, what are you people living in, out there—a ditch, or what?" Mr. Floyd asked Jody, the oldest. He added with embarrassment that he had just never encountered anyone so dirty in his life. It was about this time that Mom started referring to Uncle Harley as "Sonny's kin," meaning he was her husband's brother-in-law, not hers.

While I was a journalism student at Columbia, Uncle Harley finally gave up his architectural pursuits and moved to a ready-built house on Laurel Street. In a lilac-scented letter, Mom described this great removal to the city as a Clyde Beatty circus parade, complete with five or six mangy stray dogs, a blue mule nobody had ever laid eyes on before, and a trail of sixteen amateur musicians playing fiddles and plucking blue-grass guitars and harmonizing "Just a Closer Walk with Thee" as they stalked into Marshall. Mom considered it every bit as inspirational as *The Grapes of Wrath* or *I Want to Live*. It was, she said, the most inspiring thing Sonny's kin had ever done.

When we finally made it to Dover Street in Marshall two hours later, Uncle Harley abruptly made an Immelmann turn, locked the wheels of the pickup, skidded over the curb, and landed like a bent plane upon Dad's prize bermuda grass.

"Nice shot," I said.

Before he had a chance to spit out the window or shut off the engine, Mom came crashing through the screen door, charging Uncle Harley's sputtering vehicle like an irate rhino. As soon as she reached me, she thrust in a pair of great arms, jerked me out by the lapels, and surrounded me with massive folds of lukewarm flesh as if I were a kidnap victim being brought home by the police. Even though I always love to be taken in at home, I was unprepared to contend with this Greco-Roman death grip. Mom must have been working out with a pack of angry sumos to squeeze like that. I was so overwhelmed by her warm, good-smelling mass that I actually began to fear for my life. She certainly believed in being demonstrative in matters of the heart. Tentativeness to her was sinful and hypocritical, especially in a sixty-two-year-old woman in her prime.

"Theodore! Theodore!" she shouted while she mangled me. "Where on earth have you been!"

"Oh, good grief," my father moaned. "The boy's been in New York City for twenty years!" Dad was a gentle feed-and-seed man who still possessed most of his brown hair at the age of sixty-five. Big and homely, he looked vaguely like the offspring of Baby Huey and Bette Midler. My father was almost as stooped a person as Uncle Harley. On the lawn together, they looked like a pair of high hurdles. Dad was a good, moral guy who loved football and healthy natural phenomena, such as storms, and believed in "retail sales, above all else."

"I was talking about today, Sonny," Mother said, exasperated. "He was supposed to be here an hour ago! You had us worried half to death, Theodore!"

I tried to come up with a rejoinder, but what can a man say with his mouth full of his mother's bosom? Never had it been so hard to apologize to anyone.

"Aren't you going to say something to your sister?" she said.

As soon as I can work myself free, I thought.

"Well, go ahead—speak to her!" Mom urged.

"Hi, Teddy," Amy finally said and tugged at my arm. I was starting to believe it was useless, though; I was practically a goner. I hated the irony of trying desperately to push myself away from my own mother's breast in order to stay alive, but like most mothers, this one was perfectly incapable of realizing when she was smothering her babe—until Amy wryly pointed out that poor Teddy was near suffocation and caused her to let go at last.

After reeling for a couple of minutes, I came back. "You look good, Amy," I said. She was a tall, voluptuous, thirty-nine-year-old blonde. Although a few of her pounds were starting to hang over the rail, she was still extremely pretty, even after three marriages. It was proper in the scheme of things for her to stay as attractive as possible since she'd never been know as brainchild or anything. In fact, intelligence had played about as active a part in Amy's life as the planet Uranus. I don't know. She could be clever about some things. Then sometimes she acted as if she couldn't tell a jar of cold cream from a case of penis envy. I loved the person Amy was, but her mind was like a washing machine. Ideas went in, got twisted around and cleaned up, then came right back out, worn, but otherwise unchanged.

"And you're looking smart as ever, Teddy," she grinned. "Oh—I got your book!" she added. She meant the one I had done with Eddie T. Youste—*Fouling Off the Pitches: Baseball's Clowns.*

When it became apparent those five little words had completely exhausted her thoughts and feelings on the subject, I switched to the more familiar topic of our brothers. "Ed and Frank couldn't make it?" I said to Mom.

"They're abroad, Theodore!" she replied. "They're in Saudia Arabia now. We're all real excited about it!"

"Darned proud, too," Dad beamed. "The boys are doing some real important work for the government down there. Isn't that right, Harley?"

With his great brow wrinkled, Uncle Harley studied Dad closely for a moment. "Nobody ever told me about no oil work in Salty Arabia," he grunted. "I thought them boys was up in Arkansas."

Dad glared at him impatiently. He'd been through this confusion business before. "Harley," he said, "I told Reba all about that deal six months ago."

"That ain't telling nobody," he grumbled.

"Now, Harley—"

"Well, I never heard nothing about no oil deal, and I'm in the business myself! How do you think that makes me feel?"

Dad was angry now. "You're just being contrary, Harley," he said. "You know good and well—"

"I don't know nothing!"

"Doggone it! I naturally assumed a woman would tell her own husband something as important as that!"

"Not her. She goes days without saying a word, don't make no difference how important it is."

"Well, maybe she has good reason, you ever consider that?"

"Now, stop it, you two!" Mom interrupted and caused an instant silence to fall over the group. She was famous in Marshall for her booming voice. Cops used her to call out to criminals whenever they held hostages in the bank. "Why don't we all go inside?" she said.

We left Uncle Harley at the truck, since he is not allowed in the house except for experiments, and headed up the flagstone walk. We had to go by way of the side door because the big female cat was lounging on the steps and wouldn't allow anybody to enter the house from the front. In the kitchen, Dad pinched the cuff of my shirt and led me straight out to the back yard. It was tough going, proceeding through a modest frame house with my arm extended, but I didn't mind it. At least he wasn't trying to hug me.

"There!" Outside, he released me, put his hands on his hips, and peered eagerly into my face for signs of recognition. "You see it?"

He was always putting me on the spot. "See what, Dad?" I surveyed the yard.

Offended, he proceeded to outline for me the course of a devastating tornado which had attacked his yard in 1983. The only evidence I could see of such a calamity were a couple of cracked sweetgum limbs and a slice of pine bark lying on the ground like a big slab of bacon, but Dad made me tread softly over the grass anyway, as if we were traipsing over hallowed ground. In his mind, this tornado was as significant as the Magna Carta, World War II, and the Freedom Rides all rolled into one. According to my father, those were the major events of our history. Everything else either "led up to 'em, or led away from 'em."

"She started right over here," he said and traced the path of destruction inch by inch. He had monitored this thing the way a head guard would track an escaped trustee from Parchman. Maps, charts, everything. From the very outset, he had mustered a grudging respect for the way this particular disaster had conducted itself. He had decided to leave the piece of pine bark where it had landed on the prize bermuda, in order to commemorate its arrival and departure.

"I guess you noticed the big white oak's gone," he said.

"No."

"Then where'd you think I got all that firewood?"

"I was wondering," I said, though truthfully, I had yet to see the first stick of wood anywhere.

Once again we ambled over the grounds, this time making sure to touch the surviving tree trunks with our fingers as we went. Almost like a religious experience.

"I tell you, this tornado was a real son of a bitch," he told me confidentially. "A real, hog-strangling son of a bitch!"

Only now did I grasp the importance of the event. Dad reserved his profanity for monumental occurrences, such as political assassinations, solar eclipses, and sit-ins. Accordingly, I knelt down to examine the bark inch by inch. "Sure looks like it," I said.

He seemed pleased with his son at last. "And you never even knew she hit, did you?" Evidently, the irony of that tickled him.

I rose to my feet. "No, I never did," I admitted.

He nodded knowingly, and took it from the top again, from the moment he heard the terrifying noise of the violent storm. "It sounded like your mother calling you boys to dinner," he declared with respect. "Or almost that loud," he said on second thought.

It wasn't long before Mom herself came for me and hauled me off to the annex study in order to show me her collection of research notes on the mongoloid strain in Uncle Harley's side of the family, which originally hailed from Kentucky. She wanted to know my professional opinion as to whether she ought to go to *National Geographic* with her findings.

"I don't know, Mom," I said. "What are your findings?"

"You're looking at them, Theodore."

"Not *where*, Mom: *what*."

"My findings are that the strain is there," she said. "Real bad, in fact."

I nodded and spent some time with her work. It was a mess. "You've got too much stuff here, Mom," I told her. "Too much raw material. Maybe you ought to turn it into a novel instead."

"A what?"

"An historical saga, like *Roots*."

Instantly, she grabbed me and crushed me like an empty cigarette pack. "What a wonderful idea!" she exclaimed. "A novel!"

"Mom—" I tried to back away.

"This can be a real contribution, you know it?" she said. "I know what I'll call it, too: *Species*. What do you think of that, Theodore? *Species!*"

"Sounds good, Mom."

For the rest of the afternoon and evening, Mom plotted her novel out loud, Dad retraced the circuitous path of the tornado, and I exchanged smiles and glances with my sister. At one o'clock in the morning, Dad had a Dr. Pepper and a wedge of Mom's banana nut bread which he said tasted like sofa stuffing, and him and her, as Uncle Harley calls them, toddled off to bed together. A while later, Amy announced that she was ready to go back to her lonely apartment, which I took to mean we had about two more hours to say what we were going to say to each other.

She was surprised to hear that I was going to be interviewed on the Laurel/Hattiesburg TV station by newsperson Judy Moon. "Mom never told me about that," she said.

"Maybe she told Aunt Reba."

"I've always liked Judy Moon," she said. "I think she's real pretty and a good anchorwoman."

"I think so too."

"When's it going to be, Teddy?" she asked.

"Monday evening at six. I guess I'll be on there to comment on the hundredth win. As an ex-player, or an ex-patriate, I'm not sure which."

"Judy Moon's very good at her job," she said.

"Perfect."

Amy got up and went to the fire and wheeled around to face me. "Teddy," she said, "you're so smart and all, would you mind telling me what in the world it's all about?"

"I just did, Amy. It's about the game."

"I'm not talking about the TV show, Ted! I mean life!"

"Oh."

"I'm serious. There's just one thing I want to know,

and you're the only one I can ask. Why is it that all men ever want to do is screw you and take advantage of you?"

"I thought it was the other way around."

"I'm very serious," she said coldly.

"I know you are, but I'm not sure I know what you're talking about."

She shifted her weight as she used a minute to collect her thoughts. Then: "There's this guy I know who wants to marry me. Or so he says. Only this time, I decided there'd be no screwing around until I get the ring on the finger, you know? I mean it's only reasonable, what with all the diseases going around now and all. I thought I'd do the right thing for once, and what happens? I'm just sitting there at home, waiting for him to call. And everybody else thinks I'm with him, so they don't bother to call. . . ."

She went on with this until I was worn to a frazzle. I would have given a Pulitzer Prize to help her, but all I could do was try to listen. There isn't a lot a man can step in and do about the sex life of his sister.

After a while, she realized that and got angry about it and put her mind on the subject of kids. Mine. "If you want to know my opinion," she said, "it's a disgrace, the way you never come to see your own children. I'll bet you're not even planning to go over there while you're here."

"I thought I would."

"Well, that's something, anyway. What about Nancy? Do you plan to stay with her while you're here?"

The idea of that made me warm enough to have to get up for air. "I don't usually make that many plans, Amy," I said.

"She still loves you, you know."

"Does she?"

"She told me so. I was in the A & P the other day, talking to her in the express line, and I asked her right out if she ever thought about going to bed with you."

"In the express line?" I echoed. It was late and I was tired, and I truly did not want to be interested. But I couldn't help myself.

"That's right," Amy said. "And you know what she told me? She said, 'Sure, why not?'"

"Doesn't sound much like Nancy."

"Okay, so maybe she didn't say it exactly like that. What difference does it make? I got the impression she did. Really, Teddy, I did. Nan loves you with all her heart, and she always will, and if you want my opinion, I think you ought to come back to her and the kids!"

"How would I do that, Amy? I live in New York."

"If you really loved her, you could do it. A man will do anything for love."

I let that one pass. Too close to the quick. "Why don't we talk about something besides my ex-wife and kids?" I said. "Has Uncle Harley ever told you his theory about the decline of the zeppelin?"

She stared at me, incredibly sad, hurt, and disappointed. "You know perfectly well I don't know anything about things like that," she said with a quivering voice.

"It's a balloon, Amy."

Tears welled in her eyes. "You know," she said and started for the door. "Sometimes, you make me so mad!"

"I don't mean to," I said.

"Well, you do!" She scooped up her coat and matching brown tam, and pulled open the front door. For a minute, she lingered in the doorway, then turned around to face me. She was crying. "I just thought a person who was smarter than most everybody else would just do better by the people he loved," she said pitifully. "I guess I was wrong."

It wrenched my insides to see her cry, but I didn't know what to say to her. I didn't know how to be with her anymore. "I am going by there, Amy," I promised her. "First thing in the morning."

"But you won't do anything, will you?"

"I don't know."

She was still hanging in the doorway. "You're in for a big shock with those kids of yours, you know it?" she said. "You're going to find it mighty sad that Derek and Jennifer are not little kids anymore."

"I'd find it sadder if they still were."

She glared at me, keyed up and frustrated, but as patient as a saint. "You just wait," she predicted. "You'll see. Things aren't like they were when we were kids, Teddy. All this sex and adultery and AIDS everywhere. Everything's so awful now. Oh, Lord, if I had been the one lucky enough to have kids. . . ." She stopped, turned, and ran out into the darkness over the screeching cat leaving the door wide open behind her.

After that, I drank some milk to ease my queasy stomach and lounged in front of the fire for a while, wondering if I wasn't watching some of Dad's white oak go up in flames. Before long, I got restless and went into the kitchen for more milk, but wound up staring at the fridge instead. I guess I figured I really didn't deserve it.

I was up before dawn the next morning in order to keep from eating breakfast. Mom was a terrific mother and a crack anthropologist, but she was no cook. In her kitchen, a ribeye steak tasted like a heating pad, a pot of rice was nothing but a great crumbling ball, and you would have better luck paving a country road with her oatmeal than trying to eat it. Even so, meals were unfailingly important to Mom. When she decided it was beneficial for the family to spend meals together, we went to the table and took the count, three times a day. Only sometimes, we absolutely took a stand and refused to say grace. We all agreed that it would be nothing but hypocrisy for us to thank the Lord for what we were about to receive.

Mornings posed a special horror for us, because at breakfast, nothing came safely out of a can. Mom's policy was to subdue the food whenever possible with the application of violent heat, then try to revive it with a sauce or a twig of parsley on the side. I usually started the day with a long black sausage that looked like a murder weapon, and a platter of pancakes that could have been land mines used in World War II. I never did manage to cut into one of those things. All I could do was sear a hole into the outer layer with a spoonful of that syrup she bought from the gypsies and gouge into the marrow from within with a sturdy fork.

The first person I encountered outside the house was the chubby mayor of Marshall, who was staggering up a hill in a sweatsuit, puffing "I think I can! I think I can!" as he neared the top. A few blocks later, I hurried past

Mrs. Barnes, the piano teacher, who was so busy attacking a cat with her walker that she didn't see me, and spoke to Mr. Henry, who was out in the cold with a bare chest, hoping to show his mettle in front of the neighbors.

I lingered for a minute on Laurel Street at Uncle Harley's house to see if he'd come up with anything new. There wasn't much. He still had the wringer washing machine and the green vinyl school bus seat on the porch, the statue of a little black boy with the fishing pole in the azaleas, and the stone flamingo that had been mauled beyond recognition when the a.c. fell on it from the second floor bedroom in 1980. The only addition was a new layer of dust on the facade, the result of the combination of the autumn wind and a hundred and five dog holes in the lawn which spread out like God's Little Acre from the gazebo where he kept his old well-digging equipment. Uncle Harley came out of the front door, slouched across the yard like a great C-clamp on the move and ducked under the chassis of his pickup, which was now perched on four cinderblocks with the wheels missing. When I saw tobacco smoke rolling out from below, I hitched my sweatpants and moved on.

On the courthouse square, a gang of cops was hanging about, chewing and spitting like major league baseball players in a slump. Most Southern towns are noted for raising things like camellias or strawberries or bees. Marshall raises the police. They're all over the place: constables, sheriffs, deputies, marshals, cops, highway patrol, watchmen, and lookouts. The chief supplier of the forces is a family in the subdivision, where a man's law is supposed to be his word. Even though they're not

Irish, every Bundley male starts asking for a flashlight and a pair of Foster Grants before he can raise his hand for the Pledge of Allegiance.

In front of the house next to the old three-story high school, a middle-aged man in a green Izod sweater flagged me down with his paper. He was tall and slender, with sort of a political look about him, as if he might have been the natural son of a Kennedy or Rockefeller.

"You're Ted Miller, aren't you?" He held out his hand. "Richard Temple, School Superintendent."

We joined hands as if we were a couple of pals celebrating world peace together. Although his thin wide palm felt like a cold T-bone steak, I instinctively liked this man.

"Nice to meet you," I said.

"Listen." He shielded his eyes from the rising sun. "I read all your stuff. You did a tough, solid job on those Pittsburgh drug trials back in '85. Brilliant, really."

"Thanks."

He seemed offended by my casual air. "I'm not flattering you, man," he said. "I'm telling you, I admire your courage and talent!"

"Thank you."

When I offered to go, he squashed the idea promptly by swatting my belly with his *Clarion Ledger*. "I've got a hell of a story for you," he confided.

"You mean the one-hundredth win."

He shook his head solemnly. "This is a lot bigger than that."

"I wonder if that's possible."

"All I ask is that you come by and let me tell you

about it. Then you can decide for yourself."

"Sounds fair enough." I dodged his paper and started jogging.

"Do it, Miller!" he hollered after me. "Tonight!"

As usual, my ex-wife seemed to be in a hurry to go share something with somebody. This time, it looked like it was the Hefty bag full of garbage she has lugging out to the curb in front of the house on Beacon Street. I shouldn't have been, but I was surprised to find Nan so sexy at forty-four. Didn't matter that she was decked out in her savings-and-loan skirt and blazer. You can't cover such things with a couple of yards of designer cloth.

For her part, Nancy denied that she was anything special. "I'm not sexy," she'd say and cover her bosom. She did that because one of her breasts was smaller than the other. The left one had been stunted by an errant crosscourt pass on the basketball court which struck her in the chest just as she was entering puberty. She was always self-conscious about it. Every time she felt frustrated, she would suddenly bemoan the fact that she was only half a woman. I'd counter with the argument that she was at least three-fourths of one and off we'd go. It wasn't much fun. I have never cared much for basketball because of what the game did to Nan.

She was raising the trash bag in front of her bosoms. Whatever wasn't nailed down eventually wound up in front of her chest.

"Going on a trip?" I asked her.

"I probably would be, if I'd known you were coming," she snapped and let the bag drop.

I tried to crack a little of the ice between us. "What's going on, Nan?" I asked congenially.

She would have none of it. "Nothing's going on, Ted," she said. "I'm on my way to work."

"I know that. I meant in general."

She buttoned her blazer over her bosom. "Do you really believe you can come down here once every seven years and say 'What's going on, Nan?' and expect me to answer you!"

"I guess not."

For an embarrassed minute or two, we both stared back at the house which was a gilded-age duplex makeover that had been featured once in the *Marshall Gazette*. Originally it had been two efficient households; now it was one inefficient one, with stereo doors, back-to-back bathrooms, and the remains of a double kitchen. The whole two years I spent there, I felt like Topper, as if I were living with a second, invisible family. I expected to see George, Marian, and Neil emerging from the woodwork at any time.

"They're still in there, you know," she said, meaning our children rather than George and Marian. "And if I were you, I'd go in there and see them!"

"Thanks."

She stalked over to her car, a tan Buick Regal, with the left front bumper peeled back like an injured fingernail. "I'd suggest," she said, "that you spend a little time with them before you just . . . go off again!"

"Does that mean I can stay with you for a while?" I asked.

Nancy got into the car, closed the door, cranked the engine, and rolled down the window. I felt like a carhop. "With them, Teddy," she said. "Not with me. You'll be on the couch the whole time."

"Think that'll stop me?"

"Why are you here, anyway, Teddy?" she asked. "Is it Jennifer and Derek, or is it that damned football game?"

"Would you believe me if I said all three?"

"No." She stared at me for a moment, then slammed into reverse, backed into the street, and sliced open the Hefty bag with her hang-nail bumper. I heard her utter a "Damn!" as she straightened up, ran over it and scattered debris, and zoomed away.

I stood and watched the street a long time after her car had disappeared. My stomach felt like the inside of a hot exhaust pipe.

My daughter was in the kitchen, gnawing on a granola bar, between swigs of Hawaiian Punch. Like most girls born in the late sixties or early seventies, this one was named Jennifer. If you packed all the teenage Jennifers together, I'll bet you couldn't stuff them into Kansas. Of course, I doubt if Kansas would let you try to do that, anyway.

This particular Jennifer leaped excitedly to her feet the second I walked in. She was wearing six or seven different styles of clothes, none of which had anything to do with any other. It looked as though she'd been dressed by a bunch of malcontent orangutans or a Congressional Committee, if that's any different. Impulsively, she shrieked "Daddy!" and flung her arms around me.

As much as I care for my daughter, I found it hard to throw myself into this hug. Maybe it was because she didn't feel like my little girl anymore. Or because she felt like the laundry. Another thing, she was five or six inches shorter than Nan, so that the clear majority of her hair was positioned in my face. It was wild and unruly and obviously under a great deal of stress, as though it were being kept alive only through the miracle of electricity.

I cautiously raised my hand to touch it. "Is this stuff U. L.-approved?" I asked.

"Do what?" She backed away.

I could see her face now. Or at least, what was on her face. The actual living skin, if there was any, was latent beneath various strata of cosmetics, some of which presumably matched her clothes. The look was not particularly flattering to my daughter. She would've had better luck applying the makeup with a chimney brush and a two-by-four. I could infer only that such was the style, these days.

"Well?" She wheeled around like a model on a ramp. "What you do think?"

"Nice."

"I'll bet you never expected me to be so grownup, did you?"

"No, I never did."

She gave me a serious look. "You don't like my hair, do you?"

"No, it's okay," I said. She must have been using Armor All for hairspray.

She stiffened, making her hair seem to rise up and up, like Little Eva. "You're not making fun of me, are you, Daddy?" she asked.

"No, I'm not."

"Well, good, because Momma said you would. She says whenever people start disturbing you, you go to acting like a smart-ass."

I sat down at the table. "Got any coffee around here?" I asked.

"How would I know?" she snapped. "Since I personally would never touch anything with caffein in it, how would I possibly know where the coffee is?"

"Maybe I can find it." I went straight to the cupboard and got the Folger's Instant and put some water on the Jenn-Air.

Jennifer looked bewildered when I dumped a load of flavor crystals into the cup. All this heavy cooking probably was alien to her. She was that much like Mom, I guess. "You still think of me as a little girl, don't you?" she said in a tiny voice.

"I'm just slow," I said. "The last time I saw you, you were two."

"I was not two! I was nine!"

I nodded my head to confirm the calculation. "Then I must've missed a few years somewhere," I told her. "Maybe you'd better bring me up to date."

That idea appealed to her. "Well," she began, "for one thing, I do not go by the name of Jennifer. I hate Jennifer! I prefer Electra."

"Well, Electra does go with the hair."

"It means 'the brilliant one,' Daddy. Electra was the daughter of some Greek or other. Amagon."

"Agamemnon," I corrected.

"Oh, well, anyway," she said and let her little voice trail off. She said nothing while I made the coffee, then:

"Did you know I was the Head Lionette?"

"No, I didn't. Why didn't somebody tell me?"

"There aren't many girls that can say that."

"No," I agreed there weren't.

"And I'm Secretary of the Junior Class of Marshall High School, too," she said. "That's a real honor."

"Yes, it is."

She thought she detected a note of sarcasm in that. If there was one, I hadn't meant it. "Well, damn it," she said, "I never claimed it was like being a reporter for the fucking *New York Times*, or anything, did I?"

I decided to say nothing.

"I mean, do you think you're better than your own family because you work for that fucking rag?" she charged. All this profanity fit Jennifer about as well as her clothes. I assumed she had picked something out of the gutter one rainy day and had it ready for me.

"Look, Electra," I said, "I didn't come down here to swap credits with my daughter, okay? Why don't we both stop trying so hard?"

She chewed her cud resentfully for a few minutes. It was obvious she and Nancy had sat around the table and shared their views on Dad a few times. There was a lot of hostility in this girl. But I certainly couldn't blame her mother for the way she was turning out. Or the idiotic way I was responding to her. I guess the problem was she was my own flesh and blood but didn't seem like it.

While I drank the Folger's, Jennifer sat down and made me uncomfortable while she told me all about herself. She wanted desperately to be a splendid actress someday, instead of just another gorgeous face or, if that wasn't enough of a challenge, she was considering going into TV, as if it were a garage with the door wide open. The duller she got, the more she used profanity to make her ideas. Being unaccustomed to such hard words though, she cussed without flair and relied too much on shit and fuck to be any good at it.

Since I had been in a locker room here and there, I wasn't much shocked by any of this. What did agitate me, though, was her reference to a party she attended "at this older guy's house, outside of town."

"Where, 'outside of town?'" I asked her. "McComb? Jackson? Vermont?"

She shrugged her shoulders at anything remotely specific. Clarity genuinely seemed to befuddle her. "It was after a game, and I was kinda out of it, Daddy," she explained. "It was just a weird party, with the team and the Lionettes and all, and these nice older guys. You know."

"Tell me about the older guys."

"Oh, they were okay. I know, because they were wearing suits. They really liked me a lot. One of them said I looked like this old movie star when she was young. I think she was Eva somebody or other."

"That makes him older than me."

"Oh, he couldn't have been that old! I mean, he knew all the songs and everything, so how could he be? As a matter of fact, Daddy, he was cute. Real cute. Let me tell you, he wanted me—so bad!"

"Are you sure you didn't know any of these randy Methuselahs?"

"Well, no; not really—"

"Shut up, Jen!" Derek, my son, was standing in the

dining room doorway, blocking out the living room light.

Jennifer adjusted some of her clothes. "I was just talking, Derek!" she said.

"Well, stop talking. He doesn't want to hear that junk." He lumbered into the room and offered his hand. "Hello, Dad," he said.

This was a humbling experience, being gripped and shaken by someone who was over six feet tall, weighed 250 pounds, had a nearly-shaved head that looked like a worn pencil eraser, and arms the size of pontoons. After the greeting, he skulked across the room, reached over the fridge, pulled down a banana, and proceeded to munch it. It would have been kind of funny if it hadn't been so sad. When I left him, he was a normal-sized boy with hair who ate meat. How could I have let time change him so much?

"Go get ready," he ordered his sister. "I got practice."

"I wasn't doing anything," Jennifer muttered and left with the remains of the granola bar.

I watched Derek gulp down the rest of the fresh fruit. My son was a huge human being as yet not completely formed. He had my eyes, Nan's nose, Dad's hair, Mom's physique. But nothing of his own quite yet.

There was no question that he was a jock, though. I had seen enough of them to know. Russo would have said his salmon-colored turtleneck and thick throat made him resemble a prick. But then Russo thought everything resembled a prick.

After fondling the peeling for a while, Derek tossed it on the counter, for his mother, I suppose. "How come you never write about the team?" he said gruffly.

"I'm not sure you guys are ready for that, Derek," I said, then asked: "It is Derek, isn't it? You haven't become Randwulf or anything, have you?"

"I just think we deserve some coverage, that's all," he said. "What's the big deal, anyway? It's not as if we wasn't news, you know. *Sports Illustrated* did a spread on us; why can't the damn *Times*?"

My kids were certainly rough on my paper. At least it wasn't sexual anymore. "Damn negligence, I reckon," I said.

"Greg's first team high school All-American. Did you know that? First team!"

"I'd missed that"

"All I'm saying is, we deserve some national attention."

"And you figure Dad's the hack who can do it."

"Well, it'd be a shrewd thing to do, I know that."

"Why don't we see if the team wins first?"

He laughed disdainfully. He had bright, straight teeth. I remembered those at least. "There's not much doubt about that," he said. "We've got some real good people out there now. Real blue-chippers. It's not like it was when you were here, Dad. The thing is, now we've got us a two-prong attack: the run and the pass."

"Sounds real complicated."

"That's Coach Reed for you. Everybody says he's got a tremendous football mind."

"He's got something, judging from that two-prong business."

"He was your coach, too. That ought to tell you something."

"You're right," I agreed. "It ought to."

"Just wait till tomorrow night," he said. "You gotta admit, it's not every team gets a perfect streak of one hundred consecutive wins in a row without a single loss!"

"And one right after other, too."

Derek scowled. At least I think he did. It was hard to tell. Blue chip linebacker or not, my son the gorilla was an unhappy kid. And I had no idea how to do anything about it.

I asked him about Jennifer/Electra's party, to get off the team a while, but he wouldn't open up. "Jen doesn't know that she's talking about half the time," he told me.

I gave him a fatherly look. "Don't you ever look out for your sister, Derek?" I asked.

But he was wrestling with the concept of time on the clock over the Jenn-Air, like a math professor with a calculus problem. After a while, he managed to noodle it out. "We got skull practice in ten minutes," he said.

"No homeroom, these days?"

"Team don't have homeroom."

"How about classes? Team have classes?"

For the first time, he looked directly at me. At my nose, anyway. "What do you care if we have 'em or not?" he snarled.

"I'd like to know where my child-support goes."

I could see we had slid into the nether regions with that. Fortunately, Derek's interest in his life's work brought us back to square one. "Did you come here to write about the game or not?" he asked.

I got up, ran some water into my cup, and sloshed it around to remove all traces of the flavor crystals. "I came because it was time to come back," I said.

"Does that mean you're not living with that . . . woman any more?"

"That . . . woman left me. We couldn't get along."

He gave me a confused look. "But you are going to write about the game!" he demanded.

I carefully placed the cup in the dishwasher rack. "The *Times* pays me to cover football news, Derek," I explained. "Not football games."

The distinction eluded him. "But don't you think we ought to have some recognition?" he said. "After all, we are number one in the nation!"

I nodded my head. "All right, so you're number one. But it's a big world, son. You're still just a herd of yearling bulls butting your heads against each other."

"Okay," he said defiantly, "then how come people come to see us, huh?"

"People come to see naked ladies and grand openings of the Piggly Wiggly, Derek. It doesn't mean they make statues of them for the park and church."

That seemed hard to grasp. He wrinkled his brow and gritted his bright, straight teeth. "You don't see my point," he said.

God knows, I saw it, but I was trying to be patient. "What point?" I asked him.

"The thing is, we're good, Dad. Real good!"

"And I'm glad you are. I hope you win another one hundred in a row, all in a line, without a loss, consecutive, and so forth."

"I know what it is. You're jealous of us! Football was nothing but a lot of crap when you were here. You never won a scholarship or anything, so now you're jealous of our athletic abilities!"

"Maybe so."

Satisfied with his analysis of the situation, he alluded a few more times to the athletic prowess of all the real good people out on the field, until Jennifer finally showed up again wearing a few new layers. She looked as if she'd been hit by a Goodwill truck.

"I'm ready," she announced to Derek.

"It's about damn time!"

"Hey, look, I'm a woman, okay?" she said. "I can't just throw things on! Can I, Daddy?"

"I'd hate to imagine."

Derek puffed up. "Well, I happen to be a man, and I can't be waiting around for you all day! I got skull practice!"

"Well, we sure wouldn't want to miss that, would we?"

"No, 'we' wouldn't. So let's go!" He grabbed another banana for the road and stormed out of the house.

Electra shrugged her padded shoulders. "Bye, Daddy," she said and kissed me on the cheek. "And don't worry about all those dumb parties I was telling you about, okay? It wasn't anything. Really."

"Okay."

She grinned seductively. "I don't care what Mother says, I think you're cute."

"You, too."

At the sound of Derek's voice outside, she moved toward the back door of the kitchen. "I'm serious," she insisted. "Everybody's dad around here is either a phony, a feeble, or a fairy!"

"That has a nice ring to it."

"Do what?"

"Nothing. I'll see you this afternoon, Jennifer," I told her. "After the reception."

"You'd better be here, now," she teased. "Or else!" With another seductive grin, she crashed out the back door wearing all her rummage to school.

My poor, mixed-up children left me alone in my ex-wife's kitchen in a very cold sweat. I stood next to the bar as confused by them as I had ever been about anything. Jennifer and Derek were nothing like they sounded on the phone.

They were hurting, reaching out, and fighting for all they were worth at the same time. And all I could do was quip and make them feel worse.

I got my cup out of the dishwasher and reached for the Folger's again, but at the sound of Derek's heap cranking up, I felt a chill run up my spine. A minute later with the cup still in my fist, I tried hard to throw up in the sink.

Nothing came out but air. The dry heaves. My mouth was parched and sticky and rank. I felt like I'd been out licking a washateria parking lot.

I retched again. But I got nothing but a throbbing ache for my efforts. When I realized I had dropped Nancy's cup on the floor and broken it, I closed my eyes and wondered if I might not have been better off eating one of Mom's breakfasts after all.

When I got back home at noon, my knees were assailed by Mom's cat in the living room and my brains by Mom in the hall. She planted herself outside the door of my bedroom and gave me the plot of *Species* as if she were barking instructions to a fire brigade, while the cat, who now had acquired the taste of human blood and wasn't about to give up on me, anxiously paced the floor beside her mewling continuously.

As I packed my leather bag and changed into my business suit, I heard the outline of her breathless saga, which followed the exploits of a certain midwestern family from the Neolithic Period to the election of Richard Nixon in 1969. Mom confided through closed doors that her great human adventure would make Michener's *Hawaii* look like an anecdote and could do more to advance the cause of anthropology than carbon 14 dating and the Heidelberg Jaw combined.

The only problem was getting the novel published. (She'd heard all about these Vassar graduates and what-not they had nowadays for readers.) Ever since Max Perkins died, there had been no champion of novelists in their prime. What was the matter with them anyway? What did they have against her? By the time I came out of the bedroom, Mom was railing against Random House and Simon and Schuster for having the audacity to turn down her manuscript.

"But you haven't written a word of it yet," I reminded her as the cat saw her chance and pounced on my thighs.

"And I may not, either!" Mom declared emphatically. "I just may not!"

"Look, Mom," I said, "I'm going to stay over at Nan's tonight." I knocked the cat to the floor and shook my foot at her, but just my luck, she considered a moving target a challenge.

Mom perked up at my announcement. "You don't

mean you two are getting back together!" she said.

"No, I don't mean that." I kissed her on the cheek and promised her I'd find a balanced meal somewhere today. Then I broke away from the cat, bounded down the stairs, and managed to slip out the side door just before I heard her screech.

The six-block walk to the school was a rat maze of autumn colors, pretty and seductive, until I reached the huge gymnasium itself, which was a faded monument to the WPA, with blood-red brick and peeling white window facings and a wrinkled asphalt roof. Like a great Roman ruin, it stood between the grammar school and the new cinderblock-and-fiberglass coliseum, as a testament to the Southern reverence for the glorious past and for rubble. On the concrete facade of the old building, over the faded yellow Civil Defense medallion, was a red and white hand-painted sign:

219 - 16!
99 in a Row! Go, Lions!
We Started It All!

Before I could close the door behind me, Betty Lynn was on me like Mom's cat, pecking me on the cheek, and plastering a name tag on my lapel. I went along with the elaborate greeting and boldly kissed her on the lips. It was fun. Betty Lynn had lost her baby fat and was pretty luscious nowadays, although she did smell faintly like an old pillow, up close. I asked her about her family and acted cordial, all the time pining hopelessly for a nostalgic peek at that redwood bush of hers.

When all this longing started to wear on me, I looked around the old gym. It was roughly the size of the Sea of Japan, with two massive cliffs of back-breaking bleachers, a firmament composed of two hundred one-hundred-watt bulbs, and a dozen steel rafters beneath the sagging roof, which a person could easily climb and break his fool neck on. Arranged on the hardwood floor were three ping-pong tables in the shape of a fence staple, covered with checkered tablecloths representing either our friends the Italians, or the school colors, and loaded with Ritz Crackers and Cheezits and my daughter Electra's passion, Hawaiian Punch. Betty Lynn was now starting to stir around like Marlon Perkins, slapping a name tag on everything that moved. Although she had enough supplies to accommodate the 8th Army, only about a dozen people had shown up for the reception so far.

Everybody was dressed to the hilt in football spectator finery, except for Homer Boone, who was hanging around the ticket office in a ratty wool floor-length black coat and a rolled toboggan which sat like a hamburger bun on the summit of his big gray head. Homer was dim, cadaverous, and mysterious, and always looked as if he were waiting in the cold to bless the fleet. But he was the only decent Boone I ever heard of, in a family distinguished by an unending line of hitchhikers, political terrorists, and career lieutenants. He was standing with his long legs apart at parade rest, the same way he had stood back in the second grade, when he shocked even the school board by urinating on the floor, during a spelling bee.

Homer had a coon dick. I don't mean that he was personally hampered with a penis the size of a raccoon's, though that may have been the case for all I know, since he never went out for sports and I therefore never saw him naked. What I mean is, Homer had in his possession what he claimed was an actual phallus of a *Procyon lotor* which he had received in a plain brown envelope, having ordered it from the back pages of a men's magazine which not even his liberal mother would have approved of. It was about four inches long, close to the size of an AA battery at the base, in the general shape of a wine corkscrew, and was composed entirely of bone. Homer wore it as a good luck charm around his neck on the same stainless steel chain that he had used for his dog tags, back when they were in fashion.

Whatever charm this talisman had, it managed to give Homer Boone a lot more campus prestige than he otherwise might have expected. Every girl in school was fascinated and mesmerized by this thing. They hovered around it during lunch period, and asked to touch it, and giggled and blushed and pitied what poor lady coons must have to endure on the second date. The boys were just as curious, but not nearly so impressed. Tommy Ray Felton said he couldn't figure out how a fellow could ever get any personal satisfaction out of anything you could cut your finger on. In fact, plain old solid bone, in his view, wouldn't do anybody any good at all, unless maybe you wanted to use it to dig your way out of prison, or something.

This infamous object made its first public showing one day in algebra class, when Miss Irma Boudreaux from Baton Rouge noticed an unidentified intrusion dangling from a chain around Homer's neck, and demanded to see the distraction up close. When he brought it up to the desk, Miss Irma, a spinster lady who owned enough cats to know a few things about the way of the world, recognized her mistake the instant she took the matter into her own hands.

"Merciful Heavens!" she gasped and shrank away as if she'd just bumped into the Ark of the Covenant. Before we knew it, she burst out of the room, and came back dragging Mr. Floyd in from the hall. "There!" She pointed at the coon dick. "You see! What did I tell you! What are these kids coming to, these days!"

Mr Floyd, on his way to the chocolate milk machine, wasn't up to this. He turned a couple of shades of crimson as he jangled his dimes and quarters, and gazed in bewilderment upon Homer's offense. "Er-uh," he asked, "what's that you got around your neck, Homer?"

Homer shrugged his shoulders. "Nothing," he answered.

Of course, Mr. Floyd was perfectly willing to let the whole adventure end at that and go get his chocolate milk, but Miss Irma was the most conscientious teacher in the school. She pushed the principal toward the student and demanded that he do something, or else.

My Floyd nodded seriously and jangled his coins a while, and addressed Homer again. "Er-uh, Homer," he said, "I want you to hand over whatever you've got there to Miss Boudreaux."

"No!" Miss Irma screamed and hustled behind the coat tree for protection. "For Goodness' sake, Mr.

Floyd!" she cried. "You don't expect a lady to touch such a thing!"

The principal knew enough to turn scarlet now, though he was still quite at a loss about this business. Apparently, he had never had any cats to speak of. "Er-uh," he said.

"Just make him put it down!" Miss Irma shouted from behind the tree. "Make him put it away!" She turned her back to the class, unable to face the horror any longer.

Unlike other Boones, Homer wasn't looking for any trouble, so he dutifully unsnapped the chain and reverently laid the coon dick on the open pages of Miss Irma's algebra text and left with Mr. Floyd to discover what his impending punishment was to be, in the safety of the principal's office. We all waited in silence to see what would happen next. When Miss Irma was satisfied the school authority was gone, she turned slowly around and considered the object in question, which looked to me from my place on the front row like a ritzy book mark, lying across her verbal problems.

After pacing the floor for a while, with her eyes glued to the text, she quietly left the room and returned ten minutes later with the black janitor, Ole Mose, of the Silver Creek community. Mose was as ancient as the Marshall sewer system, as big as a second-hand Buick, and about as helpful as a dead marine. He was shaking his globe of a head before he even got into the room.

Miss Irma pointed and turned away her head. "Would you kindly remove that thing from my desk this instant!" she ordered him.

But Ole Mose said no. For the first time on record, a

black janitor had not only turned white, but had refused to heed a teacher's direct command besides. Mose had his reasons, though. This Creole lady, he maintained, had done got herself into some real bad voodoo shit with that hunk of bone, and he wasn't ready to go into no mess like that for nobody.

Neither would the maid, it turned out, who reported authoritatively that coon dicks were well-known to carry rabies, and she certainly hadn't toiled in the cleaning business for twenty years in order to catch rabies and die spitting in the streets. The biology teacher, Mr. Tucker, who was unmarried and never could figure out why, told her if she'd slip it into some formaldehyde, he might consider taking it off her hands. Her last resort, Assistant Coach Paul Ford Evans, told her he was so busy trying to build a winning football tradition and rise in his profession, he didn't have time to worry about his own organ, let alone one belonging to some dead coon.

In the end, Miss Irma had to take on the job herself, with a pair of channel lock pliers which she found in an abandoned locker in the Home Ec Department. With the whole algebra class at her heels, she marched down to the basement, holding Homer's folly out in front of her. Then, with a spectacular flourish, and a few choice lines from *Oedipus Rex*, she cast the offending organ into the furnace, pliers and all.

The odd thing was, when Miss Irma died in a car wreck on I-55 near Hammond, Louisiana, two months later, we couldn't help but wonder if perhaps Homer's coon dick hadn't been a charm which she had violated with ignorance and fire. When the long black cars passed in front of the school that gloomy day in February, Bubba nudged me and made me look over at Homer, who was solemnly and mysteriously wearing another one of those things around his neck.

"Makes you wonder, doesn't it, Teddy?" Bubba said.

Yes. It sure did.

For some reason, thinking of my friend Bubba made a strange sense of dread come over me. I felt very agitated. It was as if something were terribly wrong in this town. I looked up at the ceiling and imagined I could smell the odor of moral decay seeping down through the cracks in the asphalt.

I was saved from my flight of lunacy by my former wife, who arrived at the gym with an angel food cake she obviously meant to share with the rest of the class. She looked beautiful to me. Even sexier than before. When she walked in my direction, I took a wide stance and a deep breath and held on.

"Well?" She placed the angel food cake on a table. "Did you see them?"

"Sure did," I answered. I wished I could hug her, right there on the free throw line. For just a moment.

Satisfied with where her cake was situated on the table, she turned to me. "So what are you looking so upset about?" she asked.

"I don't know. They're just not what I expected."

"Nobody is ever what you expect them to be, Ted," she said. "That's always been your problem. You type people, and then you're disappointed when you find out they're not that way."

"I hate it that Derek is so obsessed with football," I said.

That annoyed her. "How else is a teenage boy going to impress a father who's a sportswriter?"

I shrugged my shoulders and switched the subject over to Electra. "I was wondering about these older guys Jennifer's been seeing," I said.

"What older guys?"

"She said she met a couple of middle-aged suits at a party."

Nancy looked me straight in the eye. "What party?" she said.

"She didn't have enough of a grip on the thing to identify it."

Nancy now glanced around the gym, sizing up the middle-aged suits, I guess. "Well," she said, "you can be sure I'll find out. Jennifer knows very well she's not supposed to be hanging around men like that. Christ. The girl's only sixteen years old!"

"I know."

It was good to agree with Nan for a change, if only on our daughter's age. It nearly calmed me down for a moment. I could almost nurse the idea that since we had concurred on an intimate subject, really dealt with it, we were becoming close again. I could almost feel it.

"Ever think of getting married again?" I asked her out of the blue.

"What?" she said.

"Ever consider doing it all over again? You and me?"

"Not lately," she said with half a laugh.

I should have known better than to push, but the

idea was beginning to sound so good and reasonable to me, I couldn't resist. "Maybe this time we could get it right," I said. "And maybe our kids need us. Together."
A look of astonishment crossed her face. "Why didn't you say that ten years ago?"
"I probably didn't know that many words ten years ago."
"Well, they're coming a little late now, don't you think?"
"I don't see why," I said. Lord, how I wanted to hold her at that moment. Touch her warm skin. Feel her soft breath.
"I've made my contribution to the party," she said, meaning the cake. "I've got to go back to work." Whirling around, she hurried out of the gym with her hand to her mouth—in anger, disgust, or frustration—I couldn't tell which, and I was left on my own to think about my old friend again.

I had known Bubba Henderson ever since he showed up at his dead mother's brother's house with a glossy ebony metal suitcase and a Lucky Strikes pack crammed full of all the Big Chiefs he had collected in the bus stations from Shelbyville, Tennessee, to Marshall, Mississippi. I guess you could say I loved the guy. It wasn't anything sexual, of course. Not the way I loved Judy Moon, either. She was an ideal. Her presence was an aesthetic comfort in a world of clutching inanities. When the Latin began to sound moribund and the basketball Lions began to play like ailing storks, I didn't care. I could always watch Judy Moon. She was my solace. She charmed me to my toes with her poise and elegance and a warm and exhilarating kind of closeness that could only exist in the fluent, never-never grace of television. Bubba was the opposite of that. I loved him because he gave meaning to all the untidy realities of life.

He did it with a razor edge that was created out of an urge for order, fired by intelligence, and tempered by compassion. While the rest of us bounced back and forth against the pinball bumpers, Bubba found the paths. We reacted to the days of our lives, he interpreted them, within the context of the only thing which gave them meaning: the law. Bubba was our Perry Mason, Hamilton Burger, and Judge Pigmeat Markham, all rolled into one. If he didn't know the law, he made it up, and convinced us to abide by it. I learned a lot about the skeletons and flesh of life, being Bubba Henderson's best friend.

Sonya Penski is one who should know that.

If you ever run across her anywhere, I wish you'd tell her that for me. Tell her . . . that I learned a lot from Bubba, and from her. I hope to God we all did.

Sonya was the freckled idiot daughter of Stanislaw Penski, who migrated all the way from Lodz, Poland, to open a haberdashery in Marshall, Mississippi. He was a coarse little man with glasses like ice cubes, hair as mussed as a blind man's, and a sagging body that looked like the last sack of seed potatoes on the truck. He was as bunglesome as his Slavic voice, which knocked its way through English like a dog through a neighbor's garbage. He called his haberdashery *Drzewiej*, which meant "in the old days," though everyone always called it Stan's, for short.

Since Sonya was a moron, she was passed from one grade to another every so often, in order to give her teachers a rest. By the time she made the eleventh grade, she had blossomed into a sizable girl of twenty-four, nearly six feet tall, with a nose like a banana, and teeth as big as thumbs. She had a sweet disposition and a lovely smile, but in her wrinkled blue sailor outfit, she looked like a new recruit for the Israeli Navy, or the star of a Japanese movie. It was a sad situation, but since she was enormously buxom and seldom bothered to wear a bra, she naturally drew attention from all the panting males of Marshall High.

Sometimes, the boys would discuss her after geometry. Big Roy Buck Dalton, a guard on the football team who was still trying to master the notion of sides, reasoned that it'd be a mortal sin for Sonya to die a virgin in the streets, now that the Kinsey report was out, and all. He thought somebody ought to do it for her before she turned thirty and couldn't ever do it, the way it had happened to Miss Carson and Miss Williams.

Bubba rose to her defense. "You can't do things like that to Sonya," he protested.

Roy Buck looked at him darkly. "Why not?" he asked.

"Because it's against the law, for one thing."

"Shoot," he said skeptically. "You got more laws on you than coaches got plays, Bubba. Ain't no law on earth says I can't do it to a full-grown woman."

Bubba made a gesture with his finger. "There just so happens to be a law that protects the morons," he informed us as if we were a judge. "The feeble-minded are not regarded as responsible, in the eyes of the law."

Roy Buck got out a laugh that sounded like a belch. "Don't tell me about no eyes of the law," he scoffed. "I seen the eyes of the law on that statue in Mr. Floyd's office. Got a damn blindfold over 'em."

Stunned for a minute because he'd seen that statue too, Bubba nevertheless came up with an explanation. "All that means is," he said, "the Supreme Court considers kidnapping to be a federal offense. They put that blindfold on that statue right after the Lucky Lindbergh case. What I'm saying is, in the eyes of the law, a female idiot can never be the same as a regular woman. They're considered property."

"That don't matter to Roy Buck," Tommy Ray said. "He'll screw property, too. Gopher holes, ditches, cracks in the pavement, anything."

Bubba kicked the campus dirt. "Don't you guys understand what I'm saying here?" he cried. "Can't you see, it's the same as if we *owned* Sonya Penski? Like she was chattel, or something. And for God's sakes, nobody screws chattel!"

"Mr. Heineke does," Tommy Ray said.

"Not *cattle*, you dope: *chattel!*"

"Oh."

"Well," Roy Buck said, "all I know is, if somebody's gotta do it, it might as well be me."

I could tell Roy Buck's logic was vexing to Bubba, but I didn't really understand how much he hated the idea until one Saturday night he discovered Sonya and the guard double-dating in the back seat of Arnold Coleman's '55 Ford sedan, parked behind the frozen custard stand.

As soon as Bubba realized it was Sonya in there, he

went crazy. He hauled her out of the car and dragged her screaming toward the safety of the neon lights. Roy Buck went crazy, too. He came out of the car and yanked Bubba away from Sonya and crushed him like a rotten navel orange into the pea gravel in front of the ladies' room. Poor Sonya was so ashamed of causing a ruckus, she started bawling uncontrollably and fled into the woods like a frightened giraffe.

A week later, we learned that Sonya was being taken out of school by her father. Miss Irma told us in homeroom that she was being sent to a place where she could live out the remainder of her days among people of her own kind, which meant, we assumed, she would soon be headed for Arkansas. Six months after that, Mr. Penski boarded up the haberdashery and left town himself. No one in Marshall ever heard of either of them again.

Bubba never admitted that he told Mr. Penski about the altercation at the frozen custard stand. But he never denied it, either. All he would say on the subject was that he believed the law should never be compromised. We have a responsibility to others, he said, through the law. "It's the only damn thing I got to go on, Teddy," he told me, with tears in his eyes. "It's the only thing that counts."

That was Bubba's edge.

When Bubba himself made his entrance, I noticed right off that he'd come to the reception without his wife. He was being clung to by a shapely brunette that was probably flourishing on a diet of Gerber's strained foods and evaporated milk. Then I noticed Bubba had changed. Oh, he had gained the usual thirty pounds and his hair had waxed thin and gray, but that wasn't what was so different. What was wrong was that the wonderful glint in his eye was gone. The sparkle had vanished like a star grown cold, and all those extra pounds now made him look as if he'd been seriously rolled in dough. My God. Bubba had lost the one thing that had always stood between him and the rest of us: his edge.

"Well, look who's here," he said and shook my hand. "Teddy Miller, of the *New York Times*." His grip was firm and friendly, but unconvincing. The edge was definitely gone. I could feel it missing in the palms of our hands. Bubba was now like everybody else.

"How're you doing, Bubba?" I managed to say.

He grinned, showing a slit full of teeth in a rounded face. Those eyes and ears and nose looked so damned ordinary now, I couldn't stand it. My best friend, the only one I had ever had, was another face in the crowd.

"Hey, listen," he said, "don't you go giving Cyrena any ideas, you hear? Folks call me 'J. B.' these days. Isn't that right, Love?"

Cyrena sucked in her breath, considered the question, and let it out again. "He is absolutely correct about that, Mr. Miller," she confirmed, as if she were confirming that the Phrygians had had no literature.

"Sure is good to see you, Ted," Bubba said to me, but he hugged the girl. They both seemed very proud of her, I guess because she was actually doing okay in the company of adults. Probably she hadn't been on the planet long enough to have acquired many of the social graces. "They tell me you're going on TV with Judy Moon," Bubba said with interest.

"Yep."

He chuckled and renewed the hug, squeezing off a squeak from young Cyrena. "Teddy used to be in love with Judy Moon on the tube," he explained to her, slowly, to avoid confusing her with details. "When she was on *Teen Tempos*, we couldn't drag him away from the set."

"That's cute," Cyrena said.

Bubba laughed at her wit. "I guess you think being interviewed by Judy Moon is going to be a pretty big deal, huh, Ted?"

"Yeah, I do," I said, almost defiantly. I didn't like the way Bubba was making me act.

"Well, I'll tell you what," he said. "I bet it won't. I'll bet it won't be a thing like you expect it to be." Having dished out that dollop of gloom, Bubba started off. "Let's get together and chew the rag before you go back, what do you say?" he told me.

"Wait a minute, Bubba—"

"Hey, it's 'J.B.' now, remember?"

That got me. " 'J.B.', shit!" I exclaimed, much too loudly. "Why don't you go ahead and call yourself Atlas or Achilles or Hector?"

I could tell he got the point, that he was violating a trust. But in deference to Miss Pablum, he let it pass. "We'd better go pay our respects to the head of this shindig," he said, and jerked Cyrena across the floor, by her lovely wrist. I believe she thought this was a new dance he was teaching her. Or rather, an old dance.

For a long time, I felt as if I'd been kicked around the

subway by vigilantes. I never expected Bubba Henderson, of all people, to act like an ass. Some guys take to
that sort of thing naturally, like Russo. But not Bubba.
I was outraged. I wanted to run after him and tackle
him and flog him with his nickname until he started to
bleed and the edge started coming back through the
layers of fat flesh. But I knew that was metaphorical and
dumb. I had to be realistic about this. It was possible
that, like Betty Lynn's glorious pubic hair, Bubba was
lost to me forever.

I was about ready to leave the gym and Marshall
forever when I overheard Betty Lynn, standing next to
the box of unused name tags, entertaining Julie Baskins
on the subject of Freddie Thornberry. She was accounting for the poor attendance at the reception by the fact
that Freddie had cast a gloom over the event by recently
passing away.

"He just up and had a stroke on the afternoon of the
game, two weeks ago," she said to her. "Can you
imagine that? At his age?"

"I don't understand," Julie said. "Wasn't he our
age?"

"Of course he was. We were all in the same class."

"Then I disagree. I don't think it's hard to imagine
at all. What's hard to imagine is for old people and kids
to die."

Betty Lynn frowned in confusion. "Anyhow, it
gives me the creeps to think about him lying there in the
water that way."

"Why was he lying in the water, Betty Lynn?" she
asked. Julie was a hearty girl from Milltown who
played guard on the basketball team back when guards

weren't allowed to shoot, but she never held that against anybody. Folks from her neck of the woods used to try to call her Philadelphia, because her body was shaped like the Liberty Bell, but her nickname never really caught on. It was too hard for the fans to holler that many syllables in crucial game situations.

As I came closer to these two ladies, Betty Lynn fanned her fingers across her bosom and heaved a few sighs. "Poor Freddie was cleaning out Mr. O'Ryan's catfish pond," she explained to Julie, "when all of a sudden, it hit him—right there in the dirty water! It was pretty awful. They say all the catfish were swimming around him in a circle, like kids around a popular teacher at Bible school, when he floated by Mr. O'Ryan's office. Thank God, his death was instantaneous. They didn't even find any mud in his lungs."

"I wonder how hard they tried," Julie said.

"What?"

Julie looked very intent on this subject. "I mean, did they really look that hard?" she asked.

Betty Lynn regarded Julie curiously now, as if she were truly seeing her for the first time. "They weren't actually looking for mud in his lungs, Julie," she said patiently. "They were just trying to find out the cause of death."

"I know that. I'm just saying, sometimes if you look especially hard for things, you can find them. Sometimes, where you least expect it."

Betty Lynn came up with a smile, then lost it. "Well, evidently, this wasn't one of those times," she said. "Because there just wasn't a speck of mud in his lungs, and that's all there is to it!"

Julie shook her head sadly. "I sure wish somebody would call me when things like this happen," she said innocently. "I would never have stopped looking. At least I could have done that much for him."

Before long, the others were gathering around us like a school of catfish, in order to tell a few stories in tribute to our late classmate, Freddie Thornberry. As solemn as the occasion was, we found ourselves chuckling and tittering over his persistent confusion over words. Betty Lynn said it was church that gave him the most grief. Freddie was mortally embarrassed the day the preacher asked him if he wouldn't mind tithing in public. His face turned red and he answered that he'd prefer to do it in private, if the preacher didn't mind. And practically every time the congregation sang "Onward Christian Soldiers," Thornberry, like as not, would grab whoever was beside him in the pew and demand to know, "Marching as toward what? Toward what?"

"The strangest thing was, he believed that God's name was Howard," Betty Lynn said. "He never could understand why nobody else called Him that, when it was right there in the Lord's Prayer, which started off, 'Our Father, Which Art in Heaven, Howard be Thy name. . . .'"

Betty Lynn swore to us it was true. "He really did!" she said. "I used to hear him say, 'Howard damn it!' Didn't he, Teddy?"

When I swore that it was true, a few people asked me if I would tell a Freddie story. The request made me feel so much like a member of a family for a change, I couldn't refuse. I decided to tell them all about Freddie's first sexual experience of any note, with Hattie

Barefield, in the railroad yard, in 1958. Everybody had heard the tale already, but they wanted to hear it again.

It happened that while Freddie and Hattie were enjoying each other's intimate company, there suddenly appeared in the railroad yard an unusually small migrant worker from out West. This being in the 1950's, Hattie was so startled to look up and see a man with a beard and no job above them, that her entire body involuntarily froze, causing her pelvis to lock up tight, and her uterus to clamp down on Freddie's unsuspecting organ, like a hungry python on a hard-boiled egg.

Trapped like a rat, Freddie had no choice but to ask the intruding transient to do what he could to pry them loose. Being Catholic, this fellow naturally had reservations about putting asunder what God had so obviously joined together, but he decided to give it a shot, anyway. Unfortunately, the usual aids, such as broomsticks, crowbars, and Spanish incantations, seemed to have no effect at all on the connection.

After an hour of all this gouging and sticking, Freddie began to wonder if he'd ever be able to walk the streets alone again, not to mention chase any more rodents through high cotton, or play solitaire with his Momma at home. "I gotta go to the house, Hattie!" he said anxiously. "Momma's expecting me!"

"Is she expecting me, too?" Hattie said dryly. She was a bit outdone with herself, at the moment. Why did she have to have such a recalcitrant body as this? Oh, sure, it was cute and voluptuous as the dickens, but in four and a half years as a dental assistant, she had never heard of anybody with a bite like this.

Freddie had an idea. "Look," he proposed, "suppose we get all our legs to going like a caterpillar, or something? Once we humped over the rails, it'd be smooth sailing. We probably could roll on home."

"Stop moving!" she shrieked in agony as he tried out the plan. "You're scraping my behind on the cinders!"

Freddie was no sadist, but he had it in his mind to be on his way. "I was thinking," he said, "maybe if I got on bottom for a change, we could work up some steam. It ain't more than a couple of blocks to my house."

But Hattie held her, and therefore his, position fast. "And just what do you figure we'd do, once we got to your house?" she quizzed him. "Do we lie out in the front yard and ask your momma to pull our legs apart and make a wish?"

Thornberry seriously shook his head. "She never believes in things like that," he said.

"Well, good for her."

"Momma's a real serious woman."

"I don't doubt it. Why don't you just get off!" she said, disgusted with him altogether. "Just... stand up!"

Freddie tried as hard as he could to oblige her, but it was no use. "No way, Hattie," he said finally. "I can't even budge her. She's really got me in there real good, hasn't she, sir?" he said to the transient.

"Jace," the migrant worker, a gentleman from Mexico, agreed. "*Por siempre jamas,* in other words."

"God, this is so embarrassing!" Hattie groaned. "It's not bad enough to have hips like a clam, I've got to have this perfect stranger looking on!"

From where he lay, of course, Freddie didn't consider this short, scroungy Mexican to be anywhere near perfect. "Hey, come on, Hattie," he said. "This poor guy can't even speak English!"

"So what? What difference does that make?"

"It makes a lot. It's like people are blind or something, when they can't speak English. To tell you the truth, I always feel sorry for them."

"My God."

"Well, I do!"

"I was never so humiliated in my life!"

Thornberry frowned suspiciously at her words. "You're not saying you've done this before, are you?" he asked.

"Oh, of course I haven't done it before. What do you think I am, a snapping turtle?"

"No, I don't mean that. I mean, you know—this."

"Why don't you just shut up, Freddie?"

"Because I want to clear this up before we go any further."

"Just where would we go, Freddie?"

"I want you to know," he continued, "that for my part, I have never humiliated anybody before. Never, ever. I'm a virgin all the way."

"Oh, good grief."

While the air was being cleared, the migrant worker, whose name was Marcos Valdez, was scratching his scraggly beard, trying hard to figure out how to deal with his problem of the Siamese lovers. Since he was new to this country, he wasn't sure if this complicated condition was unusual with Americans or not. All he knew was that if the gringos really wanted his help, well, then, yes, sir, he was going to do what he could. To be of aid to his powerful neighbors across the border had always been one of his fondest desires. Besides, there might be a peso or two in it for him, somewhere.

The action he took was to drag Freddie and Hattie under an Illinois Central Railroad boxcar for protection against the night air. Then he carefully covered them with a Navajo blanket which he had stolen from an Indian with the flu in Arizona.

After doing this, he began to search for a person of authority, which in Marshall, Mississippi, is like looking for evidence of the reproduction process in a maternity ward. Among the many available buildings, he selected the sheriff's office, because it was the closest thing to adobe in town, and shortly after dawn, he entered it with two stubby fingers raised high above his head, announcing in broken English that he now had *dos americanos* holed up beneath the train, nearby. Before the receptionist could take down his name, the sheriff was pulling his gun and ordering Marcos to hold his fingers just where they were, for he was now being arrested for the crime of kidnapping, the law's worst offense.

I glanced over at Bubba when I said that, remembering he'd often said as much, but there was not a trace of recognition in his face. It was such a bland face, in fact, that I wanted to maul it with Betty Lynn's box of name tags, to give it some of its character back. But I turned away and went on with the story.

With Marcos safely behind bars, Sheriff Hutson and his deputies headed straight for the I.C. railyard, like the grammar school letting out for snow. So did the city police, the marshal, the constable, the highway patrol, the nightwatchman, and anyone else who could scare up a dog and a shotgun, or spit tobacco into a Dixie cup and cuss at the same time. At 7:26 a.m., sixty-four men and eleven German Shepherds in fourteen cars and two vans, stormed the railroad yard like Normandy Beach, and surrounded the boxcar. Six minutes later, Mom was in front of the others, exhorting the kidnappers in a booming voice to come out with their hands in the air, the way their amigo Marcos had, or face a round of hostile fire, for which she could in no way be held responsible.

At first, Mom's sobering words were greeted with an eerie silence in the yard. Then all the forces scattered here and there over the rails and crossties got restless and began to cock their weapons and assume their various stances, and practice hollering "Freeze!" to each other. At last, after a shuffling noise beneath the boxcar, a Navajo blanket slowly emerged into view and began crawling suspiciously into the open. Cocking his .45 magnum beside his head, Sheriff Hutson scratched his masculinity a couple of times, took ten giant steps forward, and boldly whipped away the cover.

"Great God in the morning!" he gasped when he saw the unhappy couple. "Don't you young people ever do anything else, anymore!"

"Sir?" Freddie said, looking up.

"Couldn't you have waited til we caught the kidnappers, anyway?" he cried.

When it came to him that he was not looking at a casual embrace, Hutson ordered his stoutest and most discreet deputies to scoop up the lovers like a stack of pancakes and whisk them off to the hospital in a van, which, he noted, the Ford Motor Company had never made for that purpose. With sixteen sirens screaming in the early morning air, the entire law contingent of

Marshall raced off to Travis Memorial. Within an hour, there was such congestion in the parking lot, the Jaycees were out in droves, collecting a dollar a space.

Since Hattie turned out to be a Christian Scientist who had read most of the relevant literature in the dentist's waiting room, she warned the doctors that her body was a temple, and that included the pelvic region especially, and they should not touch anything there with any medical instruments, no matter how stubborn her bite proved to be. After a lengthy consultation in the snack bar, the Marshall authorities agreed on two separate courses of action. First, they would send Marcos Valdez down to Louisiana, where migrants were, if not exactly needed or encouraged, at least tolerated. Secondly, they would summon a psychiatrist down from Jackson, where most of the professionals in the state tended to hang out. They reasoned that a person with a degree from somewhere other than Mississippi might just feel right at home with these two.

Since Dr. Timothy D. Groden, M.D., and Ph.D. from Tulane University, had dealt intimately with cliques of New Orleans lakefront swingers in his time, he knew all about this sort of thing. Conducting himself with admirable professional dignity, he promptly cleared the room of unnecessary nurses, covered Freddie's eyes with a night mask, then hypnotized Hattie into believing she was a mother who was currently in the process of being fulfilled as a woman by the natural phenomenon of birth. Soon Hattie was in such a swing of things, she was able to gently expel Freddie's withered little fancy from her tenacious grip, and celebrated the ultimate act with tears of absolute joy.

When he was brought to his feet again, Freddie confided to the team of doctors that he honestly believed this sex business was a highly overrated deal, just as his mother had said. It took so long to do it, he didn't see how folks ever got anything else accomplished. He swore to Howard that from that day on, he would never have another thing to do with it.

When I finished the story, Bubba squirmed out of Cyrena's clutches and announced that it was his turn. "One time," he began, "I told Freddie this joke about this dumb country bumpkin named Sonny, from the Delta. When Sonny got married, he went straight to his momma and asked her what to do about the sex act, which he had never done before—"

"We weren't telling jokes, J.B." Betty Lynn cut him off. "We were talking about Freddie Thornberry."

"Hey, so was I!" he insisted. "I told Freddie that joke fifty times, and he never once understood it!"

He broke into a laugh and that made it even worse. It was clear the old class was now depressed. I could see it in every eye in the place. Maybe even Bubba's. We all felt like sacks of garbage in the street.

Most of the time after that, the subject was football. Bubba and Dr. Hewitt, Dixie Wilkins' husband, were discussing the bets on the game. I was surprised to hear that the amount of money floating around this town of two thousand amounted to over a million dollars.

There were two of these men I didn't know. One was a stumpy Italian with a plumb-bob nose and a polyester suit, who could have been anything from a dragline operator, to a salesman for Ragu. The other was an anemic man with an ugly, gaunt face that was cracked and yellow like a legal pad left out in the sun and rain. Since he spoke with a hush, every time he opened his mouth, listeners had to lean forward and cup their ears.

I didn't care for either of these guys, but I assumed that was because they had Bubba's attention, and I didn't.

"What's the current line on the game?" I asked, to fit in.

"Bookies are giving Brookhaven and eight," Bubba said. "And it's getting farther apart all the time. God damn if we don't have us a team here, boys!"

Dr. Hewitt, however, looked mighty concerned about the team. He was a fretting physician who was never able to cure himself. In his twenty-year career, he had had three massive heart attacks, a severe infection of the esophagus, and some very serious problems with his toes.

"Let me tell you something, that Las Vegas spread is killing me!" he moaned. "It never gives you any leeway! I've got five thousand bucks on this game. One lousy call by an official, and I'm dead!"

"Got any particular official in mind, Joe?" the anemic guy said in his hush.

Leaning forward, Dr. Hewitt answered, "Yeah, Douglas, as a matter of fact, I do. That damned Jack Duncan. Every judgment call he's made this year has been against us!"

"He's out of Summit, right?"

"That's right. And Mike Cramer is another one.

Remember that goal line stand in the Natchez game, J.B.? Might've only cost the Lions six points, but it cost me my royal ass. Jesus, what's he trying to do to us!"

Douglas' long fingers searched his wrinkled yellow face like a blind man figuring out looks. "Duncan and Cramer," he said, barely above a whisper. "Noted."

"Noted." That one word sent a chill up my spine.

"Hey, Teddy," Bubba said to me. "How much are you in for?"

I was still working on Douglas' whisper. "What?" I said.

"I was wondering how much a rich *New York Times* reporter would bet on the Lions."

"I didn't get rich by betting on lions," I said. The other four men stiffened like German soldiers around me.

"What the hell does that mean?" Bubba said.

"It means when I bet, I lose."

"Not with the Lions, you won't."

"I lose with everybody, Bubba," I said. "You can't beat a Las Vegas betting line."

I might as well have been a spirit telling them there were to be no more erections here on earth. They quickly switched to a discussion of the team's Ryan-type defense, which Coach Reed was shrewdly calling "The Roar." Nobody else, I was assured, could have come up with such a motivational appellation as The Roar. This was the best little call to war since Dietzel invented The Chinese Bandits down at LSU. They were convinced the man simply had a great football mind. A chip off the Ole Bear Bryant Block. Mired in all these intricate technicalities of the game, they hardly noticed when I cashed in my patience and left.

Shortly before seven, my sister Amy called me in the throes of a gripping domestic dilemma. She claimed she was a desperate woman these days, and since Mom was busy writing the dedication of her novel to Uncle Harley and other hominids, and Dad was down in the cellar with the weather maps plotting next season's hurricanes, I was the only one she could turn to for help. When she told me that Mr. Avery McWilliams of Osyka had actually asked her to go to the game, I told her I was overjoyed at the turn her life was taking.

"Yes, but the problem is, he wants me to go over to his house after the game!" she said.

"How do you feel about that?" I avoided the question by turning it around. Why not, psychiatrists do it all the time.

Amy reached down deep to consider the questions. "That's just it," she said. "I don't know how to feel! What do you think, Ted? Do you think I should hold to my guns or what?"

"Might be a good idea, with things the way they are today."

"I don't know how to act around him," she said mournfully. "I mean, with all the disease and stuff going on. Should I be chaste or what?"

"Might be safer," I said.

I could feel her nibbling at the idea at the other end of the line. "I don't know, Teddy," she muttered. "I sure wouldn't want to do anything to lose Avery."

"Then screw him, Amy," I said.

"I'm not so sure about that," she said. "I mean, it's

so dangerous nowadays, with somebody you don't know."

"Then do what you want to do and stop whining about it!" I snapped.

She was hurt. I might as well have ripped out her pulsating heart with my evil talons. "Why do you always have to be so abrupt with me?" she said. "What did I say?"

"You didn't say anything, Amy," I replied. "I was thinking about something else." My kids.

"Well, how am I supposed to compete with what you're thinking?" she cried. "You know I'm not very smart. But that doesn't mean I don't have feelings, Teddy. Christ. Everybody can't figure everything out, can they?"

"No," I said.

"I'm sorry now I even called!" she said, and hung up.

While I was considering returning Amy's call, Electra drifted into the house like a Barnum and Bailey clown sporting a somewhere-over-the-rainbow look in her dark eyes and half the Dairy Queen on her mouth. She lolled about the living room for a while and hinted that she wanted to speak to me about something, sometime, somewhere, as soon as it was convenient for one, both, or either of us. At times my daughter seemed very airy and bloated to me. Maybe as a kid she hadn't been burped enough.

Derek's arrival at 8:30 gave Jennifer an occasion to drag her tired, popular body off to bed. I have to say, I was proud of my son, the way the big guy lumbered into the living room on his own without ever once touching his knuckles to the floor. He found his balance in the middle of the carpet and stood with heavy heart and a dull, dazed expression on his face as if a gang of Huns had been brutally trying to force him to read above his level.

"Want to talk about it, sport?" I asked congenially.

"Do what?" he returned.

"Talk."

"No," he said distantly. "Nothing to talk about."

"You're probably right," I agreed.

Fully erect, he moved stiffly but surely across the floor, dragging his left leg slightly, like Kharis hunting for the princess. At last, he came to a halt, gazed dimly up the stairs toward his room, and let out a grunt.

I took the utterance as an attempt to communicate. "Team got bed now?" I asked him.

Apparently I was right, for the son actually turned around and faced the father for once. His eyes were round and sad like a mountain gorilla's. After struggling through his vocabulary, he came up with these words: "Coach believes in us athletes getting lots of sleep."

"Coach is quite a philosopher," I noted.

"Sir?"

"Coach sure knows what's good for you."

"Oh. Yeah." Since he had agreed with me, he assumed we were done and therefore all bets were off, so he began to make his way silently up the stairs. I oversaw his movements to make sure he found his room.

After a while, Nancy came home from a Tupperware party in McComb fairly loaded down with two dozen bowls and a pie-wedge saver in the shape of a plastic door stop. I fancied these were peculiar items for her to bring back to the cave since Nancy would as soon go a whole week without expressing herself as bake a cake or pie. But she handled the implements with skill and care anyway before she managed to bury them in the nether regions of the cabinets. That done with dispatch, she said she was sorry to make me sleep on the couch, but the fourth bedroom was in such disarray, it would take a soap opera year to clean it up.

"Why don't I sleep with you and save the couch for paying guests?" I offered.

"Be serious."

"I am," I said.

My heart was pounding as she seemed to consider the idea. But she said, "I want you to know, there's a Yale lock on my door and I use it!"

"A Yale lock?"

"That's right. And there's also a night chain, a chair propped against the doorknob, and a two-hundred-and-fifty-dollar burglar alarm!"

"Who are you expecting, a SWAT team?"

"I'm not 'expecting' anyone. I share my bed only with responsible adults!"

"Sounds crowded."

"Believe me," she said, "it's not."

"Then it sounds lonely."

She glared censoriously at me for a second. "No matter how I feel, Teddy," she said more softly than usual, "You may as well know, I still have principles."

"Even a principle needs a rest every now and then," I said.

"Not these principles."

"Nancy—"

"Forget it," she said and headed upstairs for her empty room. "There's just no way I'd even sleep in the same room with a man who'd choose a career over his family!"

I stood and watched her go up. After all this time, here I was in the middle of the duplex wanting and craving my ex-wife. I didn't understand the way I felt, and I didn't particularly like it, either.

Nancy was making me realize what a dope I'd been.

Not long after I dozed off on my beloved couch, I was awakened by a cacophony of eating noises in the kitchen. In my corduroy robe, I peeked inside, expecting to find at least a herd of sows at the wheat shorts, but it was only my girl Jennifer poised in the ghostly pale light of the open refrigerator, snorting and gnawing on a chicken thigh the way a hyena chews on a gazelle. She was standing on her big bare feet, draped in a sheer white negligee, with coats of makeup spread haphazardly over her face. She seemed to be waiting for Count Dracula to light on the window sill and fly her away into the romantic night.

When she recognized that she was in the presence of her father, she smiled guiltily. "I always do this when I can't sleep," she explained as if we all ought to know that before proceeding with the rest of our lives.

To be sociable, I sat down at the table. What a girl. After stalking around all day in an outfit that Pizza Hut could sell for lunch, she now stood unembarrassed before me in a transparent nightie with a pair of raisin-sized nipples peering at me through the veil like the searching eyes of an alley cat. I went from her little bosom to her big hair. How on earth had she managed to impart to a mere wad of natural follicles such a wonderful aura of other-worldliness? She must have washed the stuff in Oxydol, then dried it by yelling at it. Or maybe she sprayed it with Easy-Off and beat it into place with the *Wall Street Journal*. I really couldn't figure it out. Such a pretty baby girl she'd been.

After masticating the cold chicken, she wrenched her face enough to crack the cosmetics.

"Too many herbs and spices?" I asked.

"I'm just glad you happened to wake up, Daddy," she told me.

"I didn't just happen to wake up. Sounded like you were taking a Viking out to lunch in here."

She slammed the refrigerator door, enveloping us in a womb-like atmosphere. After waiting each other out for an eternity, a tiny voice cut through the thick darkness. "I've been wanting to give you something," it said.

"I'd settle for a little electric light."

"Take this, please," she said mysteriously.

I felt a wee hand touch my liver spots, then three soft fingers press a bill of money into my fist. "I hope this isn't for the chicken," I said.

"It's a hundred dollars, Daddy," she informed me.

Figuring the game was over, I stood up, clicked on the Jenn-Air light, and looked at the crackling new hundred dollar bill in my palm. I pretended to be intrigued by the fine quality of the engraving to give her time to form an explanation.

Finally, she had one. "It's Derek's," she announced. She always ended her phrases with a stress, to tell the listener that the final word in her sentence carried the key to the meaning of the rest.

"Why does Derek keep money in the fridge?" I asked her.

She frowned and scratched at the blush on her cheeks. "He doesn't," she said, while taking a seat at the table. "He keeps it in his room. That's where I found it yesterday morning. I know I'm not supposed to be in there, but I was looking for my Irene Cara album which he's always borrowing without my permission, and I saw that on his dresser. It nearly scared me to death!"

"Where would he get a hundred dollars?" I asked.

"You see, that's what scares me. All Momma gives us is a crummy five dollars a week allowance. Since Derek's always too busy playing football to work anywhere, I keep wondering if maybe he's started to sell drugs or something."

"Just what I wanted to hear," I said in a hollow voice. Wonder why I thought they'd be safe in Mississippi when I was facing it in New York?

"Do you want me to put it back?" she asked.

"No, I'll talk to him about it."

"I wasn't sure I ought to give it to you," she confessed. "I mean, since you don't much approve of us or anything."

Unable to endure a top-view of the hair any longer, I sat down and faced her head on. It was interesting. The last time I had seen makeup like my daughter's, it was resting on satin. "Jennifer," I said, "I don't disapprove of you. Or Derek or your mother. But I want you to tell me if Derek was at that party you told me about this morning."

She braced herself. "How am I supposed to know who was at some party?" she wondered.

"I don't know. Sometimes people notice things like that."

"Well, I never do. All I do is try to have a good time."

"Is it possible any of the other players were there?"

"I guess so. Why?"

"Because exploited high school athletes are in danger of losing their amateur standing with the NCAA," I said.

"What does that mean?"

I looked at the hundred dollar bill. "It means if they've accepted any money, they may be prevented from playing college football."

"Oh," she said quietly. "I didn't know that."

"Why were you at the party, Jennifer?" I asked.

This question was either too specific or too personal for a half-naked girl to take sitting down, so she rose to her feet. "What's so wrong about being there anyway?" she asked. "They invited me."

"Why did they invite you?"

"I told you before, Daddy. Because they thought I was attractive. They said I looked like Eva Garner!"

"Ava Gardner."

"Why is that so hard for you to believe, anyway?" she said accusingly. Right before my eyes, she was transmogrifying, like Sally Field into a Sybil. "I happen to agree with them!" she said modestly. "I think I very much resemble Ava what's-her-name!"

"Maybe around the eyes and ears."

"How would you know! You never even look at me! Why don't you go ahead and give me a good look? I've got nothing to hide!" She tried to subtly, seductively cup her breasts in her hands, but her romantic gesture fell flat. "Go ahead, Daddy," she cried, "tell me your honest opinion! How do I look!"

As I watched her assume a provocative Playmate stance, I could see the tears begin to form in her eyes. I would rather have dropped dead on Broadway than to make my little girl cry, but there seemed to be nothing I could do about it. I was an iceberg and Jennifer was the Titanic; there was no way to avoid a collision.

"For Christ's sake, Daddy!" she said impatiently. "Is it really that hard for you to say something nice about your own daughter? Can't you at least say I'm sexy?"

"I'm prejudiced, Jennifer. It wouldn't mean much."

"It would to me!"

I gazed into her big, moist eyes. Blank. Sad. Soulful as a cow's. I wanted to kick in the wall between us, but I couldn't. "I'm sure to the boys of Marshall High, you're a regular Fay Wray," I said.

She shot me a nasty look. "I don't care one bit about the boys of Marshall High," she pressed. "I'm talking about you! I want to know your opinion! Compared to the girls you see up North, what do you think!"

"I think your values may be misplaced," I said. I could almost hear the egg shells cracking beneath my feet. She was reaching out to me in agony in the only way she knew how, and all I could do was hold her at bay. Too much time between us, too little anything else. I couldn't tell her she was graceless and self-conscious, with a makeup base you could land a plane on, and a coiffeur that looked as if it had just come out of the freezer. An absentee father hadn't the right.

"Just what is so wrong with me!" she cried. "I want to know! Why don't I look like Eva Garner!"

"You're pushing, honey," I told her. "Eva Garner might have thrown herself once in a while, but she never pushed."

Jennifer was stupefied. "You are such a smart-ass!" she cried. "You believe everybody in the family is a dumb and ignorant hick! Don't you?"

"No, I don't. I love my family—"

"You do no such thing! You hate us! And you know what, Daddy? I don't care! I wish I had never brought you that hundred dollar bill. It's Derek's property, and I wish to God I had never ratted on him. I feel like I betrayed him to a stranger!"

"You did the right thing."

"God, how I hate everything! I hate this lonely, deserted old house! Mother's always going somewhere, Derek's always practicing football or doing who knows what else now, and all you ever do, year after year, is work on that fucking *New York Times*!"

"Look, Electra—"

"Don't you *dare* call me that!" she screamed. "You don't have the right to call me that!"

"Sorry."

She was in a rage now, determined to make me pay for my negligence. "I used to believe you were the world and all," she said. "I used to defend you against everybody. But Derek is right, you know it? You *are* the worst father in the world! Honest to God, you care more about that career of yours than you care about your own fucking children!"

"Jennifer, you don't mean that—"

"I do mean it! And let me tell you something else," she sniffed. "You'd be surprised at what I mean! Real surprised!" She bore down on that last syllable as if it actually had meaning, then erupted into tears and dashed out of the room like a corporate secretary in the final stages of a stomach virus.

In the cold and lonely silence of my couch that night, I lay on my back and stared at the dismal ceiling and thought about my kids. At one time in the evening, I felt a powerful urge to get up, steal into the kitchen for a final meal and promptly cut my throat.

The next morning, I ate the crusty cupcake which was languishing like a hardened criminal in the refrigerator and drank some Folger-flavored water while I stared through a glaze at the shiny knobs on Nancy's stove. I would have had better luck crunching a hunk of coral reef, but since there was no one to complain to, I consumed what I could and got into my running clothes.

Even though I have long considered jogging a crime against nature, I still religiously do about five miles a day. I got into the rut because my face has an autonomous tendency to smile and running never fails to clear that up. It's tough enough being a Southerner in New York without risking life and limb by walking into Times Square every day wearing a smirk.

My only competition on the paths this day was a slender gray blur that zipped by me so fast, I figured it was either Voyager 2 or a Thomas. Ever since Dexter Mayfield toppled off a flatcar in 1868 and landed in what he thought was Marshall, Texas, there has been one Thomas or another darting in and out of the corporate limits. Other kids grow up and run away from home, the Thomases merely change direction. Back in the sixties, Harry Tolar Thomas jogged all the way from Mississippi to Massachusetts to run in the Boston Marathon, and if he hadn't forgotten to register, he would have officially come in first. Also sixty-eighth and two hundred-twenty-second.

Two blocks from the high school, I saw what at first looked like a Jaycees' carwash but turned out to be an array of law-enforcement vehicles spread over public streets and private lawns like bumper cars during a power failure. Each unit sat with a door open and an engine running squawking into the morning air with short wave static. At the same time, potbellied men in uniforms were milling about in pairs as if they were busily planning the next teddy bears' picnic.

Most of them were hanging around the superintendent's home, which was unusually small, mainly because dedicated people, according to Mom, should always live in Pigwiggen houses and wear locally-made clothes as an example to the rest of us. This one was a post war, single family dwelling with a four-pitch roof and a stratum of asbestos siding which had apparently been nailed on by an idiot in a hurricane. Except for all those wavy shingles and a broken screen door on the porch, it was a neat and orderly place.

As I stood catching my breath, a pair of freckled deputies lunged around the corner of the house dragging with them a screaming black boy in overalls. As they hauled him by his metal buttons toward a police unit, he moaned in a high-pitched voice—which Mrs. Barnes would have loved to get hold of—that he had never done nobody no harm, ever. But they crammed him into the back seat of the car anyway like a pimento into an olive and dashed off for the jail with the siren blowing.

With all this going on, I was able to slip up to the house to see what had happened. I wish I hadn't been able, for on the second step of the porch, I ran into the sickening sight of a big, red, half-wet stain on the gray concrete floor. It looked as if an ailing Holstein cow had backed up to a flat rock and pissed out two or three gallons of blood.

Before my stomach had a chance to turn, I was yanked off the porch by D.T. Bundley, the chief of police and a resident of the subdivision. Bundley was a short, chubby man in a dark gray uniform with a black Santa belt to hold the sawdust in. He had a mushy, featureless face with glassy buttons mashed into the flesh for eyes positioned at a 25 degree angle from each other. To talk to him, you had to tilt your head to prevent dizziness while trying to follow his train of thought.

"What're you doing here, Miller?" he snarled at me. "I heard you were in town."

"Who's been shot?" I asked.

"Not that it's any of your business," he answered, "but the guy who lives here got it from a pistol sometime last night. You know, the high school superintendent."

I tried to swallow, but couldn't. "Is he alive?" I asked.

"Are you kidding me? There ain't hardly enough left in there to autopsy." He plugged his thumbs into his belt and informed me that the TV crews from Hattiesburg and Jackson were on their way to Marshall right this minute. He would sure like to know what a man from the *New York Times* had to say about that little development.

I was so stunned by all this that all I could do was tell him that I had seen Richard Temple only yesterday not ten feet from where we were standing now. After waiting to see if there was more, Bundley wryly noted that well, he sure wouldn't be standing there anymore, would he? He boasted that the killer had been apprehended while returning to the scene of the crime, which, while that was trite and all, black killers tended to do for some reason.

"I heard him say he didn't do it," I pointed out numbly.

"What do you expect him to say? He's a retard. I'm just glad we got him before he started in on somebody else."

Bundley quickly drifted from the murder back to the more interesting subject of the TV crews, which according to the reports he was getting from the Mississippi Highway Patrol, were due any minute now. He told me that since he had to attend to several responsibilities related to that, he was going to have to ask me to move on. After all, he couldn't very well tolerate unauthorized personnel cluttering up the job site. "We got enough cops around here to do that ourselves," he said.

My attention was on the damaged screen door which was easier to look at than Bundley's eyes. Usually I avoid death like the plague, but there was something strangely alluring about that house at that moment. I didn't understand the attraction, unless it was that the idea of this happening in my hometown was so unbelievable, I had to go in and confirm it for myself. At any rate, I lied to D.T. and said that I was officially covering the story for the *Times*.

Although he didn't quite believe me, he backed off, and warned me not to track my feet through the evidence, if I could help it. As I stepped inside the screen door and tried to collect my disarranged emotions, I heard him charging his men to get themselves organized for a change. Television was coming soon, and there they were, standing around looking like a herd of thirsty moose before a rain.

The mostly-dried blood on the floor was turning brown in spots, and the porch had the depressing odor of a butcher shop. Steeling my nerves, I identified myself to the deputy posted at the front door of the house and crossed the threshold.

Half a dozen lab boys were scurrying about like hotel maids with baby dusters, checking for fingerprints on tables, chairs, and lamps, while two short guys were snapping Polaroids like Orientals at the opening of an A & P. In the claustrophobic living room, Coroner Randy Holman squatted on the blood-soaked rug next to the body in a blue nylon jacket-vest, a checkered shirt, and Tony Lama cowboy boots. He was a meaty, pinkish man with a pancake face and ears like dried apple slices. Although he owned the most comprehensive collection of guns in the county, he preferred to hunt deer and rabbits with nothing but a loin cloth, moccasins, and a bow which he solemnly called "The Only Weapon of World War IV." He was hovering over Temple's corpse like a lion over its prey.

The body was an unholy mess, a badly mangled clump of lacerated muscles, shattered bones, and striped pajamas. Even though Richard Temple's exploded face had been pulverized with fragments of wire screen from the door, I could still make out from the one remaining open eye part of his likeness in the carnage. It was as though he was peeping at me from around a side of hanging beef. When a heavy feeling of nausea gripped my insides, I had to turn my face away.

Fortunately, there was Randy Holman to focus on, busily telling his tape recorder that the subject in question had received a total of five gunshot wounds from a .45 caliber handgun. The first projectile had struck the mandible and travelled through the maxilla into the paranasal cavities. The second one hit the sternum, the third the heart. A fourth had entered the abdomen just below the umbilicus, while the last had impacted the penis and scrotum at point-blank range, which, in his professional opinion, would have rendered the subject fairly useless, even if he had lived to talk about the other four.

After he clicked off the recorder, Holman pitched it to his assistant, a dapper twenty-year-old brimming with the excitement of it all. He seemed to treasure beyond words the very recorder Holman had thrown his way.

"How's it going there, Ted?" Randy greeted me with a handshake with a trace of blood on the fingernails.

I wiped my palm on my sweat pants. "Going great," I said.

Holman made a backstroke motion at his assistant. "You might as well go ahead and clean this shit up," he ordered. While the assistant hustled off for a body bag, Holman sighed at the flesh and blood on the floor and expressed his regret over the murderer's choice of weapons. "Real messy, isn't it?" he said. "It's a wonder he didn't blow up the whole house. What he should've used was a Walther P-38 with a double action trigger. I got six I could have lent him myself. Of course, a .45 revolver obviously will do the job."

I waited until he was through with the weaponry lecture to ask him how he happened to know the order of the shots.

"Simple deduction," he answered smugly. "The trajectory of the mug shot indicates it was fired from a position lower than that of the victim."

"From the yard up to the porch."

"Or a lower step. It shapes up like this to me: Temple crawls out of bed and comes to the door, and gets shot in the face, through the screen. When he falls back, the killer hops on the porch and pops off one for the heart, only hits the gut. The impact of the second shot sends Temple in here, where he is now. Then the killer calmly pumps a slug into the heart to make sure."

"You mentioned two other hits."

"Who knows? He was probably just making sure. Or it could be he was getting a kick out of what he was doing. We get them like that, sometimes."

"What about the sixth shot?"

He pulled a wrinkled hanky out of his vest and

wiped his hands with it. "How do you know there was a sixth shot?" he asked suspiciously.

"Simple deduction," I said. "If I remember my Roy Rogers, a revolver has six shots."

After scrubbing a stubborn spot of blood on his wrist with a corner of the handkerchief, he admitted there had been such a shot. He pointed at a hole in the oak strips, six feet from the corpse, then wiped his forehead with the handkerchief, like Louis Armstrong on a humid night. "Last one was a miss," he said.

A minute later, Bundley was back in the house ordering the assistant to hurry up and get the body in the bag, if the lab boys were through with it. "We want to haul her out as soon as they start the cameras," he said. "It ain't gonna look all that authentic otherwise."

Suddenly, I felt wheezy and unsteady on my feet. The air felt thick and smelled like vomit. Like a slaughterhouse.

Bundley was tickled by my pale, Yankee looks. "What's the matter there, hotshot?" he teased. "I thought you New Yorkers were used to homicides."

"I don't make that many," I said.

He chuckled. "I never would have guessed," he said.

After I lost the cupcake in the gutter, I felt better, but knew I should eat something solid soon. It was clear to me that Louise's Cafe on Main Street wasn't the place to do that when I noticed Mom's favorite cookbook resting on the shelf above the coffee urn, but since it was the only restaurant open that early, I took my chances and went in.

The dingy little place was the size of a service station john, with a beer and french fries air that hadn't been let out in years, and Old South murals on three of the walls, as bleak and faded as the past they portrayed. Under "John Brown's Uprising," the gray Formica counter stretched ten yards wide with vinyl stools so low and close, a girl would have to break her hymen to sit at one. Two older men were sitting spread eagled there now with fixed expressions of agony on their faces either from having to endure the childbirth positions or from having recently swallowed some of Louise's cooking.

The older, scraggly man in the drooping business suit was Mr. Thaddeus D. O'Ryan, who Dad claims was not only the first commercial catfish farmer in Mississippi, but the only one in America to have developed a successful strain of albino mudcats, which he called Paleskins. Dad's view is that O'Ryan would have amassed a fortune from this hybrid, if only the fishes hadn't looked so much like newborn babies that black people wouldn't go anywhere near them and white liberals from Alabama and Tennessee kept getting in the way trying to adopt them.

O'Ryan was wearing a hand-painted silk tie that consisted of a huge scene of Oahu Island, Hawaii. It was furled like a state flag and tied at the throat in a knot as big as a pillow. It's seldom you get to see a tie of that breadth anymore. It was so wide when he unbuttoned his coat, you got a view of not only Oahu, but all the other islands too, plus the Equinoctial Line and the shores of Japan. At one time Uncle Harley could have used that tie for a door.

The other customer was surly Willard Hume, a

husky fix-it man who many years ago had lost one of his opposable thumbs at an Easter egg hunt at Percy Quinn State Park. Exactly how that happened, he never said, but his guardian agreed with Dr. Hollander that since the boy had obviously been sticking his hand where it ought never to have been, perhaps he'd just better learn to live with the handicap and be the better for it. As it turned out, Willard grew up to become an ornery, restless sort who was usually so caught up on his work he wasn't looking for anymore and who very likely would have left Marshall years before, if he had only had a thumb to hitchhike with. He wheeled around on his toadstool and stared at me, evidently hoping I was bringing in something he could object to.

I ignored him and took a seat in one of the Tilt-a-Whirl booths and opened up the laminated menu. On the front page was an impressionistic drawing of the railroad depot which had withered into a ruin twenty years ago when all the trains had gotten together and agreed not to stop in Marshall any more. Faded gothic letters between the depot and the tracks said:

> *Welcome to Louise's Cafe.*
> *Serving Marshall with the*
> *same fine food since 1936.*

From what I could see around me, I had no reason to doubt the word of the menu.

The graying brunette waitress with a lively spring in her walk and a twinkle in her eye spurted so quickly toward me with a glass of water, I wondered if something wasn't on fire. She stopped abruptly and spread a paper napkin before me as if she were hoping I would sign it for her.

"Morning!" she said cheerfully. "What'll it be?"

"Coffee," I said.

"Want the stale now or the fresh later?"

"Anything."

She started to write "Anyth—" on her *Thank You!* pad then erased the letters carefully and wrote "Coffee" instead. "Say, you wouldn't be Mrs. Miller's boy, would you?" she asked. "The one that went off to Pakistan or somewhere to get rich in oil?"

"I'm the one in sports."

She flicked the erasure crumbs off the pad with the backs of her red-painted nails. "Then you must be the quarterback, right?"

"Used to be," I said.

She smiled warmly at me. "Looks like you've already heard about the murder over at the school," she said.

I nodded my head.

"Better get you the stale," she said. She tucked the pad into the pocket of her starched apron and hustled over to the counter, observing to herself how strange it was that murders always occurred when decent folks were asleep.

I buried my head in my hands and tried very hard to shape up.

While I was warming my fingers on the cup of coffee she brought, Tobie Mayer, a squat little orderly at Travis Memorial, burst into the cafe in such close-fitting white clothes he looked like a giant roll of Charmin. He announced in a shrill voice to all that would listen that he'd been following this murder very closely because he had been wounded in that area himself once, and thus understood exactly how the victim must have felt.

Actually, Mayer had been shot six inches below the navel with a .22 hollow point by his adopted brother So Lin in an argument over whose turn it was to go out into the cold and prime the pump. Picked up off a rare snowfall and rushed to Travis Memorial by Mr. Alton Hinds, who was supposed to be delivering milk in another county at the time, Tobie came out of the crisis with his life intact, but with his pubic area shaven clean by Mr. Haywood Phillips, the barber, who happened to be in the bed next to Tobie with colon trouble and needed the practice to keep his hand in. Unfortunately, for some reason, Mayer's manly tuft never grew back, which made him reconsider his lifelong dream of becoming a male dancer on the road. He didn't figure he could do anything nearly that bold now that he was different from other men. It was dangerous enough to go hopping around a stage in tights like a girl without being as smooth as a balloon to boot where it really counted. With his mind set, Tobie went to the principal, with the idea of being exempted from all physical education which required any form of full frontal nudity.

Mr. Floyd considered this request to be embarrassing to say the least, not to mention unwise. He thought Tobie looked pretty healthy, and while he nervously rattled his change, he told the boy right out that he considered him to be actually pretty fit for such a little tyke. He could easily see him going on to lead a perfectly normal life as a jockey, maybe, or one of the people who worked on those tiny foreign cars. "But, er-uh, in order to succeed in this man's world," he advised, "you've got to participate in various team activities, and take your showers with the other guys."

"But you don't understand, Mr. Floyd," he cried. "I've been plucked!"

"Er-uh, now wait a minute there, boy—"

"But it's true! I was shot up like a deer by my brother So Lin, and they laid me on the bed and plucked me clean!"

As soon as Tobie launched into the details of the situation, Mr. Floyd silently went rummaging through his files for a medical exemption form to get himself off the hook. Settling on one that looked right enough, he hurriedly wrote under "Reason for Being Unable to Participate" the words, "Shot and plucked," which was all he could think of under the circumstances. Then he thrust it at Mayer and begged him to tell no one where he happened to get it.

The next day, Coach Higgins promptly returned the form to Mr. Floyd with a note attached: "What in your life or mine does 'Shot and plucked' mean? Who's this cutting my class anyway, a man or a duck?" After an asterisk, he added: "I demand a pow-wow."

Two weeks later, Mr. Floyd called for a meeting with the coach along with Miss Alice Cross, the guidance counselor who had hoped to enroll Tobie in a small junior college, and a representative of a rival class-ring manufacturer who had been requesting an equal-time audience with the school administration for seven years. While they conferred on the Mayer business and drew up a statement advocating freedom of choice in the selection of class rings, Tobie dropped out of school and took up a career as an orderly with a five-year mission to straighten out the place that had ruined his life.

He had been there ever since.

Tobie plunked down a quarter, ordered a shot of Donald Duck orange juice, and worked his stout legs into a split that would accommodate the counter. In the grip of suspense, the others sat like draftees awaiting a short-arm inspection until Mayer again broached the subject of the murder of Richard Temple.

"Boy, talk about your gross sights!" he gasped. "Mr. Temple came into E.R. looking like a hog hanging from a tree in November!"

"Well, I reckon that makes two of 'em," O'Ryan noted with a pair of fingers.

"Sir?" Tobie said.

"Death always comes in threes," Thaddeus explained. "It's just like women going to the restroom. Always in threes. First there's Freddie what's-his-name in my pond, now here's this school fella in his own damn home. Who's gonna be next, is what I'm wondering?"

Willard Hume rubbed his chin with his thumb nub. "Didn't they arrest the guy who did it?" he asked.

"It was the colored boy that used to work around the school," Tobie answered. "They say Mr. Temple fired him because he tried to get friendly with his daughter."

Hume sneered. "Can't see why even a colored boy'd want to get friendly with a gal that homely. She must be adopted, huh?"

"I don't know if she's adopted, but what happened was the colored boy come back and shot Mr. Temple right where it counts."

"Well, good riddance, I say," Hume declared. His

opinion was that this egghead had been asking for it from the start, the way he kept throwing around his liberal notions, trying to turn Marshall High into a little Harvard or Yale. "You think this state needs another hotbed like that?" he challenged the others. "No sir!"

"But why would he shoot him below the navel?" Tobie asked. "Why do people do that?"

Hume didn't particularly care where he was shot. "Remember the day Temple took over the school?" he said. "The bastard took out all the old desks and burned them behind the Ag building. Call that responsible behavior? Hell, some of those desks had my own name carved in them!"

"I figure Sarah Huddleston will be the next to go," O'Ryan said. "Of course, Sarah is a widow woman, and widows are tougher to kill than the mange."

"You guys want to know what a woman thinks about it?" the waitress offered.

"Not hardly," Hume told her. "Murder's man business."

But the waitress insisted. "I don't think he did it!" she said. "It doesn't make sense. What colored boy would shoot a white man in his own home? Even if he did, he'd never open the door and go inside the house and shoot him again!"

Hume stirred on his stool and wiped his nub across his burly chest. He was as suspicious of cold logic as he was cold women. "I'm just saying they should never have hired him," he maintained.

The waitress pointed her pencil at Hume. "You'll see what I'm talking about when they locate the gun," she said. "Ballistics will prove he's innocent."

" 'Ballistics,' bull. There won't even be a gun," he grunted. "Nobody keeps a murder weapon anymore."

"So what do you figure a retarded boy's going to do with it, Willard? Hide it in his tinker toys? Stick it in his rear end?"

"I figure he dropped it down an abandoned well," Willard said.

"And where in the name of heaven would he find an abandoned well?"

"Hell, I don't know. That's his problem!"

"Oh, for God's sake!" she exclaimed. "You men wouldn't have enough sense to go to the potty, if a woman hadn't taught you how!"

Tobie was now gazing upon the waitress as a true madonna figure close to nature with all the answers. "Do you know why he shot him where he did?" he asked her.

"It's simple, hon. Whoever shot him was getting him back for some evil deed he'd done with that thing."

"Ma'am?"

"It's perfectly obvious, Tobie. The person who killed Mr. Temple was a woman!"

"Really?"

Hume let out a groan. "Now that's just sick," he declared.

"Why? You said he deserved it, didn't you?"

"He deserved it all right, but not because of what he done to some woman!"

As they went on, so did I, with no more taste for any more details of murder than I had for the Louise's coffee in my cup.

I was surprised to walk into Nan's and find my censorious daughter tearing toward me like an appliance salesman in a financial recession. It was as if I'd just agreed to a convenient purchase plan, the way she flung her body and clothes against me and squeezed with a wild and unsettling passion.

"Hi," I said. I felt like a game show host being mauled by a contestant.

But this one wasn't happy. "Oh, Daddy, isn't it awful!" she cried. "They've got the school all roped off and everything! They even gave us a holiday!"

As soon as I was able to worm my way out of the half nelson, I escaped to the living room. While Jennifer reamed out her purple eye sockets with her thumbs, I picked up my suitcase and lugged it into the bathroom. When I came out in a tweed coat and dark slacks ten minutes later, she looked at me as if I had been plowing up a grave. "You're not going away!" she whined.

I grabbed my leather attaché from the coffee table. "With all this going on," I said, "I thought I'd hang around Hattiesburg until the TV show."

"But why? I don't understand."

I zipped the case as she came toward me. She was wearing an entire fall collection of sweaters, vests, blouses, pants—enough to outfit a guerrilla army. Her hair was different today covering a wider area than before. It looked as if it had been yanked on for a week by the third grade. "I don't like it here," I told her.

"You mean, you don't like us."

"It's not you, honey. It's this place."

"You mean you're leaving because it's a duplex? That old business again?"

"I mean the town, Jennifer."

She unsheathed a fingernail and attempted to penetrate her makeup down to the source of an itch, but she couldn't quite manage it. All she did was to leave a scar on the finish. "In other words," she said, "you're going to run away. Just like you always do."

Although that hit me like a Gooden fastball in the nose, I kept calm. "Where's Derek?" I asked her.

She used the nail to scratch at one of her garments, testing for some indication of life underneath, I guess. Again apparently unsuccessful. "They're having a skull session in the gym," she told me. "Coach didn't want them to get all upset over what happened to Mr. Temple."

"Coach is considerate."

Jennifer seemed worried. "Daddy," she said, "what am I supposed to do about the guy who called a while ago?"

"What guy?"

She shrugged her shoulders. "Some older man. He said you'd know who he was."

"I wonder if I would?"

"Sir?"

"Did he happen to mention who he was?"

"Yes, but it was a real stupid name, I thought. Mr. Magoo or somebody."

"How about Agnew?"

"Maybe," she allowed. When she sensed my impatience, she defended herself. "How come I'm supposed to remember his name, if you already know it?" she asked. "It was for you, after all, not me!"

Searing logic like that I couldn't contest. After

debating a minute on whether to leave or stay, I flung the attaché on the sofa, snapped up the phone, and called the number of the managing editor of the *Times*. I didn't look forward to talking to him. My boss Jason Holmes let me go my way, but Sam Agnew, the Great Developer, considered me a negative which had not yet been properly developed. This ex-pro basketball player (six years in the NBA) kept a close eye on the sports department and delighted in reminding me that I had never explored my potential. I had never committed myself to my talent was the way he put it. In that husky, Andy Devine voice which always needed clearing, he asked me casually what I was doing in Mississippi.

"Losing weight, mostly," I told him.

"Is that right? Maybe I should've gone down there with you."

"That would've been fun."

After this dose of small talk, he abruptly switched to his business tone and his voice smoothed out a bit. "Ted," he began, "I'll put it to you straight. Jason and I are agreed on this: we want you to cover this school superintendent's murder."

"I'm in sports, Sam," I reminded him.

"I know what you're in, Ted. What I'm telling you is, this is damn good material. 'Educator blown apart in a Southern town famous for its football team,'" he said in headlines. "Has a lot of appeal. Sounds to me like a splendid opportunity for you to develop your potential and break into hard news."

"I'm not sure I like hard news."

His voice was settling like cement. "This can be explosive stuff, Ted," he said. "And damned important. Am I right that the sixteen-year-old boy who's been arrested is black?"

"You're right."

"Do you think he did it?"

"Doubt it."

"Then you must believe the police down there will conduct a thorough and unbiased investigation until they uncover the real murderer?"

"Not likely."

"So why are you sitting on your butt, Miller?"

"I'm not sitting on it. I'm about to take it to Hattiesburg for a TV show."

"What about your obligation as a reporter for the *Times?*" he said indignantly.

"Come on, Sam."

"This could be a hell of a story for you, Ted," he predicted. His words chilled me to the soul for they were exactly the same Richard Temple had said to me the day before. "Listen to me," he said. "This is a chance to wrap around a sensational crime a lot of important issues we've all been guilty of neglecting lately. Like, what's it like down there, these days? What's happened to all the social tension of the sixties? Is there still a dangerous polarity of the races? Or is the South now a *Dallas,* all white and rich and sleazy? I need you on this, Ted."

"You need Bertrand Russell, Sam."

Agnew paused for breath, then tried another tack. "Don't forget these are your people, Ted," he said. "And that means you are uniquely qualified to write a story that can knock this country flat on its complacency. I really don't see how you can pass it up!"

"It's not my field!" I said flatly.

But he was undaunted. He told me I was a literary coward who had never been able to face who he was or where he had come from. "Tell me," he said, "when are you going to look yourself square in the face, for once? When are you going to stop trying to escape your roots!"

I turned away from the tree analogy to Jennifer, who was busy counting her clothes on the sofa. I had to admit that the same idea coming from such different sources as Electra and Agnew must have some truth in it. That was a reporter's creed after all. Maybe they were right. Maybe instead of staying away all those years, I had been running away.

"I realize you've done a fine job on drug abuse and recruiting violations, but tell me," he said, "do you have the guts to face a few grisly facts about your own background?"

I had to struggle with that and ask myself how many times I could keep letting my children down. But the background seemed so close, I resisted.

"Are you listening, Miller?" Agnew pressed.

"I'm listening," I told him. But what I was really hearing were Temple's words to me. And Jennifer's. And Nancy's.

"I don't believe in pushing any man, Miller," he said, "but if you refuse to do a story for which Holmes and I believe you are perfectly suited, then we are obviously wrong about your qualifications."

"In other words, either I do it, or I go back to writing up the box scores of the Mets games."

"I'm not saying that. I'm just asking you to tell me yea or nay, Miller. I've got other things to do."

I kept staring at my daughter. She sat sniffing into a handkerchief, with her knees curled against her chest, looking so small and vulnerable, I wanted to hang up the phone and take her into my arms. But I knew I couldn't. There was too great a vacuum between us. I had resisted my children so long there wasn't enough between us to cling to.

"I'm waiting for an answer, Ted," Agnew said.

"I know."

"All right, I'll send Dave Holdenburg down there—"

"Never mind. I'll do it."

"That's more like it."

"I wonder."

"I know what kind of job you can do with this, Ted," Agnew said. "Just keep it personal and objective. Dig down to the roots and pull them out if you have to. Even if they turn out to be yours."

"I'm looking forward to it."

"Who do you want for the stills?"

"Nobody. I'll do them myself."

"Fine. Just send us some copy soon. And look: thanks, Ted. Rest assured, you won't regret it."

Hanging up the phone feeling as though I had just been squeezed through Aunt Reba's wringer washer, I took a step toward Jennifer. "If you have any more clothes to put on," I told her, "do it, and let's go."

She eyed me suspiciously. "Do you mean you're staying?"

"Long enough to eat, anyway."

She cocked her head. "Just you and me?" she said.

I headed for the door. "We'll give it a try," I said.

After I rented a Thunderbird in McComb, Jennifer and I attended a McDonald's where I punched holes in my styrofoam burger package while she wolfed down two fistfuls of cheeseburger and a hefty order of fries. Even surrounded by the smell of mayonnaise, a hundred percent beef, and Lysol Spray, my daughter transmitted all the fragrances of a national beauty pageant. She must have been wearing a dozen or so layers of perfume to match the makeup and clothes.

While she ate, I gazed out the window at five or six kids strangling each other on the Ronald McDonald playground equipment outside and tried to get myself organized. Although I was afraid of what I would find in an investigation of Richard Temple, I was committed to doing it. The circumstances of the murder were curious and compelling, but at the same time, I was plenty leery of tripping over my roots. I kept feeling that I would soon be ripping up bits and pieces of my own past.

Following the gulp of the final fry, Jennifer stared at my half-eaten quarter-pounder, with all the pity of a social worker beholding a starving child. "Aren't you going to eat any more of that?" she asked me.

"I was saving it for the Chinese."

Like a hammerhead shark after bait, she lunged across the table for the food.

"I would've thrown it to you," I told her.

She arched her eyebrows over the chunk of burger which was momentarily stuck in her painted cheeks. "Do what?" she said.

"How often do you have meals, Jennifer?" I asked.

"Just as often as they come," she answered confidently and chewed happily away.

"It's a wonder you're not a heavy child," I observed.

"Oh, believe me, I would be, if I didn't make myself throw up every once in a while."

I winced. "Do you think Eva Garner ever fingered her gullet in order to flip her food?"

After seriously considering my question, she stuffed in another segment of beef. "How would I know?" she said. "It's not like I studied her in class or anything."

"I suppose it's enough to look like her."

"It is for me." In a series of hectic pants, she demolished the rest of the burger, then wiped her hands on the paper napkins and brushed her teeth thoroughly with her tongue. I counted myself lucky she didn't lean back in her chair and belch a few times to put an end to it.

"Good, huh?" I said.

"It was okay."

"Could've fooled me."

"I prefer sweets, actually," she confided and scanned the McDonald's for possible supplements. "Do you think I could have an apple tart?" she asked me.

"No."

"Why not?"

"I wonder if you could forget about the fodder for a minute and answer some questions for me."

"Maybe. If they're not too hard. Actually, I'm not really all that good with questions and stuff. As you know."

"You might be able to handle these."

"Okay, then, shoot! Oh, Jesus, I'm sorry! How could I have said such a thing! God, it's just so unbelievable, Daddy. What happened to poor Mr. Temple!"

I allowed her some time to conquer her grief and remorse and recover her natural poise before I asked her how a man as dedicated as Richard Temple could be so unpopular with the crowd at Louise's. After a few slurps of her Coke, she guessed that I must have run into some pretty ancient people because the older folks were always the ones that hated him.

"Why was that?" I asked.

"I don't know." She squinted her eyes as she scouted the tables around us for fugitive burgers. "Maybe because he's so sexy," she said. "Oh, Lord, I mean 'was'. It's so awful, I can't get used to it!"

"By 'sexy,' you mean he fooled around."

She found that worth a chuckle. "Honestly, Daddy," she moaned condescendingly. "You're as bad as Aunt Amy. Nobody says 'fooled around' any more. Sounds like an old dictionary or something. Say, 'He had sex.'"

When I staunchly refused to repeat after her, she resumed her search for forage. As soon as she sighted a handsome middle-aged man in a business suit, she began to suck on her straw provocatively and flutter a pair of Lolita eyes at him as he carted a load of fast food and cardboard clowns out to the chimpanzees on the playground equipment.

"Did Temple fool around," I said stubbornly, "with anybody in particular?"

"Of course," she said and gave me her full attention, for a change. "I know all about stuff like this. Take Miss Douglas, for instance."

"Who's she?"

Jennifer had to work on that one for a minute. "I guess she must have been his secretary or something,

Daddy," she concluded. "I know she had this desk right outside his office, and she was always carrying these file folders and things around."

"Let's be wild and say that was what she was."

"Well, anyway, the important thing is, she fell like a ton of you-know-what for Mr. Temple. Hook, line, and sinker. They say she was carrying his child when she took off with that truck driver to Iowa or wherever it was. I know it was one of those states that start with an 'I.'"

"Who else?"

"Well, there's Mrs. Trager. Jesus, was that a case! All Mr. Temple had to do is open his mouth and Mrs. Trager would cream in her pants. And her a married woman, too. It was funny, really. If you just said his name to her, she'd get all hot and flushed and go up on her lines and everything."

"You mean she was an actress?"

"No, Daddy, honestly. Where's anybody going to act around here? This is not New *York*, you know. Mrs. Trager was the home ec teacher."

"Ah."

"She was a good one, too, before she decided to go back to school for some more degrees and what-not. All I know about homemaking, I owe to her."

I let that one pass. "Give me another name," I said.

She gave me a curious look, instead. "Don't you think this is kinda morbid?" she said. "I mean, here we are, sitting around this place not even eating, talking about a man who's not even in his grave yet!"

"I'm not too crazy about it myself."

"You're not really going to write about all those

women Mr. Temple screwed, are you?"

"I'm just digging at the roots," I said. I could have told her I was following a lead provided by a waitress, but I wanted her to know as little as possible about what I was doing. Fortunately, that wasn't hard to do with my daughter.

"I'm glad you're not going to expose anybody," she said. "Because it just so happens, one of Mr. Temple's ladies is one of your old haunts."

"One of my old flames," I corrected.

"I'll make a deal with you," she said. "I'll tell you who she is, if you'll buy me an apple tart."

"No deal."

"Please?"

"You've had enough. Who was it?"

She dumped a load of suck-cleaned crushed ice between her gums and ground away at it. I could see she was endeavoring to show with exaggerated facial movements just how inferior in taste the ice was to the tart. But I held my ground. "I'm talking about Mrs. Henderson," she finally announced in frustration and grimly contracted her throat with the cold of the ice. You'd have thought she was a pelican swallowing her young.

For some reason, the name didn't surprise me. Bubba's wife. Now it made sense that Marian had chosen not to come to the reception at the gym.

"I'll bet you didn't expect to hear that!" she teased. "Mother says you went out with her a lot."

"I went out with her four times, if you count the field trip to the Esso plant."

"Well? Did you have any luck?"

"Not at the Esso plant, no."

"Well, Mr. Temple sure did, I can tell you that. They say he loved Mrs. Henderson best of all. Which was real strange, Daddy. I mean, she's not exactly gorgeous or anything, and she has these real tiny bosoms. Jesus! All this stuff is really making me nervous, you know it? Can't I please have something to eat?"

"I never pay my sources, Jennifer."

"Jesus. What kind of father are you?"

"I wonder if, amidst all this adoring gossip about Mr. Temple, you ever heard of his being involved in gambling?"

She clamped down on some more ice, to show further disapproval. But in spite of her defiance, she was interested in the question. "You mean gambling like in cards and stuff? Like strip poker in the rec room?"

Strip poker. Now there was Electra's game. No losing streak could last long enough to get this girl through all those layers to her undies.

"More like football," I told her.

"Oh. Well, I do know Derek says Mr. Temple didn't even like football. He went to some hick college or other where they didn't even play it. In one of those states that starts with an 'I' again. There really are a lot of them that start with an 'I.'"

Having had enough food and information for a while, I rose to my feet and picked up my tray. "Do you have a good camera, by the way?" I asked her.

She took a shot at being seductive again. Missed it by a mile. "What'd you have in mind?" she cooed.

"Thought I'd take some pictures."

"Of me?"

"Sorry. Business before pleasure. Come on, I'm taking you home. I've got some work to do."

"What about my apple tart?"

"They look like they'll keep."

I emptied my refuse into the plastic trash can, deposited my tray on top of a stack, and headed out to the Thunderbird. When Jennifer showed up at the car a few minutes later, she was feeding on a confection of sugar, crust, and gooey fried apples paid for, presumably by her own allowance.

After I left my teenage gourmet at the duplex, I bought a Minolta 35mm camera at the drug store, took a few shots of the school and Temple's house and drove the Thunderbird to Stanley Haymon Ford Co., to talk to Bubba. In the shadow of a magnolia tree across the street from the car lot, I waited while he craftily talked a toothless farmer and his shy wife into a previously-owned F-100 truck with gumbo mudders, a C.B., and no bumper. Watching him blithely cut through their grass-roots resistance depressed me so much, I felt an urge to head straight toward Hattiesburg and Judy Moon. But after taking out Derek's one hundred dollar bill and staring at the picture of Franklin for a while, I was able to keep from doing it. This time I was determined not to run away.

The Ford dealership on Elm Street was located on the perimeter of the black section of town called Nairobi and consisted of about twenty-five new cars and twice that many used. The business was begun after the war by Stanley J. Haymon, who was what was then called a closet homosexual, who was always driving up and down Main Street in brand new demonstrators, hopelessly trying to ferret out prospects for the evening. He usually rode with the dome light on to emphasize what he considered his best asset, a black toupee made with his own hair and as thick as one of Mom's pancakes.

Since Stanley Haymon was not an aggressive man, all you had to do to get along with him was put up with a little casual bawdy conversation about things such as tap-dancing naked on top of a glass table with him underneath, or climbing on top of the grand piano in the formal parlor and squeezing chlorophyll toothpaste into places it didn't ordinarily go.

The most he ever did was to waft you off to Magic Casements, his one-bedroom house on Blueberry Hill, where he'd serve you some hot Postum, sit down with you on his floral Danish modern sofa, and discuss some of the prevailing issues of the day such as bomb shelters, individual expression, and Spanish fly. Whenever he felt particularly bold, he would slink over to the parlor closet, fling it open, and whip aside a row of clothes to reveal an iron pair of nude Greek wrestlers fastened securely to the back wall with impressive erections serving as hat hooks for a couple of New Orleans Pelicans baseball caps. "This one's resting on its Laurel," he would announce and flip away the first cap. "And this one's on a Hardy!" Once he stopped laughing at his joke, he'd ask you if you liked upright wrestling or pancratium the best. The trick was to say you had violently straddled a plow once in your formative years and didn't care much for either as a result, and

Stanley would go back into the kitchen for another round of Postum.

Stanley Haymon was a good person, but everybody was so concerned with figuring out the right way to react to him, they never noticed.

With my heart caught in my throat like a crabapple, I wandered behind the dealership to the shop where Bubba, having shoveled off the farmer, was now overseeing the detailing of a half-dozen white, gray, and black used Lincoln Mark VII's. As soon as he recognized me, he hurried across the oily cement, shook my hand like a salesman during Closeout Days, slapped me on the back, and informed me that for a Yankee, I was looking real good these days. When he noticed I was interested in the chubby Italian who was running back the odometer on one of the Marks, he chuckled and assured me that this sort of thing was standard operating procedure in the car business.

"Technically illegal, but no big deal," he said.

While the Italian bumped his big nose on the dashboard and fumbled with a 007-type machine in a brown leather case, a black boy in Lee overalls pried a Metairie, Louisiana, dealer shield off a trunk lid with terrific care as if he were defusing a nuclear device in a Penney's store.

To spare me from the banalities of the used car business, Bubba led me past the cashier's office into a showroom larger than the parking lot outside, then down the hall to Stanley Haymon's old office, where he offered me a doughnut that was as big and hard as a lawn mower tire, and coffee that had been brewing on a scuffed-up old table since Reconstruction.

"Thanks," I said, turning down the pastry but taking a chance on the coffee.

Bubba straightened up in his swivel chair and showed me the proper way to stretch and breathe from a sitting position and survive. Then, as casually as he could, he asked me what I was up to. "You wouldn't be trying to get the game cancelled because of this killing, would you?" he asked.

"Wouldn't think of it," I told him. A single reckless swig of that coffee left a precious layer of my tongue in the cup. Why didn't I find a burning fireplace and lick the chimney clean and be done with it?

"Rotten thing, Temple getting shot like that," Bubba said. "But that game's the biggest thing to ever hit this town. I sure hope nobody's going to try dickering with it."

"I'm not much on dickering, Bubba," I told him.

He pulled out his display handkerchief and re-stuffed it into his coat pocket while I slyly got rid of the styrofoam cup in the waste can. "Just because that colored boy goes and does something stupid," he said, "is no reason the rest of us have to stop living."

"You think he did it?"

The handkerchief taken care of, he commenced to play with the top of the desk with his manicured fingernails. It made such a racket, he had to know he was doing it. Even without a Cyrena hanging on him like a barnacle, my old friend was no more delightful now than he had been at the gym. What I was looking at was an inflated, plastered-over, re-issued version of him.

"Makes no difference to me whether he did it or not," he said.

"Why doesn't it?" I said. "It made a difference with Sonya Penski." Not very subtle, but classier than ramming my knuckles into his face.

Bubba infuriated me when he casually brushed aside our mutual past. "We were young and ignorant in those days." he said. "I thought I was going to be a lawyer. But how many law degrees do you see on this wall, here?"

There was nothing special on his wall but three Ford sales citations, a Jaycee's certificate, an award for shop safety for a thousand years or so without a single boo-boo, and a faded color picture of Stanley Haymon himself, in his Mark VII-shaded toupee, handing over the keys to the dealership to J. B. Henderson. He was holding them away from his body as if he had a couple of nasty mice by the tail.

"You don't need law degrees to be sympathetic," I told him. I knew I was being pompous and self-righteous, but I didn't care. I was so annoyed with him, I couldn't help it.

Bubba cocked his head, still trying to figure out why I was there. But I was enjoying letting him squirm. I let him guess. While we sat there eyeing each other suspiciously, a twenty-year-old girl with enough hair to stuff a library chair stuck most of it into the office door and announced that "Mr. Ames" was on the phone. It might have been another Ford citation, the way Bubba instantly popped up from his seat. "I'll take it down the hall," he said and hurried off.

Trapped within the confines of Bubba's office, I sat

and listened to the old Sunbeam coffee pot which hissed and growled like a restless spirit offering to come out from behind the veil. Maybe it was Stanley Haymon trying to make contact with someone, the way he never had in real life. Or the other residents of the duplex, finally agreeing amongst themselves to reach out and touch someone. While I waited for a clearer sign, I stared at the lighted button on Bubba's phone and considered picking up the receiver. But I couldn't do it. I couldn't violate his privacy that way. As angry as I was, I still respected him.

I was sighing wistfully over the oak-framed Olan Mills portrait of Bubba and his blushing Marian when he came back from his phone call with Mr. Ames.

"Now I see what you're up to," he said sourly.

"What?" I said, replacing the picture on the desk.

Bubba gritted his teeth unattractively. "You're wondering if you can pin this on me, aren't you? Damn Yankee. You heard Temple was banging my wife, so you figured I just might have gone gunning for the son of a bitch!"

"Is that what you did?"

"Screw you, Miller," he snarled and swept past me to the desk. Grunting like an old sow, he whipped open the top drawer and rooted out a Tampa Nugget.

I hoped he couldn't see the two or three tears I was attempting to blink away. I've always considered it a waste of time to let yourself become disappointed with people at every turn, and yet there I was, desperately trying to think of a way to change this crass J.B. back into my old friend Bubba. What I should have done was to turn around and walk out of Haymon Ford right then and head toward Hattiesburg. But I didn't.

I couldn't.

"But Temple was having sex with Marian?" I said. I used Jennifer's modern phraseology so there would be no mistake about it.

After peeling the cellophane off the Tampa Nugget, Bubba puckered up and shoved the stogie straight into his round face and fired it up with a paper match. As he puffed and spewed the smoke my way, he leaned back and tried to look lean and philosophical like Robinson Jeffers. He was more like Mr. Toad of Toad Hall. "She left me and moved to the Medallion Apartments," he said. "I reckon that was their little pig sty."

The cold, sneering way he said that made my flesh crawl. While it shouldn't have mattered to me whether Marian was training to be a Mother Superior or screwing a Mack Truck on weekends, somehow it did. "What happened between you two?" I asked.

Bubba quietly thumped his cigar on the edge of a glass Haymon Ford ashtray, appeared to be about to spit, then swallowed hard. "It was all pretty damn sordid, Ted," he told me and curled his lip to show just how damn sordid. "She got all messed up because she couldn't give me any kids. Even started liking girls, if you can believe that. The bitch. After all I gave her."

"I wonder what she saw in Temple?" I led him.

He didn't follow. "Who knows?" he said. "Screw them both. As far as I'm concerned, he was welcome to her. I couldn't've cared less who it was, plugging her."

"Any old finger in the dyke, huh?"

He glared at me through the smoke, the fire in his eyes. "Don't push it, son," he warned. "And watch your mouth. Technically, that woman is still my wife." He formed a hole with his lips and blew the smoke out with his tongue like spittle. I parted the cloud with a wave so that I could see his dull face. "This happens to be my home you're stomping around in," he said. "Nobody likes Yankee hotshots diddling with their town."

"I can understand that."

When he self-righteously pointed his finger at me, I cringed. I hated the way he was, more than I had ever hated anything. "Let me tell you something, old buddy," he said, "don't think being a reporter for the *New York Times* gives you the right to exploit the people of this town. I don't care how backward and ignorant we are around here, we're not animals in a lousy zoo, okay? Do you understand me?"

I watched him crush the cigar, tug at the thin belt on his thick body, then lean forward carefully in his chair. Soon he was whipping out a wrinkled handkerchief and mopping his fevered brow. It was obvious I had untied his bundle of nerves.

"I'm beginning to," I said. "You're in this town so deeply, you're starting to choke on it."

"You're way off base, Miller. All I do in this town is sell cars and trucks."

"You also bet on high school football games, associate with men who bribe officials and fix scores; you run back odometers, sell stolen cars—"

"All right, that's enough."

"Was it something Richard Temple knew, Bubba?

Was he threatening to expose somebody?"

"Listen, Teddy," he said, "I know it looks bad to an outsider, like yourself, but all we're talking about here is economic necessity. You don't realize how poor we are down here. Hell, if I didn't fudge a little every once in a while, I'd be taking up residence across the street with the other niggers. Nobody likes to sell his principles for a few bucks, but what choice do I have in this dumb, ignorant place? Tell you what: spread a little industry and money around this county, and I'll sell you a car with a three hundred dollar markup. I'll give you five percent financing and carry the paper myself. Otherwise, I've got to work on the fringes just to stay alive!"

"Temple might not have seen it that way."

"You're scrounging around under the wrong rocks, bud," he told me. "How many educators do you know that have any idea in hell about business? The guy was nothing but a whoremonger, I tell you. And Marian wasn't his only whore either. Why don't you do something useful and go checkout that colored woman of his, huh?" He had to laugh at my open-mouthed silence. "Yeah, you didn't know about Mrs. Essie Curtis, did you?" he taunted. "Well, I wouldn't feel bad. Temple might not have known much about people, but he did know better than to let that little business out. Let me give you something you can take back with you to your beloved North, Ted, regarding the great progress of integration. We may call these people 'blacks' now, and we may let them piss in the public urinals, but nothing has changed since you lived here twenty-five years ago. It never will, either. The only reason we let the niggers in our schools is to get that federal money which we've got to have nowadays to get along. And we're not putting our own money into the schools, until they're out of them. But make no mistake about this: you don't have an affair with a person of the Negro race any more now than you did in 1950. Not if you expect to live very long, you don't."

"And that's why Temple was killed?"

"I'm not saying that's why he was killed. I'm saying it doesn't matter to me who did it."

Having had enough of J.B. Henderson for a lifetime, I headed for the door. One last question, and I was done with Bubba forever. "Where can I find Essie Curtis?" I asked.

"She's a schoolteacher at Marshall High," he said. "Her husband's a truck driver or something. Lives over in Nairobi."

"Thanks," I said. "I'll be in touch."

"Teddy?" He held up a thick, cautionary index finger. "As one old buddy to another, watch where you're stepping, you hear? You can act superior all you want to, you can go stick it in Marian, or poke around colored town till you're as black as they are, I don't care. But goddamn it, man, keep your nose out of my business!"

Silently, sadly, I turned around and left J. B. Henderson and his bitterness in Stanley Haymon's old office in the Ford dealership and walked across the street to my car.

Even after all these years, Nairobi was still a mass of unpainted houses with warped front porches and creaking rockers for the old folks to shell their peas on while they waited for the postman to deliver the welfare checks or the son-in-law to bring home the government commodities. I was as antsy as an adolescent driving the family car to pick up a loose date as I dodged the potholes of the washboard streets in search of Essie Curtis. I was beginning to feel, in fact, pink and naked, like one of Mr. O'Ryan's albino mudcats squirming around on the bank out of his element.

When I asked about the schoolteacher, I heard one solemn oath after another that no black woman since the American Revolution had ever been known by such a name as Essie Curtis. A rangy woman in a dingy T-shirt never stopped digging up a boxwood as she told me she knew Essie Coleman once, who ran off to Chicago, or maybe it was Detroit, with a Choctaw Indian in 1972 in order to work for good money in a battery plant. Of course, I could call up that way to find out about her, but since that Indian boy never had been much good to begin with, chances were she'd be moved on by now. The only help I got was from a grizzled and disgusted old man who had fallen into a vat of hot kreosote at the sawmill thirty years before and was still plenty sore about it. Looking like a badly exposed Uncle Remus, he came out of the house and started complaining about today's youth as if he were picking up a conversation we'd been having for years. Standing on his porch in the bright sunlight, he finally directed me down the road a piece.

"Want to find her old man, go down there," he said and pointed at a rectangular whitewashed cinderblock building down the street. "If he ain't on the road some place, he's down to the Fallen Inn, drinking with the rest of them."

The Fallen Inn happened to be a dirty, windowless lounge which had "Ladies Welcome" printed in blue paint on one side of the door and "God Loves You. Jn 3:16" scribbled in what looked like blood on the other. In the gravel driveway was an abandoned Cities Service gas pump and a cracked and warped pine bench turned on its end and leaning against a faded Royal Crown Hairdressing sign.

Still bristling over my talk with Bubba, I blithely yanked open the door and stepped into a stifling little abyss of heat, beer, and total obscurity. As the thick odor of alcohol, cheap cologne, and human sweat gathered around me like a wad of wet cotton, I tried to get organized by moving in the direction of the dim red Schlitz sign suspended over the bar. This was a mistake. Two steps into the journey, I crashed into a hard body that let out a stiff grunt and withdrew immediately. I apologized quickly in case it was human and backed away.

Gradually, I began to sense the presence of other life forms around me. Soon they began to make discernible human sounds: first a muffled cough, then the "pu— et!" of a healthy tobacco spit on the dirt floor, and finally a few actual English phrases, such as "white guy" and "What's he doing here?" and "motherfucker." When the front door suddenly clanged open, a dramatic shaft of light poured into the darkness long enough to reveal a monstrous yellow-eyed bald man looming nearby. I could tell he was forming the shape of a head with paws as big and flat as flounders apparently practicing the art of taking the life of an intruder into his hands.

The door closed, there was mumbling and hissing all about me. Then, abruptly, out of the darkness, an iron claw clamped down on my unsuspecting wrist, and a deep-throated male voice growled: "You Miller?"

When I offered to go without answering, he tightened his grip, shook my wrist as if he were trying to put out a match, and repeated the question.

"Yes," I confessed through a knot in my throat.

"Let's get out of here," he said. "Too crowded."

Crowded? How could he tell that? All I could have sworn to was one glowing beer sign and a couple of hands the size of Dumbo's ears.

But taking him at this word, I slipped out into the blessed light, where I noticed the tallest black man that I had ever seen without a number on his back. He was slender and homely, with a broken nose, bulging marble eyes, and a row of lip fuzz that looked more like a third eyebrow than a moustache. His complexion was as dry and rough as a plate of Mom's oatmeal. His skin was almost corrugated, as if it had been chewed on regularly by an animal—likely a giraffe, for no other could have reached up that far.

Knocking off six feet of gravel at a time, he strode over to his Chevrolet Caprice, folded his body like a wilted sunflower stalk, and crawled inside. Through the window, he hollered at me to follow in my car; otherwise, my T-bird would be nothing but a picked carcass when I got back.

With the image in my mind of black men as condors and me and my rented Thunderbird as prey, I followed him into Nairobi, down a winding gravel road, to an immense old dwelling back in the trees on the hill. It was a yellowed, cracked, and gabled house that only needed Tony Perkins loping around in the azaleas to complete the picture. When I got out of the car, a round, fifteen-pound black and tan male dog rolled out from under the porch like a bowling ball and instantly tore into my right calf. Curtis didn't seem to notice that anything was amiss as he bounded like a gazelle onto the porch and disappeared into the house.

I had managed to drag myself up to the porch by the time Duke, as I later found out he called himself, returned with a six-pack of Pabst Blue Ribbon beer. About the time I flipped the top of my can, the dog dug in.

"Damn!" I yelled and poured my Pabst on his head. After a minute, he let go, shook the foamy liquid out of his eyes and nose, backed up, and looked up quizzically at me. When I offered to have another go at it, he hastily beat his retreat to the safety of the yard.

"That's my boy's dog, Ann," the black man said and guzzled his beer.

"Ann?" I said. "Are you sure you heard him right?"

"That's what he calls him, so that's what he is," Curtis said. He dropped his long frame into a camouflage canvas butterfly chair next to the banister, effectively splitting his legs like a boiled hen or a customer at Louise's. Since he seemed to be oblivious to the bone-chilling mistral that was whipping viciously across the porch, I pretended not to notice it either.

Having nothing else to go with, I kept Ann in sight and gave the other butterfly a try. It must have been waiting for a donor for a long time, for the moment I let go, it wadded me up like a wet Dixie cup and held on to me like a hug from Mom. Knotted up into a fist in that canvas, I came to see at close range certain areas of my body I had forgotten a long time ago.

"Nice place you have here," I observed through my knees.

Duke Curtis had already gulped his first can and was commencing his second. "Anybody tell you I used to play ball?" he said.

I tried to straighten up. "Is that right?" I said.

He nodded, drank, and swallowed. "That was back when there was a colored school here," he explained. "Averaged 26 points and 11 rebounds a game. Ball players around here never got much publicity in those days though."

"I guess not," I said agreeably. I was more reconciled to the chair now that I realized it was shielding me from the wind.

"Nobody offered me any scholarship, either," he said. "Had to go to college on my own. But I keep up. That's how I know about you. Read that magazine story you did on black athletes using drugs and all." He widened his legspread in order to accommodate the Pabst can on his crotch. We must have looked like two mothers-to-be awaiting delivery on that porch. "They tell me you've been nosing around about my wife," he said to me.

Unable to lean forward successfully, I stayed within myself and tried to explain that I was following a story for my paper, possibly a book. All the time, he stared into the hole in his beer can, either puzzling over the role of the hops in the brewing process or sifting through his thoughts for the right way to say something to me. I had no idea what to look for. The last thing I expected was for a Southern black man to want to discuss with a white reporter from the *Times* his wife's interracial affair. But Duke Curtis surprised me. This was no airhead jock that was spread out before me like a Sunday newspaper. There were brains and sensitivity wrapped together in this man.

"I figure if I don't set you straight," he said, "you're going to screw us up good. You think my wife had something to do with that mess over at the school, but she didn't. Even if she wanted to, she'd never have been able to cock that .45. Not with that crooked arm of hers."

"All I wanted to do was interview her," I said.

"Now you listen to me, man," he said sternly. "You let me talk, all right?"

"Go ahead: talk."

"What I'm saying is, Essie's got this bum arm, because I broke it myself a while back. I took her to the emergency room, and they worked on it for a while and put it in a cast, but it never healed right. Looks like a damn chicken leg. Won't bend right. You see what I'm telling you?"

"No."

"Then you're not as smart as I thought."

I set my beer on the floor and tried to raise up, to ease a pain in my lower back, but for the moment, the chair had me. "Why did you break her arm?" I asked.

After a noisy suck on the can, Curtis swelled his cheeks with beer then collapsed them like rotten lungs with a deep, gurgling sound. "Because she was being a little bitch, that's why," he said. "But I reckon you wouldn't be here now, if you didn't know that already."

"I couldn't know much," I told him. "Until an hour ago, I had never heard of your wife."

He put the Pabst between his legs again. Whether it was to warm the beer or cool the parts, I couldn't say. "You know, I'm a Jackson State graduate," he said. "And the only job I can get around here is pushing an eighteen-wheeler up and down I-55 for twenty cents a mile. Same thing kids with high school educations do. But that's all right. It's my work, and it's fine with me. The thing is, Essie never looks at things that way."

"I wonder how she looks at them?"

"She's always got to have her intellectual stimulation. She's got to read her books and get all worked up over something somebody wrote a hundred years ago. That's why she hung around that school superintendent. It sure as hell wasn't because he was white."

I probably would have left this domestic drama unresolved if it hadn't been so tough to get out of my chair. Anyway, Ann had hunkered down into a low crouch on the bottom step and was watching me, ready to pounce like Mom's cat at the slightest provocation.

Curtis, on the other hand, was a veteran in those chairs, so he was able to move about at will in his. He could even lay his left ankle on his right knee without fear of permanent injury to his posture. "She told me all about it," he said, "and I beat the hell out of her, and that was it. She's been pretty good ever since as far as I know. But I'll tell you this: nobody around here knows a thing about that mess. And that includes Tommy. I'll swear to God on that."

"Who's Tommy?"

He turned his head to spit over the banister. "Shit," he said. "And here I thought you were so smart."

I couldn't imagine where he'd gotten that idea. I was still blind and naked and groping in the dark. "He must be the boy they arrested," I guessed.

"That's right. Tommy's my son. And sooner or later, they're going to be telling him he committed murder to protect his momma's honor. And he'll get all confused about it and say he did it, just to protect us. That's how he picked up that dog there. It got hit by a car over on Pine Street, and they were going to take it off and shoot it, but Tommy wouldn't let them. He stood up and lied to them. Claimed that old stray dog had been his since it was a pup, and they'd better not lay a finger on it. Made me set the bone and put a splint on it and everything. That's the way that boy is. He'll do the same thing to protect me and his momma, too, you watch."

"Didn't Tommy resent Temple for firing him?" I asked.

Curtis launched a load of spittle over the banister, reaching a new low for the struggling azalea bush. "Temple didn't fire him," he said. "I made him stay away as soon as I heard about this stuff with Essie."

"How much of this have you told the police?"

He laughed. "Man, I wouldn't show a policeman a commode if he had the johnny trots," he said.

By coiling and springing forth like a rattlesnake, I was able to extricate myself at last from the butterfly chair, and Ann began to snarl. Naturally, now that I knew the history of his leg, I was more tolerant of his belligerence, but I couldn't forget I had a leg, too. Using slow, deliberate movements, I eased over to the banister and gazed down the hill at the unpainted houses. It wouldn't have surprised me to see in every window a telescope trained on me. What a twist it was, after all these years, to go into Nairobi and be maneuvered from one front porch to another then tricked into assuming the posture of a father-confessor to a beleaguered black family which I had never heard of the day before.

Stiffening my body to the frigid breeze, I faced Duke Curtis and asked him just what he wanted from me. For the first time, a faint smile crossed his scarred face.

"Maybe you're wising up, after all," he allowed.

"I doubt it."

"All I want you to do is help my boy," he said. "Get him out of jail."

"Is that all?"

"The thing is, the kid's real slow when it comes to brains. It's not that hard to trick him into saying anything you want him to. He's just like old Ann there. Whenever he gets scared, he makes a whole lot of noise and starts being something he's not. You need to pull Tommy out of there before they get to him."

I took a deep breath. "I may have grown up in this town," I told him, "but I've been away a long time. I don't have any influence here."

"Come on, man. You've got the greatest influence there is! You're on the paper. You write books. It's just what Essie is always saying. The only difference between folks like Martin Luther King and a million others is the words they use. It's the words, that's what changes things!"

"Yes, but I'm not a crusader," I told him. "I'm doing

a story and that's all."

He curled his lip. "If that's true, you're not even worth crapping on, are you?" he said. Angrily gritting his teeth, he hurled a can of beer over the banister at the azalea bush. Then he looked me squarely in the face. "You know how it makes me feel to admit my old lady's gone off with some white dude while I'm out busting my ass on the road? Well, I'll tell you: like shit in a sewer, man. But I was willing to tell you about it anyway, in order to help my boy."

"You need a lawyer."

"Listen, I had me a lawyer up in Hinds County. I got two years in Parchman prison for housebreaking because I had me a lawyer." He stood up. "Come in here, I want to show you something."

He led me into the house. It was hot and dreary inside the living room with plaster walls the color of a tongue, the kind of Danish modern furniture that goes with Gideon bibles and Christian network talk shows and thin wall-to-wall carpet as cushiony as roofing shingles. There was a new television set and a spinet piano and small birch bookcases filled with Dickens, Austen, James, and Hawthorne and a larger one jammed with works by Ellison, Baldwin, and Whitney Moore Young, Jr. Hanging over the spinet was a framed needlepoint sign which read:

"When elephants fight, it is the grass that suffers."
Kikuyu Proverb.

In the kitchen, Curtis stopped to finish his beer. I shied away from his bobbing Adam's apple and took a look at the black-and-white picture of a fiery Vietnamese village over the refrigerator. Typed on a strip of paper beneath the shot was a quotation:

"It became necessary to destroy the town in order to save it." *Vietnam, 1968.*

"Had a brother-in-law killed in that war," Duke said. He set his empty can on the counter and walked into the den. What a claustrophobic place that was with an archive of pictures strung out over the walls: hundreds of personal photographs from weddings, reunions, basketball games, mixed with glossy poses of Rap Brown, Malcolm X, and Martin Luther King joking with Southern Christian Leadership Conference members in Montgomery. Curtis punched me in the belly with one of them, the same way Richard Temple had slapped me with *The Clarion Ledger.* It turned out to be a photograph of a pretty young black woman with high cheek bones, perfect teeth, and a bright, cheery smile. She was joyously cradling a grinning baby in a hospital bed.

"That was before they told us my boy was screwed up," he said. "I don't figure Essie's smiled much since then. At least, not around me."

"Good-looking boy," I said.

"That's probably the only kid I'll ever have," he said sadly. "They had to cut out all her female organs when Tommy was born." With a glazed expression on his rough face, he stared intently at the picture. "Looks real fine there, doesn't he?" he said helplessly. "Wonder what could've happened?"

"I don't know," I said.

He looked and nodded. "You got any kids?" he asked me.

"I have two."

"I figure both yours are normal, huh?"

"As far as I know."

"That's good." He cleared his throat. "You're lucky on that. I reckon your old lady's good to you, too, huh?"

"Pretty good. We're divorced."

"Probably lucky on that, too. I never knew a woman to want the same thing a man wants. And then they do this stuff like Essie. Don't even much care for it, and they do it with somebody they're not married to."

At that point, a car drove up outside, crackling the gravel in the driveway and causing Ann to bark excitedly. When Essie Curtis swept into the house a few minutes later in a wrinkled black skirt and red sweater, my attention was automatically drawn to her arm. Duke was right about it; the thing looked like it had been used to pry open crates.

"Where've you been?" Curtis said to her. His tone was sharp and impatient.

"Where do you think I've been?" she shot back. "I've just spent the longest morning of my life in jail talking to my son. Trying to do something for him!"

Curtis took the picture from me. "Sucking up to the police won't do him any good," he said and reverently hung the photo back on its place on the wall.

She glared at him, ignored me. "Do you think standing around here talking about football and basketball is going to do him any good?"

"Now look, woman," Curtis said. "Don't come in here giving me lip, you hear me?"

"My God, you don't even care! How can you just stand there and talk when your own son is crying his eyes out in a jail cell!"

"Hush, damn it!"

"If he were Gregory Lewis or Johnny Davis, you'd care, wouldn't you?"

"What the hell do you want me to do, Essie? Huh? You want me to crawl over to the jailhouse like some poor, desperate, starving nigger? Well, forget it. I won't do it."

"Is that what it is? Are you too proud to go in there? Are you so ashamed of him, you're willing to risk his life? Are you willing to just turn him over?"

"Get out of here, woman."

"Just tell me how you feel, Richard. Tell me what to do! We've got to do something to help him!"

"I am doing something."

"No, you're not, Richard! You've got to see him!"

"I said, get out of here, goddamn it!" he commanded. Essie held her ground for a second, before she unconsciously grabbed her elbow and burst away in tears. When the bedroom door slammed with a bang behind her, Curtis clinched his teeth. "Damn woman falls apart at the least little thing," he said.

The tension in the house was so galvanic, I felt as if I were caught in a maze of lightning rods in a thunderstorm: trapped in the heart of darkness with deadly sparks of adultery, miscegenation, jealousy, revenge, and murder flying wildly about. And yet, in the middle of all this sizzling electricity, Duke Curtis stood tall and straight as a grounded tower patiently trying to sort it all out. It was obvious he saw me as a Southerner who had access to the authorities of the town, and a Yankee who would be sympathetic to blacks. He saw me as one of the few chances he had of getting justice.

"I'd better be going," I said. The moment I stepped out on that cold, windy porch, Ann scrambled to his feet and assumed the attack position.

Curtis kicked the front door shut behind him. "That girl will never understand me," he said. "I don't give a damn about Gregory Lewis and Johnny Davis. Hell, she ought to know that."

"Lewis and Davis must be the stars of the football team."

"Oh, yeah, they're stars, all right. Way up there in the sky. Spending hundred dollar bills and driving Pontiacs all the time. They tell me, every once in a while they even ride through here to show off. If I ever catch them going by my house, I'll bust their heads with a tire iron."

"Why?"

"Because they're dangerous, man. They're like a herd of mean, spoiled stallions. When they get horny, the coach gets them a gal. When they get hurt, he gives them dope. When they want to move around, he gets them wheels."

"Where does all the money come from?"

"Wherever it comes from, it ruins them. Take that Lewis and Davis. Their mommas raised them as pretty good boys. But I tell you, I wouldn't piss on either one of them if they were on fire. All they ever talk about is their average yardage and the big thrills of the NFL. Gregory Lewis once told my boy all a colored man needed in this life was some bills in his pocket, and all the white women he could eat. You try to explain that to a kid like mine."

"Is gambling the source?" I asked.

He considered that for a second. "All I know is," he said, "there's a hell a lot of money these days all over the place. Even down here. My old man bets part of his welfare check on every game because he believes in that Gregory Lewis. Thinks he's some kind of black savior or something. Trouble is, he can't understand the point spread, so he's always losing money. But he doesn't even care. Thinks it's all for a good cause. I've told him he's not doing anybody any good playing in that white man's game, but he won't listen."

"Still, where would boys like Lewis and Davis be without it?"

"Maybe they wouldn't be anywhere like me. But at least they wouldn't be owned by a bunch of greedy white men, would they? Ever see that movie *Mandingo*? Ball players are just like that poor ignorant nigger in that story. They'll bite and claw and get horny and screw anybody the white folks want them to. They figure the only way to be respected by white men is to be on top, to be *Big Number One*. It's stupid, man. They haven't made it to the middle yet. They don't even have my respect yet."

"They make a lot of money in the pros, and money brings respect."

"Envy, man, not respect. Anyway, it's still *Mandingo*. The pro draft's nothing but a slave block and you know it. White men buying and selling and trading black bucks, the way they used to before the Civil War."

"You don't think playing for the Dallas Cowboys is

better than living here in Marshall?"

"All I know is, I've been watching black boys come up for a long time now, and I've never seen all this do shit for good. It turns you into a scared nigger, when you get down to it. In high school, you're scared nobody'll notice you. Scared you won't get a scholarship. In college, you're scared you won't go high in the draft. Scared you're not getting enough publicity. In the pros, you're scared you'll get hurt. Scared you're getting too old to play. When you live like that, you can't be much use to anybody."

An inadvertent flex of a muscle set the black-and-tan to growling. "What could they do instead?" I asked Curtis.

"They could find out what they can do instead of spending all their lives playing white men's games."

"That's a tall order."

"We're a tall race."

I smiled. "You're an unusual man," I said.

He leaned against the banister. "It's just that having a boy like Tommy makes a man think," he told me. "Essie knows I always wanted my boy to grow up and play ball like me. So she thinks I'm disappointed in him. But I'm not."

"Tommy's lucky to have parents like you," I said.

Curtis laughed nervously. "I don't see how he's lucky to have a truck driver for a daddy and a whore for a mom."

"His parents take him seriously enough to be truly responsible for him," I said. "That's a hell of a thing."

If I had been accustomed to seeing the red in the black, I might possibly have seen Duke Curtis blush. As it was, I nodded at him, turned away, and met a double row of flashing canine teeth, on the bottom step. "Easy, Ann," I said.

"Reach down and pet him," Curtis told me. "He'll shut up."

"Sure."

"I mean it. He's just like a kid. He's bad till he knows it's okay to be good."

Having no other choice, I stepped down to the dog's level and reached over and stroked the short black hair between his ears. He offered no resistance, but plopped down on the concrete as if he'd been shot. Then he rolled over on his back and laid bare his vulnerable underside.

I could hear nothing but sighs and moans of contentment from his relaxed little round body as I knelt down and rubbed his tender belly.

* * *

New York Times

BOOK EXPLORES GAMBLING, VIOLENCE IN MISSISSIPPI
First in a series

EDITOR'S NOTE: Noted New York Times sportswriter Theodore Miller describes his personal involvement in the case of Richard Temple in this five-part series excerpted from his book, *Life on the Line*, which will be published in April.

Bookmakers in major American cities are busily taking bets

A wizened, 60-year-old Italian grandfather named Mario cups his hands behind his head and props the heels of his glossy alligator shoes on a scarred, tobacco-stained desk in a cozy back room of a pizzeria in San Francisco's North Beach district.

Across the slick hardwood floor, through a dense cloud of cigarette smoke, his 35-year-old son busily answers the telephones and jots down numbers in a book. He writes and speaks at a frantic pace. Half a dozen lines flash on and off as Super Bowl Sunday draws closer.

Mario has a calmer temperament than his son. He lights another cigarette and reflects that while he's been making pizzas for over 11 years now, he's been making book for most of his life.

"I started back in '48," he says. "Never forget that first college football season. Michigan won the Rose Bowl, Georgia Tech won the Orange, and Texas won the Sugar.

"And if SMU had beaten Penn State in the Cotton Bowl, I might even have made a few bucks straight out of the gate. As it was, I lost $250 and had to make it good myself because my backer left town."

Mario estimates his total income this year will exceed $260,000.

"I guess I'll have to pay taxes on about $80,000 of that," he says. "Which is what I'll earn from the pizzas."

In Chicago, a former star high school quarterback and junior college coach now makes book above a 1930s-type neighborhood grocery store.

This tall, black-bearded man in a solid white turtleneck sweater and designer jeans refused to allow me in his "wireroom" where his wife and sister-in-law take calls.

"They've got enough to contend with in there as it is," he tells me.

But downstairs in the grocery, leaning against an old-fashioned white enamel meat counter which his father once owned, he's very friendly and talks freely about his trade.

"I only take bets on college and pro basketball and on football, and major league baseball," he says. "I'm in touch with a couple of line makers out of Las Vegas, and I subscribe to a sports information service which pretty much keeps me up to date.

"That's costing me about $350 a week, but it's worth it. Sometimes, CBS and ESPN just aren't enough."

In an Atlanta suburb, a retired baker runs a bookie operation out of a second floor bedroom in his split-level brick home.

He's paunchy, bald, and wears red-and-white polka dot pajamas and gray fuzzy slippers all day long.

"I never see nobody," he says. "Oh, I recognize the voices all right. But they never use their whole names, so I couldn't tell you who they are, or anything.

"Anyway, a lot of them use runners," he explains. "Which are guys that make the calls and collect or pay off the debts. That's unusual for Atlanta, but that's the way I like it. I'd rather deal with a runner any day."

Does a bookie always make money?

This one pats his stomach as he contemplates the question. "Put it this way," he says. "It's like a bank. Today, maybe not. Tomorrow, who knows? But in the long run, you've got to make money. Remember, the bettor's always betting $11 to get $10, and you're taking bets on both sides of the game. Over a stretch, the odds have to go your way."

In New York City, The Establishment employs ten full-time clerks who take bets which may total as much as $5 million a week during peak football season. This amount is called the "handle."

This may be the largest such operation in America.

"It's true, we do generate a lot of business," admits a corporate lawyer who manages the operation on a five-hour shift three times a week. He is impeccably dressed, soft-spoken, and polite. "I'd say that state-wide, the yearly handle comes to a billion dollars," he claims.

But being located in a state that traditionally has been a haven for gamblers has its drawbacks.

"The problem for my partners and me," he contends,

"is that our volume amounts to only about a 10 percent share of the market. With all this heavy concentration and without the benefits of advertising, it's extremely difficult for a New York company to expand its profit margin."

These are examples of illegal gambling businesses in major American cities, which specialize in sports (non-horseracing) betting. Just how many of these small but highly profitable concerns exist is hard to judge. Since the usual sources of financial information, such as the Internal Revenue Service, have little to offer, data must be culled from independent surveys, President's commission reports, congressional investigation findings, and from files of the U.S. Department of Justice and individual police departments.

Information gotten this way is seldom meaningful.

Estimates on the volume of business nationwide range from $2.5 billion guessed at in a survey in 1977, to maybe ten times that amount today. But it could be as much as fifty times that estimate.

Sports betting claims a long history

The idea we're dealing with here is nothing new, of course. There has been gambling in sports ever since Cro-Magnon man first picked up a stick and brained a rock instead of another skull.

The seamy side of it crawled into the public eye in 1920, when eight greedy players on the 1919 Chicago White Sox were discovered to have made a $100,000 deal with a New York gambler to throw the World

Series to the lowly Cincinnati Reds.

The infamous Chicago Eight were Chick Gandil (1B: .290), Fred McMullin (2B; .294), Swede Risberg (SS: .256), Buck Weaver (3B; .296), Happy Flesch (OF; .275), Joe Jackson (OF; .351), Eddie Cicotte (P; 29-7), and Lefty Williams (P; 23-11).

All eight of these "Black" Sox, who received a total of $20,000 for their dishonest labor, were suspended from the team, and a dark cloud descended over the game. Spirits went down. Morale sank in a mire of shame. Gloom began to spread like a disease over the game. Fans became sour, players performed badly. A Cleveland Indian, Ray Chapman, was struck with a fastball by Carl Mays and died the next day.

It was the only such fatality in major league baseball history.

The modern era has had its share of gambling scandals, too. In 1961, the Dixie Basketball Classic in Durham was wiped off the slate forever when several North Carolina State players were accused of fixing games. That same year other blue-chippers, such as Larry Graves of Mississippi State, were lathering up the sport by shaving points right and left.

In 1985, John "Hot Rod" Williams and two of his teammates were accused of cutting points for gamblers at Tulane. There have been many others, but the pattern is always the same. Discoveries are made, controversies flare up, individual careers are forfeited.

But the sport remains, the games play on, and the bets continue to be laid.

Sports betting is becoming very popular

Once horseracing was the sport of kings. Now it's the game of the rich and destitute. For mainstream America, sports betting has far more appeal. For this development, bookies are extremely grateful.

"Bookmaking's much simpler with a game like football," said one of the partners of The Establishment. "The handle may be the same as the races, but the volume is significantly lower. Horseracing has a lot of winning combinations, whereas football has only one. Which makes it easier to work with on both sides of the fence.

"There are fewer events to follow, too. It requires less personnel to cover 50 games on a weekend, than to cover 150 races in a day. Naturally, a reduction of staff can increase the profit margin."

This reduction of overhead, plus the proliferation of instant-access equipment such as television, computers, and sophisticated telecommunications systems has attracted many neophyte bookies in the past few years.

While anyone who wants to can become a bookie, he is usually someone who has had close connections with a gambling operation as a runner, a clerk, a lender, or a bettor.

Even though his motives are essentially those of a banker or insurance executive, he is regarded by society as an unsavory character who works in the shadows of the law, exploiting the human weakness for gambling. Since he is bound to be a social pariah, the bookie is often either a person who believes he has no hope of ever gaining respectability or simply doesn't care to have it.

For a new bookie to set up shop is fairly easy. Once his phone number has been passed on to local bettors, he takes their calls, registers their bets. After the games, he pays the winners and receives money from the losers. The difference between those two amounts constitutes his profit or loss. Because all transactions are in cash, no money gets reported to state or federal agencies, and no troublesome taxes have to be paid.

However, to meet other expenses, such as line maker fees, sports information costs, local law enforcement bribes, and worst of all, losses, a bookie must have a backer. Since losses sometimes fluctuate radically, there must always be available a sizable store of capital or else he has to resort to borrowing from loan-sharks at a distinctly unhealthy rate.

On a typical day during the football season, the calls pour in, the bookie answers the phone, cites the odds, takes the bets, and notes every penny in a ledger. On a given weekend, he may end up owing his bettors $20,000. Next weekend, he may clear $20,000. Eventually, if the accounting is accurate and the financial backing is solid, he will turn a tidy profit from—"the general public." According to Mario, of San Francisco, "Anybody with a dollar in his pocket is subject to play."

Sports betting is a simple operation

Here's how the process looks from the bettor's side.

Let's say you're a pharmacist in Chicago who likes the Bears. You like them so much, you're willing to wager a few bucks on their upcoming game with the Washington Redskins.

If you lived in New York, you'd contact a runner who would make all your bets for you ("This is Tim calling for No. 16"). He would also collect and pay your wins and losses. But this is Chicago. Here you may deal directly (by phone) with the bookie himself.

Nervously you dial the number you got from a dentist friend. A clear, slightly hurried voice answers, "Hello." Never any more than that. No identification is necessary.

"This is Ed," you say. "What's the line on the Bears game?"

"Chicago plus 3 1/2," the bookie replies. This means if you bet the Bears, they must win the game by four points or more or you lose.

You seriously consider the odds for a moment. You know the Bears better than you know your own kids. You figure they're a lot more predictable, too. You feel in your bones they'll take the skins by at least four points. No way to lose. "Put me down for five dollars," you tell him. The dentist has already warned you a dollar is slang for a hundred.

"Anything else?" the bookie asks.

"Nope. But then, if I win, I may branch out."

"Right," he says, matter-of-factly. "Excuse me. I've got another call."

Now you've done it, taken the plunge. With a pounding heart, you sit on the edge of your divan on Sunday afternoon and drink your Bud Light and pretend to your wife that nothing is on the line while you watch the Bears methodically demolish the Redskins by three touchdowns. On Monday, you call that number again half-expecting some flak. But the bookie surprises you. He's downright friendly. All he wants to know is where to send the money. Come Wednesday morning, five crisp new hundred dollar bills arrive at your post office box in a plain envelope.

In your car you take out the currency and look it over. Making money you're used to. Anyone who dispenses drugs these days earns chamberpots full of money. But this is different somehow. Those new bills positively send a chill through the body. You have instantly discovered the thrill of winning.

"It's like something for nothing," said a restaurant owner in East Manhattan. "No matter how much you lose, you feel like you're ahead of the game when you win. I know that's dumb, but that's the way you feel."

"It's a real high," claimed a hotel manager in Brooklyn. "There's nothing like it on earth. It's not like being paid for your work. You expect that. It's like you're beating the system. When you win, you're somebody. You matter."

"It's better than sex," beamed a waitress in the Waldorf. "Infinitely better than sex."

Winning heightens your awareness of the possibilities, of course. Before you know it, you're liable to start taking an interest in other teams, other games, other sports. Soon you're calling your bookie and laying down bets on three, four, five games at a time. It doesn't take long to realize you're losing money. But since all of this is entertainment for you, so what? If you do happen to win, you've gained. You have created something out of nothing. You have in your possession the ultimate philosophers' stone.

Bookies love bettors who think this way.

Gamblers are different folks

Although sports betting is illegal in most states, it is part of a vast network that is supported by the many different kinds of people who gamble.

The *casual gambler* has some extra money to spend and takes a chance. When he wins, he's elated. When he loses, he backs away from gambling for a while. Researchers have found that such a person rarely invests more than 5 percent of his income on the outcome of a game. Probably 90 percent of all sports bettors fall into this category.

A *percentage gambler* not only loves the game, but has an instinctive feel for it. Whether he does the sport for a living or not, this rare person is a pro. Think of Minnesota Fats in pool, and the Cincinnati Kid in poker.

I talked to a chic middle-aged woman in Queens who regularly plays bridge with bankers, lawyers, and judges—for money.

"I play the odds and the people as well as the cards," she explained. "When I see I can win, I press. When I see I can't, I back off."

"How much money do you earn playing bridge?" I asked her.

She shrugged her shoulders. "As they say, it's a living," she answered casually. "I don't know, maybe forty or fifty thousand a year."

A *compulsive gambler* is the most psychologically interesting type. The American Psychiatric Association claims there are at least 8 million of these in the United States, and they're laying down their money every day. This person is one who usually makes at least $30,000 a year: bright, educated, resourceful—and out of control. Compulsive gamblers are like compulsive smokers, alcoholics or drug addicts. They have low self-esteem, borrow wildly, write rubber checks, let businesses and marriages go slack, and are inclined to depression and suicide.

A 38-year-old woman in Mississippi told me: "I'll bet on anything with anybody at any time. I'll go out in a thunderstorm and shoot craps against a pine stump. I've lost two husbands because of all this gambling, but I can't help it. I've just got to roll those dice and see what comes up!"

Compulsive gambling isn't a disease. At least judges don't think so. Recently a court—United States vs. Torniero, 735F.2d725 (3d Cir. 1984)—ruled that compulsive gambling is not a mental illness and therefore cannot be considered the basis for an insanity plea.

Most psychologists agree. Dr. Richard McCormick, in *Journal of Psychology*, stated the consensus when he determined that people gamble compulsively for the same reason they use drugs—as a relief from the feeling of impotence in modern life.

There is no reason to call the phenomenon of sports betting itself a disease, either. Rather, it seems to be a convenient outlet for the peculiarly human desire to gamble, and the irresistible urge to combine play with pay.

It's also a way for desk jockeys to participate in sports. Some psychologists claim that the current rash of betting information on television constitutes a concerted effort on the part of networks to keep viewers actively involved, and therefore glued to their chairs.

Active viewers, the thinking is, tune in more often and buy more advertised products than the passive ones.

In spite of this rising tide of popularity of gambling on sports, most of the professionals involved in football, baseball, and basketball persist in the belief that we should somehow dam the flow. At a sports betting hearing in Washington back in 1975, owners of pro football teams altogether denounced the notion of legalized gambling. Art Rooney, owner of the Pittsburgh Steelers at the time, claimed it would change the structure of the game. Even Jimmy the Greek opposed it. In 1984, in a survey in *Sociology of Sport Journal*, practically every coach and athletic director who was contacted was against mixing gambling with sports.

And yet, the mixture does exist, it does work, and the volume is growing fast. Millions of American want to take part in this diversion, and the rest of America apparently wants to permit it.

Such a liberal view of a criminal offense evidently stems from the widespread feeling that sports betting, after all, isn't much different from playing the stock market or investing in TV pilots or condominiums, not even as a matter of degree.

As one occasional gambler, a watch repairman in Brooklyn, put it: "What's all the fuss about here? Hell, everything I've ever encountered in life has been a gamble. Except maybe Tide detergent."

* * *

Feeling more and more as though I'd just been squeezed screaming through the wrinkled, yellowed rollers of Aunt Reba's wringer washer, I left Nairobi and drove over to the high school to find out more about the team and Richard Temple. As unhopeful as I was about my prospects at the moment, I figured it'd be as good a way as any to get back on track after having my emotions grabbed and twisted dry by the likes of Richard Duke Curtis. It wasn't enough to be ordered by a Manhattan Greek to do a root canal on my Mississippi background; now I was off on a mission of mercy on behalf of a black moronic kid who had a tendency to pick up stray dogs and tell lies.

Although a pair of Bundley's bulkheads were standing like a 7-10 split on either side of the murder porch, nobody was bothering to guard the school. After girding myself to the task at hand, I drifted up the concrete steps of the three-story red brick building and shoved open the front door. The huge foyer was big enough to play jai alai in and almost as dim as a French restaurant. Over the creaky oil-stained floors, the peeling pea-green walls were plastered with testimonials of another day.

As I looked around me, I saw a thousand school pictures grinning back at me through the veils of faded generations. What a crew my class was! Simpering mooncalves off on a spree. You'd have thought we'd just been let out of the bomb shelter and were tickled white about it. The girls were evidently trying for an Eva Garner effect in strapless bras and black boudoir lace—at least they knew what to shoot for—and the boys were wearing pencil-thin black ties and looking as if we were solidly entrenched in the commercial business of growing ears. In the top left-hand corner of the picture frame was the oval image of one of our beloved sponsors, Mrs. Byrd, also known as Mrs. Bird, because of her habit of saying "Cah! Cah!" whenever things went wrong in class.

Before Mrs. Byrd was struck down by a Checker cab during an arts festival in Birmingham, she had a doting husband who collected porno films and made periodic trips to New Orleans in order to buy his wife spicy underwear, and a mother who insisted on going along with him to help pick out the right bras and panties and to keep herself abreast of what the girls were wearing these days. She also had a waterhead son who was psychic and played the spoons as well as the jew's-harp and was said to hold long conversations with creatures from cartoon movies and Asimov novels. Every so often in assembly, Mr. Floyd would suddenly call upon young Donnie Byrd to rise up and twang his jew's-harp like an apostle or something and sing "He's Got the Whole World in His Hands" in F Minor, not so much to entertain the crowd, as to remind us that we had the Good Lord to thank for the shape we were in that day. Although young Donnie's tearful renditions moved us all, (except The Gospel Accordians, who were professionally jealous), as far as I know, no one ever made the first sound during or after the performance, since we considered it sacrilegious to clap at any song that had "Christ" or "God" or anything with a capital "H" in the lyrics.

Our other sponsor, Mrs. Hannah Green, was an English lady with a grimacing smile and a beartrap of vicious-looking teeth to back it up. She wore a pleated wool skirt that reached down to her heels and a black felt beanie that made her puffy little face, when it wasn't smiling, look like an acorn. She also entertained a mysterious, unbridled passion for slow-witted men. "They're not always trying to act smarter than you are," she explained once. "Which means a lot to an educated girl like me."

Mrs. Green taught American history with a cool defiance (after all, it wasn't her history), and kept her nose in the air and her arms across her bosoms while she took issue, one after another, with the famous people in the book. I remember her pacing back and forth in front of the blackboard, fussing about all the frantic doings in the colonies, and referring to all the historical personages by their first names as if she'd grown up with them back in the U.K. After a quietly contentious life, she died in a nursing home in 1975 trying to the end to convince one of her former students that George Washington had unsightly wooden teeth and therefore was in no shape to be anybody's father, let alone a whole country's. In her dying declamation, according to Mom, she said that if the American economy was ever going to get back on its feet again, these stubborn Yank farmers were just going to have to return to some of the more traditional crops such as your maize and your indigo.

On the third floor of the school building was the Mammoth Cave where we used to gather to witness Mr. Floyd's demonstrations with the commode. It was also where the girls saw films on self-rising flour, and the boys saw black-and-white movies on V.D.

When I was in the tenth grade, Mr. Floyd came in and announced as solemnly as a flag at half-mast that we were now going to view a genuine U.S. Army training film concerning various reproduction-related maladies. We may have been blissfully ignorant in those days, but we knew pretty well what he meant by that. We leaned across the aisles and nudged each other with our elbows and somebody cracked a joke about girls being clap-traps and about these being rubber movies since they were being shown for the prevention of disease only. We squirmed and giggled with anticipation while Mr. Floyd told us he'd rented the film from the New York Public Library, which meant the thing was bound to be good for us, and not particularly funny. "So, er-uh," he said, "I'll thank you not to find any humor in the unfortunate individuals which you will see on the screen."

His impassioned warning made us fidget even more, of course, and encouraged us to believe we were in for two or three naked bosoms at least before the day was over. While Mr. Floyd threaded the film through the projector with all the finesse of an elephant learning to sew, Jake Simmons became so excited, he began to cuss uncontrollably. Homer Boone simply couldn't take the suspense; he hustled off to the restroom without even bothering to get permission.

At last, though, all was quiet and all the ducks were properly on the pond. The lights went off, the projector clicked on, and the square silk screen began to flicker with grainy images of a gallery of men who were obviously in some mighty dire straits. It was a very sad movie. The story may not have been much to go on, but the actors were notable. They looked like a collection of very old hoboes that somebody had found curled up in some newspapers in the back of an art theatre somewhere. The flesh on their ears and cheeks and noses was crumbling to pieces, and their complexions were puckered with oozing sores which would have scared Job. For twenty-seven minutes, we sat in the dark and winced at one gruesome mug shot after another, until we finally became convinced you caught V.D. with your face.

During recess, we hung around the campus in clumps, avoiding girls like the plague, and worrying a lot about our future. Bubba said his uncle told him the only way you could get V.D. was either from an older woman or from a commode. In one way, this was comforting news, since none of us was planning on getting our faces anywhere near a commode, but in another, it wasn't. There were still a lot of older women to consider with all the family reunions and all the kissing going on.

As far as I know, the only member of our class to successfully contract a social disease was Johnny Dale Landers, a freckle-faced loner who lived on the edge of both town and distraction in a cozy house trailer with a thirty-five-year-old mother and three sexy teenage sisters. When he just couldn't take another padded bra hanging like a pair of open hands on the shower rod, Johnny Dale hitchhiked up to the McDermott Hotel in downtown McComb and paid the desk clerk four dollars and asked what such a sum might bring him on a good day. After conferring with a wizened gray-haired bellhop who fired off a couple of off-color jokes about cradles, the clerk sent him up to Room 238 on the mezzanine where he was cordially greeted by a woman old enough to be his aunt. In fact, when she stood in the light a certain way, she even looked like his aunt.

Like a ravenous bullfrog snatching a fly off a lily

pad, this lady quickly grabbed Johnny Dale where he was ready and promptly admitted him to the fraternity. After a ten-minute performance, which she probably held a patent on, she proceeded to wash him good in the sink with Oxydol, while she rhythmically tapped her heels and toes on the linoleum floor and sang "Gary, Indiana," two or three times without stopping. Johnny Dale was shocked, of course, but so intrigued with all this post-operative attention that he kept taking a renewed interest in her work, every time she did it.

Two to four weeks later, Landers located a chancre in the shower instead of a padded bra and then discovered when he tried to urinate, a painful, swelling sensation in the neighboring lymph nodes. After missing school one day, he arrived on campus bragging that he was the only fifteen-year-old ever to pass the Wassermann test at the Davis Health Clinic. He admitted, though, that the doctors were making him take some penicillin in order to prevent something that was going around these days called *Tabes dorsalis*, or possibly a case of general insanity.

Bubba chuckled at the very idea. Anybody horny enough to have to go to the McDermott Hotel to begin with was already legally insane in his book, he said. There wasn't a company in the United States or Canada that could make a pill strong enough to fix something which was that broken.

When I walked down the hall to the superintendent's office down the hall, I discovered a bald little man with a Tootsie Roll belly wrapped in a tight short-sleeved shirt, perched on a volume of the DNB and typing on an IBM like a chicken pecking corn. It was Francis Poole, the principal, successor to Mr. Floyd. Poole had been my eighth grade English teacher, an elfin, tongue-tied, battered husband, who hung around the coaches and tried to mimic their masculine manners with such tough-guy actions as digging the lint out of his belly button in public and sticking his leg out of his car and skidding the pavement with the soles of his combat boots before it came to a stop. For a while, he even gave spitting tobacco into a Dixie cup a try, but with his harelip, it got to be too messy to fool with, and he had to give it up. I remember Mr. Poole used to stand behind the home team bench at the baseball game and slobber that tobacco juice and try to cuss a blue streak while he cheered. He'd holler, "Hit that hell of a ball!" or "A damn pitch, Teddy! A damn pitch!" and set everybody's teeth on edge. His profanity was more humiliating to the coaches than it was to the parents. The coaches figured if a man couldn't cuss and chew at the same time, he ought not be allowed to do either.

As I entered the room, Poole sprang up, or rather, he sprang out from under the typewriter, since he was roughly the same height standing or sitting. He was a good deal rounder and chubbier these days, and seemed at least a foot shorter. He looked like something you'd win by having your weight guessed incorrectly at the fair. Or something you'd sleep all curled around if you were insecure.

"Jesus!" he exclaimed.

I let that go and looked around the place. Richard Temple's office was immaculate, which meant he had been either clear-headed or seldom very busy. There was a single gray file cabinet, a color picture of the man and his family struggling with a picnic lunch at the petrified forest in Flora, and a commercial black-and-white portrait of the new capitol in Jackson on the plaster wall.

Poole's thin, rubbery lips were shaking. "I guess this looks bad, doesn't it?" he said and ripped the paper out of the machine.

"I don't know. Maybe it just needs revision."

He looked at the torn paper with chagrin. "I mean my being here," he corrected.

"I thought you worked here."

"I do work here!" he said. "I mean, being in Richard's office on a day like this! Jesus, don't you know what's happened!" Before I could hammer out an answer to that, he came up with one for me. "Of course you know!" he said. "That's why you're here, isn't it? You're doing a story!"

I watched him fumble around with his sheet of paper for a while. At first, he tried to fold it into a neat square, but it kept coming out with two extra corners that protruded like terrier ears sticking out from under the covers. Resting in both his hands, it reminded me of a failed party hat. After working with it some more, he became so panicky about it, he started to sweat and had to give it up as a lost cause and resolutely stuffed what he could of the whole business into his pocket.

"That's good enough for it," I said.

Before I had gotten these words out of my mouth, he was making a bee-line for the door. "You're not supposed to be in here, Teddy," he said nervously. After frantically checking the corridor for possible intruders, he quickly shut the door and mumbled something about the halls having ears. Since I had seen the school photos, I knew exactly what he meant. Mr. Poole's harelip was still bothering him a bit—he was still Elmer Fudding his r's—but I thought he'd improved his way of talking considerably since the seventies when he took elocution lessons in Jackson.

Pulling away from the door, he wiped his spacious forehead with a wrinkled handkerchief and tried to force it into the same pocket as the party hat. It wouldn't go. Since he evidently was determined to do something with it, he resorted to the job of dusting off the desk of the deceased. I watched him labor at that for a while, but when he came to the picture of Temple's wife and girl, I interrupted to ask him where the dead man's family were when the murder occurred.

"They were in Durham, North Carolina," he said curtly. "Where else would they be? That's where they always are. Jesus! Why was he so obstinate about things like that! Why couldn't he have sent his girl to school here?"

"I don't know," I said.

If Mr. Poole could have endured any eye-to-eye contact, he would probably have taken the chance and glared at me. As it was, he kept his gaze on the floor, the way Mr. Floyd undoubtedly taught him to when he was grooming him for the job. "He was always going against the grain," he said. "I kept warning him, but he wouldn't listen."

"Sounds like you hated the guy."

"Jesus, no! Goddamn. I didn't hate him, even if the

whole faculty did disagree with him. How could we help it? He wanted too much. When our kids couldn't do as well as the blacks he had in Florida, he decided we should change the rules. But you can't do that!"

"I wonder how much he expected of our kids?"

He seemed to realize that dusting the furniture with his hanky was stupid, but since it was calming his nerves, he extended his work area to the file cabinet. "He wanted them to be smarter than their parents," he answered.

"And the parents didn't go for it."

"You don't understand."

"Tell me."

Apparently, this appeal to his professorial side made him itch, for as soon as he heard the challenge, he began to scratch feverishly at his groin. After a time, he'd dislodged the tick or chigger and was ready to go on. "Richard was wrong about a lot of things," he said. "He was too idealistic. He believed people down here hated being more ignorant than everybody else. But they don't. They know exactly what they are, and they're resigned to it."

"Jesus," I used his favorite word.

"It may sound dismal, but it's the truth!" he said. "Why should they want their kids to learn ideas that challenge theirs? What good are sexual equality, evolution, and integration going to do them, except to create dissension in the family? Don't forget, Teddy, in Mississippi, the family is the very core of the community's existence. It means everything!"

I thought of my own family: me, Nancy, Jennifer/Electra, and my simian son. Some core of the community we were. "So your job is to keep them bemused and benighted," I said.

My job is to create viable alterations in the educational climate."

"With what—dry ice?"

"Now wait a minute! Just because we opposed Richard doesn't mean we're any less dedicated than he was. We just realize how slow the community has to move on these things. Temple was like a herd of wild horses. Nobody could understand why he was always in such a hurry!"

"Could be, he wanted to raise the state up to 48th."

"Damn it, the state doesn't want to be 48th! People down here are happy with being last. It's familiar and it's comfortable. Nobody expects them to be any better than they are, and that's fine with them."

I don't know why all these tales from the dark side depressed me so much. It wasn't as if I expected any Great Enlightenment from this cueball from Missouri. After all, I already had a handle on Poole. The only way you can find out what size people are is by stretching their spines, and Mr. Francis Poole's spine had been drawn and measured a long time ago. It happened the day Bubba, Roy Buck, and I ran up to him after school and confessed that on a trip to pick up some federal turkeys for the cafeteria, we had accidentally left poor Freddie Thornberry stranded at the United States Frozen Food Locker in McComb.

After nearly upchucking his new wad of tobacco, Mr. Poole began to shake his head vigorously and fell into citing one feeble reason after another why he couldn't get involved with us on this crisis. He was all tired out from paddling students all day, he had a cyst which he was planning on scraping off his butt that night, he had to stop by the 7-11 for some ice cream and curry for his pregnant wife. But we would have none of that. We told him Mrs. Poole could get her own curry and encouraged him into his station wagon which was parked behind the Ag building.

On the way to McComb, Mr. Poole squirmed and fidgeted and became so fearful of what lay before us, he finally gagged on his Sweet Man cud and had to pluck it out of his mouth like an offending eye and hurl it through the vent window at a passing semi. After trying to eject a round or two of saliva through his harelip only to have it come right back at him, he announced that he couldn't say how much actual help he could be in a situation like this. He never liked the freezing cold all that much. In fact, of all the college graduates he knew, he probably hated the cold more than any of them.

"I wonder how Freddie's doing in there?" I said from the back seat of the station wagon when we reached the Five Points intersection.

Mr. Poole wiped his harelip with a handkerchief and glanced at me in the rearview mirror. "How long has he been in, Teddy?" he asked me.

I thought over the question as I studied my wrist watch. "Let's see, it's about three-thirty now," I said. "I guess it's been quite a while."

"Yes, but how long?"

I shrugged my shoulders. "When was it, Bubba?" I said. "Friday?"

"Friday!" Mr. Poole groaned. "Jesus! What a damn

thing! What is the matter with you! Don't you realize he could be dead by now!"

"I hope not," I said. "I'd hate to have to chop him out of there with an ice pick."

Roy Buck had a thought on that. He figured we could hire the ice truck and some tongs from Mr. Adams and haul Freddie back to his momma. But Bubba didn't think it'd work out. "Wouldn't be much point," he said. "His momma's cheaper than Jack Benny. She wouldn't even accept the charges."

All by himself, Mr. Poole fretted over the possibilities so much that by the time he parked the station wagon in the alley next to the food locker, he quietly placed his wide forehead on the steering wheel and muttered softly that what he needed now was to stay with the car, if it were all the same to us. Since it wasn't, we coaxed him out by reminding him that he owed Freddie one because of that "F" he'd given him in English the year before.

Reluctantly, Mr. Poole agreed, and walked with us like a constipated elf on the way to the john to the locker. He even bowed his head with us as Bubba placed his right hand on the bar of the door and solemnly intoned some legal Latin, the way a priest with nothing better to do blesses a fleet of boats. "Feels like we're about to open up a tomb," Bubba noted.

As much as Mr. Poole hated that idea, he had no choice but to press on and make the best of it. When Roy Buck flicked on the locker light, we saw stacks of ice cakes rising from the floor, frost covering the walls and ceiling, and chunky beef quarters suspended in the air. I thought the scene looked like the Liberty football team playing on a jungle gym in the snow, but Roy Buck thought less of it than that.

"This place looks like hell," he said.

Mr. Poole, meanwhile, was surveying the room with a suspicious eye. "I don't believe Freddie's in here," he concluded. "All he'd have to do is open the door from the inside!"

"That's all a normal person would have to do," Bubba said. "But remember, Freddie ain't all that smart. Anybody that'd fail your English class. . . ."

"Jesus."

"I'm betting he's still in here somewhere." Bubba pointed toward a darkened corner of the locker. "The last time I saw him, he was right over there," he said. "Playing with the pullets. There's no telling what's happened to him by now."

We all regarded the frozen chickens a while, until a great noise like the start of an avalanche cracked in the cold air and reverberated off the beef quarters. Suddenly, a block of ice the size of an Amana home freezer came sliding across the slick floor like the Panama Limited running late for New Orleans. We managed to cast our fragile bodies out of harm's way just as it rushed past us and crashed into the metal wall with a resounding thud.

After checking his heart for a steady beat, Mr. Poole drew close enough to inspect the block. Even though the spooky object inside the cloudy cake of ice was barely visible to the naked eye, it was clear enough to him that he was gazing upon a human body. It lay there as long and as stiff as an assembly speech with a blank white face peering up forlornly through the ice like

James Arness in *The Thing*.

"It's Freddie!" we all cried at once.

"Jesus!" Mr. Poole exclaimed.

Of course, it wasn't Freddie; it was the top half of a one-armed mannequin we'd found in the trash heap behind the Penney's store, and had carefully frozen the day before; but Mr. Poole didn't know that. In his agitated state, he naturally assumed this pale reflection of youth was none other than the poor soul he'd flunked in tenth-grade English. He was so flustered, he began to babble what sounded like lines from the odes of Keats, then crashed through the open door clutching his genitals for all they were worth.

"Mr. Poole!" Bubba called out to him. "What do we do about Freddie!"

In no mood to answer, he raced down the alley as if there were a printed T-shirt saying he did it waiting at the other end. In just a few moments, he had vanished from the alley.

"What a dope," Roy Buck laughed and nudged Bubba's side.

What a coward, I thought.

The next day, Thornberry, who didn't know about the gag, waltzed into the school just as Mr. Poole was slinking into Mr. Floyd's office to report a death in the student body. When he saw his former student alive and kicking, he was beside himself. "Freddie!" he shouted. "Jesus! You're not dead!"

"Do what?" Freddie said.

"I can't believe it!" He grabbed the boy's biceps and shook him like a bottle of root beer. "Look at you! Hell in the morning! Are you all right? Are you warm enough?"

"I thought I was." Freddie glanced down at the plaid wool coat his mother had laid out for him that day. All of this attention was befuddling, because the coat looked perfectly efficient to him.

"I don't understand!" Mr. Poole said to Bubba. "What happened?"

"We revived Freddie," he answered. "Nothing to it. All we had to do was read him a couple of pages of *Peyton Place,* and all that ice just melted off!"

It was then Mr. Poole realized everybody in the hall was laughing at him. He tried to pretend he was amused, but he wasn't. He knew our joke had exposed him. It had shown us the measure of Francis Poole. I'll never forget how small he looked as he receded to his car. I knew I was seeing the back of a man who'd run out on you if he ever had the chance.

The back of a man you could never count on.

While Mr. Poole was searching his trousers for a pocket that would accommodate his handkerchief, I paused with my fingers curled around the handle of the file cabinet. To my surprise, he wasn't moving a muscle to stop me. "They tell me Richard Temple was research-ing the football team," I baited him. When he declined to bite, I yanked open the top drawer with a clunk finding it as empty as a country church. So were the other three. "Looks like he travelled light," I said.

"If you're looking for his papers, the police took them," Poole told me.

I kicked the bottom drawer shut. "Why?" I asked.

"Ask them."

I was trying hard not to let that old business with Freddie and the locker annoy me now, but it was doing it anyway. I hated the way Poole kept doing nervous things with his handkerchief. At the moment, he was polishing his forehead with two fingers in a corner of the linen.

"Why are you looking at me?" he said defensively.

"I was just wondering why you're here," I said. Actually, I was wondering why he looked like he'd just been caught with his hand in his diaper.

"I was typing a letter," he said.

"On Richard Temple's typewriter."

"That's right." With a show of self-satisfaction, he whipped the crumpled paper out of his pocket. "If you don't believe it, here." He handed it to me. "Read it. Go ahead!"

I straightened out the spitball and found a formal-sounding application for a job of assistant principal in the Alabama public school system. The idea caught me by surprise. And it turned my stomach.

"So much for viable alterations," I said.

Poole snatched the paper out of my hands. "This is the only IBM typewriter in the school," he said. "I wanted to make an impression."

"Well, you made it," I said and headed for the door.

"Jesus, Teddy! Do you think it's easy for me to leave these kids after all these years?"

"I think it's always easy to run."

"Well, what are you so sanctimonious about? Didn't you run, too?"

He had me there. Having nothing to say to that, I turned around and left the room.

Outside the school building, I stopped and peered around me and found Mr. Poole at the window of Temple's office. I swear to God, as snotty as I had been to him, the poor bastard was actually standing there waving goodbye to me with that damned handkerchief.

That made me feel like something a wino had disgorged into the Hudson River.

One thing I was sure of—this man could not have murdered the superintendent. Imagine Francis Poole with a .45. It strikes horror. If he managed to figure out which end you were supposed to cock, his next move would probably be to blow off his penis with the thing.

I crossed the middle sidewalk of the campus, weighted down by that same oppressive feeling I'd had ever since Betty Lynn's reception. There was something ugly and ominous hanging over this town. I could almost see it. Hear it. Taste it. I trudged heavily through the cold wind toward the gymnasium. I was too weary to fight the signs anymore. They were all leading down a one lane road—to the football team.

Which meant they were also leading me to my son.

That fact kept sinking into my tired brain like a craggy rock into a gob of mud.

The Lions had been let out of their cages and were running around on the gymnasium floor as if they were being chased across the desert by Hottentots. Standing next to the bleachers, I watched the Big Four and my gifted son Derek try to settle down on the sideline by bowing their heads in what looked like a humble prayer for a count of ten, holding their gazes low as though they were contemplating the miracle of each other's feet. Then they exploded into a five or six word incantation that served to spur them into action, and hustled out to center court to the rest of the team. I wondered if they planned to use the ritual against Brookhaven that night. From what I could tell, it was the best play they had.

The leader of this outbreak was Johnny Davis, a tall, black quarterback with a bump of a face that looked like a pothole that had been recently paved over. His main man was running back Gregory Lewis, who bobbed coolly up and down the court saying "Man" a lot, trying in his own way to figure out, I suppose, how anybody was supposed to play football on a basketball court. The only Caucasian in the backfield was a rust-colored Italian boy who had a pizza face, a zucchini nose, and a thick, squat body with a low center of gravity that scooted across the floor like a sack of wet peat moss. The silent center, Jackson Smith, had all the verve of a roll of Boston bread; but he did have the talent of being able to squirt a football out from under his rear end without so much as a grunt. As far as I could tell, the boy did not possess the gift of language.

Davis ran plays the way Mom makes Sunday dinner. As soon as he got the ball from the center, he wheeled around and thrust it into Lewis's gut like a roast into the oven. That done, he promptly flung his arms into the air to indicate he had done his part; now everybody else could do theirs, because he didn't want any more to do with it. By this time, Lewis had stayed within himself long enough to burst into the line like a fist into a pile of rising dough. The defense sagged, then crumbled under the force of impact, enabling Lewis to burst into the secondary where he abruptly tripped over his size thirteens and punted the ball with his face across the free throw line.

"Damn!" he growled in frustration, and slammed his fist to the floor. "Whoever heard of playing ball on shit like this!"

I felt the coach come up beside me. "What do you think of our All-American?" he asked me.

"Really puts his nose into it," I said.

Coach Wilson Reed shot a spray of Day's Work into his Dixie cup. "What you're seeing is the result of a momentary disorientation," he said knowingly. "This Temple thing has them all screwed up. They're acting more like pallbearers than ball carriers."

I thought the analogy was pretty grim, but I said nothing.

"Jenkins!" he yelled at the offensive guard. "You cretin! You're supposed to take him to the right, you idiot! Look—it's this hand! The one you hold your fork in!" Getting nothing but a "Huh?" as a response, he ran out on the court to straighten Jenkins out.

Wilson J. Reed was what sportswriters call a coach with "class"—meaning he won scads of games and yet was never so lumpish as to say in an interview that they were just going to play them one at a time. We sportswriters greatly admire coaches who rise to the top of their field while being at the same time as humble as piss in a bucket about it. We especially dote on the ones who say things like, "Hey—you fellas have your jobs to do, too, right? Just like I do!" Except for possessing this kind of class, Reed had no distinguishing marks or tattoos of any kind. All he owned was a serious face with a profile that looked so much like the kind you see on coins that people trusted him with anything they had. He used his looks to persuade the school board to fund his pet projects, and his brain to transform mediocre players into winners.

"Don't act rural!" was his motto on the field, which meant players were not allowed to wear parti-colored socks under their uniforms, or strap survivor knives to their hips during workouts. He even converted the catcher on the baseball team to smokeless tobacco, because whoever saw Yogi Berra with a smoldering Pall Mall hanging out of his mask, for God's sake? Coach Reed got things done. He single-handedly convinced the board to purchase two electric scoreboards from his brother-in-law and had the dressing rooms moved out of the attic of the gym into the basement. His argument was that no winning tradition could exist where players went to dress like a bunch of Rhode Island Reds headed up to roost for the night.

The way he got the football team to win games was to channel our concentration by encouraging us to adopt a conscientiously applied program of regular sexual self-gratification.

This was a screwy idea he had acquired either as a by-product of a part-time job in a maximum security prison in Ohio or from a Yankee Methodist preacher he knew on the way up. If he could line up the gears of the sex drive of his athletes, he figured, he could race his team into first place in the conference.

At first, he was very subtle about all this. He began by calling us into the supply room where he told us that he wanted us to start thinking of our healthy male sex organs as sentries of the soul. He made tears come into his eyes as he traced the poor, pathetic history of the penis through the ages. This poor device of nature had been maligned for centuries by artists and clergymen alike, when in truth, it was a lookout for the spirit, assigned by nature to perform certain critical duties for the body and ready to discharge them at practically any time especially when you first got up in the morning.

"Don't look now, but there's a penis on every man in this room," he informed us. "And from now on. I want you to consider every one of them as individual members of the team. We will think of first place as Babylon, right? And these as our Hanging Guardians."

As familiar with penises as we were, we truly had no idea in hell what Coach was talking about. Not knowing whether to cheer his pep talk or shrink out of the equipment room with our heads bowed in shame, we let inertia be our guide, as we were accustomed to doing in a game, and hung around the shelves and rolled up the socks and unpacked the toilet paper, until he ordered us to go out and play our hearts out for Marshall High.

Thereafter, he caught us unawares with impromptu speeches, such as the one after wind sprints, when we usually hied ourselves to the sidelines to throw up and wave at the girls who were watching practice from the stands. On the fifty-yard line, he reared back and lectured us for twenty minutes on the curse of the wandering eyes and concluded with a quotation, more or less, from Valentine Blocker: "Put your faith in God, my boys," he told us, "and keep your peckers dry."

Privately, we happened to believe this football coach

of ours was a man who had himself a problem. But the ignorance of youth is never a match for a coach with class. Before long, he had indoctrinated us with hand painted signs which he appended to lockers and doors and taped on commodes in the head. Things such as:

"People may need people, but a wise man lopes his own mule."
Granville Dubois.

And:
"Know thyself. Know girls after graduation."
Mayor Cleveland Lyles

And:
"I want to be alone."
Greta Garbo

By homecoming, we were sufficiently brainwashed, had sworn off girls and were rallying our energies around our individual flagpoles. As soon as we did that, we miraculously acquired that tunnel vision which is necessary to win football games.

As I watched Coach Reed shouting out rude instructions to my son Derek, I wondered what sly and sophisticated techniques he was using these days to control the team. As he directed these boys like extras in a Tarzan movie, I tried to imagine young Miller coming to grips with lectures and quotations. The idea wouldn't quite wash. I loved my son, but I wasn't convinced yet the big guy could noodle out a pull tab on a Diet Coke.

After firing up the team a bit, Reed came back to herd me into his office in the gym. It was a hot, close room in pine paneling trimmed with off-pink wallpaper roughly the color of a runny nose. The whole place smelled like Clorox. As Reed plopped down at his desk and massaged his lizard neck with the tips of his fingers, I decided he must have been washing his face in the stuff.

"What I like," he told me, "is to keep the press out on the day of a game. I don't want sportswriters breaking their concentration."

"I suppose anything's possible," I allowed.

He scratched his Adam's apple. "This group'll be all right though," he said confidently. "Fortunately, they don't have enough sense to worry about two things at once for very long. All I have to do to get them back on track is to talk pro for a couple of minutes before kickoff. They may look like they're playing around in a sewer out there right now, but you can count on them coming through in the end. That's what makes everyone love the Lions."

"Everybody but Richard Temple."

Now he switched to his nose. "What do you expect?" he said. "Nothing but a damned intellectual. Didn't understand the importance of sports, did everything he could to sabotage my program. Hell, the guy even tried to get my kids to take a literacy test!"

"Bad idea?"

"Idiotic, is more like it. Tell you what, Miller. Go out there and ask Greg Lewis to comment on the Germanic prose style of *Sartor Resartus* and see how far you get. Hell, the boy's still working on getting his dong out of his pants without getting the prepuce caught in the zipper."

"Maybe Temple wanted smarter athletes."

He laughed scornfully at the idea. "Not even Temple was that naive," he said. "Listen. Just between you and me, the only kid who'd be willing to tear up his knees and thicken his neck and walk around in a lard-ass body the rest of his life on the twenty thousand-to-one shot of making a living playing pro football is either a nigger or a moron or both. If you quote me on that, I'll deny it, but it's the truth."

"You make a father feel proud, Coach."

"Hey, don't blame me. I don't jerk them out of the classrooms, you know. I hold practice, and the little dolts show up. Temple wasn't like me, though. He never could deal with the facts of life. Never did acknowledge a damn thing we accomplished. No surprise, though, a guy as immoral as he was. I guess you've heard of about all those women of his."

"So you figure he got what he deserved."

"Off the record, that's just what I figure. There was a man so obsessed with his genitalia, he couldn't see straight. He didn't have the objectivity to realize how much we need the game of football in this country. Lot of people don't realize football is our national trust. We've got to have the outlet. It's part of our Puritan ethic to need a winner and a loser. Sometimes, in real life, we have to let things slide all to hell like we did in Korea and Vietnam. But we'll never let that happen in football. It's too important to the national psyche. Temple was too much of a egghead to see any of this."

I waited for the patriotic fervor to cool down before

I went on. "Do any of your great players use drugs, Coach?" I asked.

He ran a fingernail over the wrinkles in his forehead as he considered how disappointed he was in me. "What is it with you guys?" he said. "Why do you always want to bring up drugs? People don't want to know how football works, Teddy. Joe Blow in the grandstand couldn't care less if you've got to have painkillers to keep up the high level of performance of a player. I'm not kidding about this being a national trust, you know. The fans are dead serious about it, especially when there's no war to lean on. They need these guys. They depend on them. They bet good money on them. And by the Lord Jesus, they expect them to play. A twisted kneecap or distress in the lower tract just isn't good enough reason for them to lose money on a game."

"So our guys will play tonight, even though their beloved superintendent is wadded up in a body bag."

"Of course they'll play. There was never any question of that."

"Real troopers you've got there."

"That's right. That's why I believe in them."

"Do you also believe in all these dead-serious fans betting money on the game?"

"Come on, now. You know as well as I do, gambling's always been a part of the profession of football."

"I thought it was a sport."

"Oh, get your nose out of your armpit, man," he said. "We're living in the computer age here. These kids are dancing around to synthesizers while Madison Avenue and Pennsylvania Avenue are filling their heads with statistical crap, and experts are telling them we could all be nuked to death any day now. They may be as dumb as cows, but they know ten times more than you did at their age. Gambling's just another gritty little reality they have to face."

"Like puberty?"

"Beats me how a guy from New York can act so simple. Don't you realize nobody plays organized football for fun anymore? Too much pressure, man. The days when a high school coach could feed himself and his wife and his two-point-three kids with a five-and-five season are dead and gone!"

I hesitated a minute, and then decided to leave. Coach Reed got to his feet and gave me a parting suggestion for my story though, before I reached the door. "Play up the courage angle on the thing," he said. "That's something the guys from *Sports Illustrated* ignored completely."

"Can't believe they were so negligent."

"However you do it, forget the drugs and the gambling, huh? Try giving these boys their due for a change, why don't you? Let me tell you something about these kids. To a man, they were all turned inside-out over this Temple thing, but when I asked them if they wanted to play tonight, you know what they said? Just as I expected: they begged me to let them play. Take Davis for instance. He'd cut his throwing hand on some glass or something, but that didn't stop him. 'I've gotta play, Coach' is what he said. 'I gotta play!' "

"I'll bet he says that to all the coaches."

"All right, it may not take any brains to play this game, but it sure as hell takes courage. And that's what this team has in abundance: guts."

"Plus, they believe in the First National Trust of Football."

"Damn right. That's what it takes to win a hundred in a row."

I didn't know whether to inform Reed that he had become a jerk in recent years or promise to vote for him in the next election. What I ended up doing was thanking him politely for his cooperation and promising not to harass his players on the way out.

Fat chance. Just as soon as I escaped the office, I ran into one of the pillars of the football community, the Italian running back, fronting the exit door of the gym like a stone on the Mount of Olives. When I nonchalantly made a go at slipping past him, he folded his aqueduct arms, puffed out his rust-colored cheeks, and solemnly held his ground.

"They must have you running out for a pass," I said to him.

Not a crack of a smile. I had a serious one here. He let his enormous arms fall and dangle at his side. Wilson Barbio was a compact fellow, but those arms were as long as fully grown boa constrictors. He and my son must have spent their off-days pulling each other across the wide Missouri.

"We wanted to know what you were writing about," he said.

Since this kid was about as close to royalty as Uncle Harley was to a seat in Congress, I inferred by the "we" he meant he and his teammates, with whom he apparently often discussed such vital issues as my career. "The usual stuff," I answered him. "You know, the game of football equals the game of life. That sort of thing."

He was not impressed. "We wanted to know if you was writing us up in the *Times* or not," he said. He followed that with a pecking motion toward the floor with a taped index finger, as if he were pointing out to me the exact location of the tell-tale heart.

"Look, Barbie—" I said.

"Barbio!" he corrected, and promptly launched into the correct spelling of his name for my benefit. Did a fine job of it, too. Might have faltered a bit on the vowels, but nobody's perfect.

"Look, Willie," I said. "It's been fun—"

"Nobody leaves this gym!" he declared.

I looked around the place. "Looks like everybody already has," I said.

"I'm just saying you can't."

"Ah. Well, I have to tell you, Barbio, I do have a few plans for the evening."

"Better listen to the man, *Mr.* Miller," said a coarse, sarcastic voice behind me. I turned to see Gregory Lewis looming over me like a black bear in springtime. "Nobody's going nowhere, till you hear all about the Lions," he said.

"I've probably heard enough already, Greg," I said.

"You hear that? He's making fun of us!" said Johnny Davis the quarterback. He and the silent center were hanging close by. "You got no right to make fun of us."

"Shut up, man!" Lewis told him. "I'm handling this!"

"Well, look at him! He's scorning us! He thinks just because his son's on the team, he can say any damn thing he wants!"

Encouraged by the show of strength around him,

Lewis edged closer to me. When he got near enough to bump my elbow, I felt my nerves begin to tighten like piano wires. But I said nothing. Children require patience. "What about that, Miller?" he charged. "You wouldn't be making fun of us, would you?"

I was starting to get anxious now with the Big Four crowding in on me like folks around a car wreck. Too bad I wasn't a football. From what I'd seen on the court, the safest thing to be around these guys was a football.

"Maybe you'd better tell us what you told the coach," Barbio said.

"Why would you want to know that?" I wondered.

That must have been a tougher question than I imagined, for it fairly set Barbio back on his heels. "Because we just do, that's all!" he countered.

"Are you sure you fellas aren't the debate team in disguise?"

"Listen to him!" Davis cried. "I tell you, he's making fun of us!"

Ordinarily I'm a patient man, but I had had it to the gills with this one-on-four dialogue with the rising generation. I was being detained and badgered in a drafty old gym by the Sportsman Quartet, and I was ready to explode. Besides, it was getting harder and harder to breathe properly with all the subtle smells of active youth around me. Barbio reeked—like a men's room at an old library. The silent center must have been swigging at the iodine. I didn't even want to guess what the others had been up to. As a last civil appeal before I resorted to breaking their butts, I asked Barbio if he would mind moving out of the way.

I might as well have asked him to scan a couple of

lines of Pope. "Are you going to write us up in the *Times* or not?" He said.

"We only print the news that's fit to print," I said.

He scowled angrily at me. "What about one hundred games in a row, huh?" he said. "You think that ain't fit enough to print?"

"You ain't won a hundred in a row yet, Barbio."

Lewis was now close enough to start sharing his life with me. I could hear his shortened breathing as he talked. "This guy's really getting on my nerves," he told the others. "It's like Derek said. Just because he lives up in New York, he thinks he's some kind of genius or other."

"You obviously don't know New York," I said.

"Well, I do!" Barbio scored a point. "And I can tell you this: that paper of yours ain't even giving the Lions the time of day yet! Now are you going to tell us what you're going to write about or not?"

I was now tightly clinching my fists to keep from breaking them on somebody's face. Wouldn't look good, lashing out at minority teenagers. "Look, kid," I said, exasperated. "I don't know what your problem is, but let me give you a few of the highlights of mine. I'm a very perverse person. I don't like where I am, I don't like what I'm doing, and I sure as hell don't like who I'm doing it with. Besides which, I am tired, hungry, constipated, disillusioned, middle-aged, and at the moment, highly pissed off. Now, hasn't your sainted mother ever told you not to mess around with somebody like that?"

"You leave my mother out of this," Barbio grunted.

"You tell him, Will," Davis urged.

"I'll tell him, all right," Barbio boasted. "This old guy don't scare me none."

That did it. I looked straight at him. "Maybe that's because you don't understand me," I told him. "Let me put it to you this way: if you don't move out of my way right now—this minute—I"m going to kick your scrotum into your esophagus and squeeze your balls through your molars like pits out of a prune. Is that clear enough for you?"

"You just try it," he puffed.

"If that's what you want—"

"Now you hold on there, old man," threatened Gregory Lewis. "If you start pushing one of us, you got all the others to deal with. We do everything as a team, right, men?"

"Right!" they all chimed in.

I stared into Lewis's glaring yellow eyes, deciding where to start with the cleanup. I was at the point of taking aim with my right shoe at the widest coccyx I could reach when a familiar voice called a halt to the proceedings.

"Leave him alone," Derek told them. Although they heard him well enough, they had to be yanked away from me and shoved out on the court to mind his words. "Go on!" he ordered. "Get the hell out of here!"

As soon as the boys were back safely on the oak, I looked upon this haggard boy—tall as a water tower, but with tired, puffy eyes, a sagging mouth, and a low-hanging chin. He looked heartsick, as if the trainer had come and taken his stepladder and tire away. He vainly searched his mind for sentences, while he nervously fondled the blood-stained bandage on the index finger of his right hand. Since that was an area we could both concentrate on, I figured I could help matters along by asking him what he had done to his finger to make it bleed so.

"Nothing," he muttered. "I just cut it shaving."

I gave it a good look. "I wonder if it really needs shaving," I said.

"What?"

"What I mean is, nobody notices a man's hands these days."

His cold, dull, pained expression was hard and steady. "What are you doing here anyway?" he asked me.

"Thought I'd get to know the team," I said.

He gritted his teeth. "You don't care about this team!" he charged. "You don't care about anything I've ever done!"

The truth of that cut made me flinch. It was as obvious as the nose on Barbio's face there was a wall between us. I don't know why I wanted to believe good fences made good fathers.

Dumb, I guess.

"I do care, Derek," I said. "Why do you think I"m here? I sure didn't come to rake over the coals with ole Coach Reed."

In his anxiety, he involuntarily squeezed his wound, producing a visage of agony that would have scared the wits out of Geronimo. Such an emotional kid. "It's just that everybody's so messed up right now," he said. "The whole team's messed up."

"Why?"

"I don't know why, we just are!" he cried. "You

don't want to talk to me anyway. All you want to do is live in New York and be famous."

While he was allowing that powerful dig to have its effect, I retrieved the hundred dollar bill from my pocket and handed it to him.

After giving me a curious look, he took the money and stared at it in his fist as if it were his first discharge. "What's this supposed to be for?" he asked.

"I was hoping you'd tell me. Your sister found it in your room."

"Son of a bitch!" he said and swore he had never laid eyes on a hundred dollar bill in his whole life. "And what's more, I don't want to!" He held it out to me. "Now take it back!"

"Whose money is it, Derek?"

"How should I know whose money it is? Nobody's."

"In other words, one night a strange C-note wandered into the duplex and hopped on your dresser?"

"Damn it, Dad!" He crumpled the bill and flung it viciously against my chest. I watched it bounce off the pects and float harmlessly to the floor landing in exactly the place Barbio had designated with his finger. When I looked back at my son, blood rushed into my face.

"Derek, I want to know where you got that money!"

His huge body shrank back and he begged me through his teeth to stop showing it to everybody. Solemnly, I picked up the bill, crammed it into my pocket, and promised him to forget I'd ever brought it up.

But it was too late for amends. Derek was already shaken to the core by all this. Beads of sweat were

popping out on his forehead, and the color was draining rapidly from his face. As he wiped his eyes with his
palms and struggled with a few deep breaths, I could
see the boy was beginning to weaken.

"Why don't you go back to that whore of yours and
leave us alone?" he whined.

"I told you, the whore is gone. I'm all alone now."

"Well, you're wrong if you think that matters to
me!"

Before I could say anything else stupid, Derek wheeled
around and raced toward the dressing room at full
speed. Ten feet from the door, he came to a sudden stop,
groggily seized his stomach, stooped over, and threw
up his bananas the way Greg Lewis bobbles a football.

Although I was the first to reach him, I was quickly
blocked off from my son by his buddies. While I stood
helplessly by, Wilson Barbio waded through the mess,
tangled his arms in Derek's, and led him toward the
locker room. As aggravated by the Lions as I was, I was
impressed with this show of loyalty. How many men
would step through vomit for a friend?

"Ain't nothing wrong with him," Lewis told me.
"He's always like this on the day of a game."

"Yeah, he does it every time," Davis said. "Doctor
says it's his nerves."

Even the silent center nodded his medicine ball
head in agreement, but I knew better. This was not my
son's ordinary behavior.

But what could I do? Feeling frustrated and guilty,
I lingered in the gym until practice was over and the
floor was clear of football players, then I left. Outside,
I was too rattled to feel the cold, too numbed by this

idiot project of writing a story about Richard Temple to feel any discomfort. But I knew I couldn't back away from it—now that the mystery was finally beginning to clear.

To save my shins, I parked the Thunderbird in Mom and Dad's driveway and waited until the family cat felt the urge to go make an evening deposit in the neighbor's yard. As soon as the Yellow Peril had gotten herself into a transaction, I sprang out of the car and dashed across the lawn to the house. I must have been getting the hang of the game by now, for I believe she never even saw me enter her domain.

Mom was in the kitchen burning supper. With all the paraphernalia for her epic novel thrown around her, you needed a library card to get into the place. Books and magazines were scattered on the cabinets and appliances, legal pads, and spiral notebooks were hanging like whores over the window sills. With hundreds of copies of *Science, Current Anthropology* and *National Geographic* strewn this way and that, it looked as though the anti-humanists had finally bombed the Smithsonian. The fledgling author herself was leaning against the dishwasher in the grip of William Howells' *Mankind So Far*, frantically scribbling notes in the margins of a first National Bank calendar.

"Theodore!" As usual, as soon as Mom recognized an offspring, she felt obliged to charge it like a camel in heat. Bracing my body for high impact, I remembered an old Indian trick and relaxed my muscles at the moment of assault, and thus was able to avoid serious injury. Even so, I was as helpless as a dumpling in her hands. She grabbed and squeezed me as if we had just discovered due North together, pounded my clavicles with *Mankind So Far*, and sucked a hickey on my right cheek the size of a candied apple ring. "What on earth have you been doing!" she exclaimed. "We've been so worried about you!"

"I've been doing a story on Richard Temple," I told her.

I should've confessed the fact sooner, I guess, for at the sound of his name, she set me free. "What a terrible shock that's been!" she said. "Why does something awful always happen to a man like that?"

"A man like what?"

"You know what I mean, Theodore. A man that acts like that! People in Marshall naturally expect an educator to be a certain way."

"And he wasn't," I concluded.

She looked at me with exasperation. "Well, if you've been writing a story on him, you certainly don't have to be told by your own mother about all his women."

"Do you think all his women got together and did him in, Mom?"

"I don't know who 'did him in,' and I don't want to know. It may be your job to think about it, but I don't have to, so why don't we talk about other things? Such as your family, for instance. How did the reunion go?"

"Went about like one of Dad's tornadoes. They all seem to be on edge over there. Even Jennifer."

"You mean she's suddenly turned into a young woman."

"I mean she's suddenly turned into an 'Electra.'"

Mom dismissed that idea with a wave of the hand. "Oh, that's nothing but a silly phase she's going through," she said. "Girls go through phases the way Sonny goes through shorts. But what about Derek? Isn't he something? I'm thinking of putting him into *Species!* I see him as the perfect prototype of Aaron Hopely in the Galley Hill fallacy section. What do you think?"

"I don't know. Does Aaron live in a tree?"

For a while, I listened to Mom run by five or six plots of the novel for my consideration. She assured me she valued my opinion on literary matters, even though she couldn't say much for my physical prowess these days. To be frank about it, she believed I currently looked like a hard case of the walking death.

"Must be something I ate," I said.

"Theodore, I want you to stop feeling so badly about all this, do you hear me? There's no denying this thing is a tragedy, but Chief Bundley will eventually catch whoever did it, and then it'll be over."

"Mom, Chief Bundley couldn't catch his thumb in his teeth."

She took *Mankind So Far* to her enormous bosom. Poor Howells. I knew exactly how he felt—as loved as a puppy, as surrounded as Custer. "We have to learn to take things like this in stride," she told me.

The image of striding made me feel guilty all over again about Mr. Poole's reminder that I had run away from my responsibilities once before. Out of the mouths of harelips. . . .

"I've done too much of that already, Mom," I said.

"Oh, that's New York City talking, not you," she said. "It's just like I've been telling Sonny. 'Theodore's only problem is he needs to move closer to home. Closer to his roots!'"

"Dad would like that," I said. "He likes roots."

"Well, if you think about it, I'm sure you'll do the right thing." With that, she kissed me hard and wetly on the lips, catching me unprepared again. It's hard to hold your own with a big, affectionate mother in her prime. "Now, why don't you go into the den and watch the TV until supper's ready?" she said.

As I turned to go, I noticed a dark curl of smoke rising ominously above the electric stove. Quite a display. A clutch of Comanches with a damp blanket couldn't have done any better. "What are you cooking?" I asked her.

"Beef and beets," she answered, and opened her book. "Amy gave me the recipe. I think one of her boyfriends is a gourmet cook."

"Great."

"Theodore, you really are looking thin," she observed. "Are you sure you're eating properly?"

I told her I was doing what I could and headed toward the den.

Dad was in his La-Z-Boy recliner looking as if he were about to be ejected and catapulted across the room toward the Sony TV set feet first. He was watching the Weather Channel through his shoes, which stood upright like a goal post. Dad was in his element, believing as he does that life itself depends on atmospheric conditions. Like those Comanches, he's always on the lookout for them. When there's no violent storm on the Mississippi horizon, he'll settle for a tropical depression off the coast of Cuba or even a high wind in the Ukraine.

Right now, he seemed to be caught in a doldrums between low pressure troughs.

"How's it going, son?" Sociably, he waved his right foot at me. "I was wondering where you were."

"What's on the tube?" I asked him.

"They just had a special on subterranean fissures that was real good," he told me. "Did you know there are more than a thousand earthquakes around the globe every year?"

"It's a wonder we don't all fall off."

"Ain't it the truth? Well, don't just stand there, Ted. Come in, have a seat. Watch the news with me. They'll probably have a film on the murder by now."

Overjoyed at the prospect, I crossed in front of the TV and plopped down hard on he sofa. For a man in the throes of an intestinal strike, this was a mistake. The cushions on this sofa were as hard as stone and as rough to the touch as a detour off the interstate. "What do you keep in this thing?" I bounced up and down on it. "Skulls?"

"That's Ed's divan," he said, as if that explained it.

"Then why isn't Ed sitting on it?"

"He left it here when he moved to Saudia Arabia. They wouldn't let him take it in."

"I can understand that."

Dad was wielding the remote control unit like a pistol, firing relentlessly at the Sony screen. "What channel you want, son?" he asked me. "Three? Twelve?"

I let him have his fun for a while, before I suggested the Laurel/Hattiesburg station. While he played with his module, I sought a place on the road bed for my aching back. Useless. For sheer comfort, Ed's divan was in a league with a seat at a rock concert or an outdoor john. Two minutes in the same position and your butt started going numb, and all your precious tissues began to meld. I wondered if I hadn't solved the great family mystery of Missing Person Uncle Silas Harper. This could be it. The old fellow had crawled inside Ed's divan and died.

"Let's see if I can find that station," Dad was saying. "I hardly ever watch it any more with all these new cable deals." He flicked his way through sixty million syndicated re-runs, which spliced together and stored in a time vault the size of Pluto, would comprise a fairly good history of our time, if anybody truly wanted one. I was starting to have the sensation of going down for the third time, when he finally allowed the screen to come to rest on Channel Seven. "There you go," he said, as if there had been nothing to it. "The news'll be on right after the commercials."

"Mind if I tape it?" I asked.

"Heck, no. That's what I bought that thing for. I'm glad for somebody besides Amy to use it. Go ahead, use that blank tape in the machine."

I started the VCR on top of the television set and returned quietly to Uncle Silas's remains. On the Trinitron screen, a man in a dog suit was putting Dad in mind of the fact that one of these days, he was going to have to break down and get himself an Irish Wolf Hound or maybe a St. Bernard. "Something big enough you can see it from the house," he specified. Mainly, he needed this dog to keep the cat in line, the way they once brought the nutria into Louisiana to eradicate the raccoons or whatever. "When it gets to where a man can't get out in his own driveway for fear of being mugged by a fraslin cat, then something has to be done!" he declared.

During the next barrage of commercial messages, I leaned back on the skulls and let my mind flash like Dad's TV over the events of the day. My psychic selector automatically stopped on that gut-wrenching scene in Nairobi. It didn't need to. I hadn't forgotten that Tommy Curtis had been whisked out of Temple's yard into a jail cell where he was now sitting bewildered, heart-broken, and terrified. "All I want you to do is help my boy," Duke Curtis had said to me. "Get him out of jail."

Sure. Burst into Marshall from the cold north and spring a black kid out of a white jail and go on about your business. At one time, maybe, Bubba Henderson and I could have huddled together and figured out a way to do that. But the times were different then. Now Bubba was nothing but a lifeless myth, like the black and white ghost of Robert Young churning out advice to Bud and Betty on Dad's Trinitron. Time had swept my friend Bubba into the corners of the past like a wisp of dust in an Uncle Harley house.

"This is it," Dad announced as a WDAM-TV logo flashed on the box. "The news is coming on."

The next image to appear was that of a stunning blonde woman about forty years old, as tall and elegant as a mythical queen. She was seated at an oval desk wearing a high-neck beige silk blouse and a chocolate brown wool scarf. How lovely she looked! Emanating a quintessence of grace, she projected a soul full of human warmth into every inch of the room through a clear, commanding voice that resonated with strength and confidence, yet throbbed at the same time with all the storied smoothness of Southern feminine charm. For the space of time that Judy Moon smiled, the world seemed perfect again—bold and alive and bracing and provocative and full of infinite promise.

I felt tears start to cloud my eyes as I sat in the house I had grown up in and gazed upon the woman I had grown up for.

I had loved Judy Moon for over half my life, after all, since the day she walked in front of those wrinkled drapes on *Teen Tempos* on Channel Three, all of fourteen years old, with a Pepsodent smile and a voice like mayonnaise. In this very house, I watched a gawky girl blossom into the essence of womanhood, first as *Teen Tempos'* pretty, nervous hostess, then as the beloved weather girl on WAPT. Dad and I never missed a show. To face the dew of the day without first checking Judy and her meteorological map was inconceivable.

To the dismay of my wife, in later years, I tuned in on *Coffee with Judy* whenever I had a chance. "My God, she's only a woman, Teddy!" she loved to point out. "It's not like she's a goddess or anything!"

Nan was wrong, of course. It was exactly like that.

Squirming now on top of Uncle Silas's bones, I wondered if I should have tried to explain my obsession with an image on the television screen. But how would she have ever understood it? Nancy might not understand her own enticing sexuality, but she could, at least, deal with it. But this was beyond her horizon. She refused to believe a man needed an image of the ideal to grow up with. She could never see how the unfathomable clarity and purity of Judy Moon could convey the light of hope into thousands of dreary dens, such as the one I was in.

"A prominent educator in Marshall has been killed," Judy Moon was saying on the screen. "The body of Richard Temple, Superintendent of the Pike County Public School System, was found in the living room of his home early this morning. He had apparently been shot to death with a .45 caliber pistol. Don Fairly was on the scene shortly after the body was discovered and filed this report."

From Ed's divan, I watched the old brick school building appear on the screen, followed by an array of wildly parked cars, then the murder house itself, where six dozen rotund little men were rolling around the lawn like croquet balls. The camera zoomed in on the porch, just as the chief of police and his wrecking crew burst through the wicket into the morning light.

"All right, folks, give 'em room!" a deputy yelled, as four young fellows dressed like Maytag repairmen lugged the stretcher out of the house. Even though Bundley was straining to look in the game, it was obvious he considered this death business as something possibly contagious, and thus gave the corpse all the room it wanted. At the end of the sidewalk, the camera perched behind a human ear and showed us how to stuff a body into a police van.

Meanwhile, faces in the crowd were gasping in horror and surprise to see something so dramatic happening on the school grounds. An elderly lady in garden gloves wept into an embroidered handkerchief. A black man peeled off an LA Dodger cap and bowed his head. A mother of many covered her face with one of her kids and bawled uncontrollably.

As the camera moved toward the chief, the crisp

voice of the Channel Seven reporter called out to him, stopping him cold in his tracks.

Bundley responded to the summons with a look of austerity. "Excuse me, Don," he said. "We're mighty busy here."

"Chief Bundley, can you tell us what's going on?" Fairly asked.

Bundley paused and stared into the camera. "I can tell you this much," he said. "We got ourselves a real situation in there, and we're doing everything humanly possible to deal with it."

"Does that mean you expect to make an arrest soon?"

"Matter of fact, we have a suspect in custody now."

"Who is it?"

"Sorry. No comment."

"Could you tell us about the victim's family?"

Bundley started for the car. "The victim's family has been notified," he answered. "That's all I can say."

"Chief—"

"Sorry, Don. That's all I got to say."

"One more question, Chief," Fairly insisted. "Will the Marshall High football game still go on?"

This brought Bundley to a stop, made him hitch his trousers, and patty-cake his belly. He was obviously glad to have a fact to report. "As far as I've been told," he said, "the football game is on."

"Is that official?"

"That's right. As of this moment, that's official."

After a shot of the police van pulling away, we were spirited back to the Laurel/Hattiesburg studio, where Judy Moon sat at a crescent desk with a good-looking, dark-skinned man who looked like a recent signee with the Houston Astros.

"Judy," he said, "to follow up on that report, we now know the identity of the suspect the police have arrested. He's Tommy Curtis of Marshall."

"And he's a minor, isn't he, Don?"

"He's sixteen. One more thing," he said. "Just before we went on the air, an official in the police department in Marshall called us to confirm: the alleged murder weapon has been found."

"That was awfully fast work."

Fairly nodded eagerly. "The chief of police down there is pretty confident he'll wrap up the case in a few days, Judy," he said. "In any event, we'll stay on it and keep you posted."

"Thank you, Don," she said and turned to the camera. "We'll be back with more news after this." Seconds later, Judy Moon was transformed into an attractive bowl of Hormel Chili.

My knees felt like two quarters of warm oleo when I got up to stop the VCR, but Dad was as calm as a gourd. "Isn't that the girl we used to watch on the weather?" he asked me.

"That's her," I answered. "Same one who'll be interviewing me on Monday."

"I'll be. She's a real looker, isn't she?"

"Yep."

"I wonder how a girl can be that pretty with all that ugly stuff going on around her all the time? If you ask me, she'd be better off doing the weather." He ruminated while I rewound the tape. "I'll bet you in real life, she's nothing like that," he decided. "I'll bet in real life, she's as sour as a quince."

"She doesn't look sour."

"Yes, but you see, Ted, that's the way TV is. Folks get themselves all worked up and fixed up for TV. That's why most of what you see on there isn't real."

"Judy Moon is real."

"I don't know about that, now. Sometimes I think the only thing that's not phony is the weather, because nobody's figured out a way to change it to suit the needs of the public. Everything else, you've got to take with a grain of salt, because most of life these days is nothing but show biz."

I was squatting in front of the Sony, watching the replay. On the screen flashed the WDAM-TV logo. Judy. Marshall High School. Cars. I stopped the VCR, backed it up, and froze the frame on a pair of gray Lincolns parked beneath the American flag on the campus. "Dad," I asked, "whose cars are these?"

He squinted through his bi-focals. "Let's see," he said. "I believe that one on the left belongs to the mayor. The next one to it is one of Dr. Hewitt's. He's also got a Jeep and an R.V."

I stared at the Lincolns for a long time. "Why would Mayor Moore and Dr. Hewitt be at the school?" I said.

"Beats me. Maybe because they're on the board."

Although the idea of seeing Temple's corpse wasn't all that titillating, I ran the next part of the tape anyway in slow motion. As I had hoped, the perspective was different. As the faces began to grow harder and more desperate, I switched to the single frame advance and inched the picture ahead, a lick at a time.

Then I saw someone I hadn't noticed before hanging back among the others. His gaunt, yellow face sent a shiver into my bones. "You wouldn't happen to know this character, would you?" I asked Dad.

He pressed his lips together thoughtfully and shook his head. "Nope," he replied.

"First name's Douglas," I prodded. "I met him at the reception."

Dad waved his feet back and forth. "Never saw him before," he said. "Looks kind of sick to me."

"How about this one?" I pointed at the stumpy Italian man next to Douglas.

"Don't know him, either. Maybe he's one of Vince Scarlotti's men. Every once in a while, he'll bring one of them up from New Orleans to work at the cleaners."

With the bright image of Judy Moon on live television in the corner of my eye, I got up and found the number of David J. Moore in the telephone book.

No answer.

When I tried Hewitt's home, I got his wife Dixie, a plump little girl with buck teeth and a hardshell Baptist father who wouldn't let her dance, date, canoe, or watch color movies. For some reason, though, he did allow her to become a strutting Lionette, soon after which she eloped with the sousaphone player to Biloxi. She came back home two months later with a tan, a divorce, and the makings of a little stranger in her womb.

"Dixie," I said. "This is Ted Miller."

"Well, hello, there! How nice to hear from you. How are you, Teddy?"

"I'm fine. Dixie, do you think I could speak to your husband?"

"Well, sure. If you don't mind holding for a minute."

While I waited, I heard a man's muffled voice mixed

with Dixie's mousey squeak in the background. "Teddy?" The girl finally returned. "I'm sorry. He just went out."

"Out where?"

"I'm not sure."

"Care to give it a shot?"

"I really don't know, Teddy," she told me. "I'm sorry. All I can tell you is, he's gone."

"Good enough. Thanks." I sidled over to the window and searched through the twilight for a sign of the cat. "Dad, where are the Medallion Apartments?" I asked.

He muted the TV with his remote control module. "That's that big complex out toward the state park," he said. "What do you want to go out there for? They tell me it's nothing but single folks and divorcees out there."

I spied the cat curled like a Polish sausage on the front steps in the pale glare of the yellow bug light. Here was my chance. If I could steal out the back door now and bolt across the lawn, I just might make it.

"Tell Mom I sure hate to miss the beef and beets," I told Dad and started to go.

"Where are you headed, this time of day?"

"I'm going to see an old flame about some used cars."

"Before supper? Look, if you're looking for transportation, your Uncle Harley knows some folks—"

"I'll see you at the game later on," I told him.

Having outwitted the cat again, I settled back in my rental car and psyched myself up for my encounter with Bubba's wife. The two miles to the Medallion Apartments were longer than a hot summer night at Aunt Reba's house. My stomach ground noisily like old wooden gears, and my throat was as dry as Utah. But the thought of Mom's simmering pot spurred me on past two Burger Kings, a Popeye's chicken, and a local Bar-B-Q stand.

The new, near-adobe apartments stretched along a wide clay bank like a string of Mesa Verde cliff dwellings with every niche facing south, as if the tenants were all poised and waiting for the ancient astronauts to return. One of them, in fact, a big guy sporting a wrinkled "Property of UMAA" sweatshirt, appeared to be surveying the heavens for his ancestors the very minute I drove up.

I stopped at the copper-colored mailboxes stacked beneath a Medallion sign as big as a glacier and shaped like a Roman coin. It was embossed with an artist's conception of what the Emperor Caligula might have looked like with porcelain crowns and blow-dried hair. After I located Marian's apartment number, I drove over and sat a minute to pull the drawstrings of my nerves together.

Everybody had always called Marian "The Gibson Girl," not so much because of the way she looked, but because she came from Gibson, Indiana. But the other part of it fit, too. On the first day she appeared in the seventh grade, she was wearing the largest set of pre-teen bosoms anybody in a rural area such as ours had ever seen. In truth, these darling buds were about the size of a couple of Roman noses, but they were still pretty big sail for such an early age.

Unfortunately, Betty Lynn's best friend, Becky

Holland, noticed our fascination with Marian's chest right away and showed up after Christmas holidays with an admirable set of her own, an inch superior to Marian's. From that moment on, the race was on. After every vacation, one of them would show up with a bosom which was slightly larger than the other's. Of course they pretended all this ballast was the real McCoy and would screech like an owl with the fits if anybody happened to bump one with an elbow or a ruler. But we knew better.

Marian's brother J.D. told us the truth. Behind the Ag building one day, he confided that if we wanted to know, Sister's boobs weren't hardly no bigger than a damn M & M Peanut. He had mighty good reason to know that, too, for once, as he was plundering through Marian's dresser drawers for Hershey's Kisses, he discovered a whole shoebox full of store-bought falsies. J.D. admitted for a while he was plenty taken with all these foam rubber cups in various sizes. After squeezing them in his fist for a while, then seeing if they'd roll along the floor okay, and finally testing them aerodynamically near the window, he decided to tease his sister by spreading them out on her bed, where she'd be sure to find them when she came home from cheerleading practice.

It tickled him to remember the scene. "All them cones on the bedspread looked like a bunch of pyramids on the desert," he told us.

That evening, Marian stormed into J.D.'s room and fussed at him for twenty minutes for messing around with what she called her science fair project, over which she had been slaving for weeks. Her story was, he had no right to get out all these miniature houses for her American Indian display, and if J.D. didn't keep his filthy hands off her wickiups, he'd be living the rest of his rotten life with nothing but nubs for fingers.

Even after that discovery, the war went on. By the time Marian and Becky were in the tenth grade, things had gotten so far out of hand, teachers had to put them on opposite sides of the room for balance. In geometry class once, while Marian dozed, Eddie Freemont took one of those little flags you tag bones and muscles with in general science lab and quietly stuck it into the foam cushion of Marian's left breast. When Miss Boudreaux asked Marian to rise and comment on the significance of the side-angle-side relationship, she muttered a startled "Huh!" and sprang to her feet, causing half the class to come to attention, salute the flag, and recite the Pledge of Allegiance.

The battle came to a ceasefire in the eleventh grade, with a peculiar but touching announcement by Becky Holland. With a long, somber face, she rose in front of the class, fired up a Diamond kitchen match, stared wistfully at it, and sadly noted, "You all have never seen this flame before." After ceremoniously blowing it out, she added, "And now, you will never see it again." As soon as we had recovered from the weight of that, she added the clincher: "The same will now be true of me." In her own way, Becky was telling us she was about to pull up stakes and D-cups and move the hell out west. Tearfully, she explained over her bosoms that her daddy had gotten a job managing a cafeteria in Fort Smith, Arkansas, as well as keeping wayward Oklahomans from drifting into the state, and since her mother hadn't been heard of since the Civil Rights Act was passed in '54, Becky had no choice but to accompany Daddy across the big river, where, she informed us, grungy farmers ate corny cereal out of dust bowls, and the wrinkled old Apache Indians drove Lincolns and Cadillac DeVilles all over the place because of all the oil.

I had a fling with Marian the next year during her French period when she inhaled Viceroy cigarettes through her nose, wore black-and-white striped blouses and fuchsia berets, and believed the sexiest way for humans to kiss was for the female to do it with the mouth held as firmly and roundly open as a hole on the eighteenth green. By the time I got to her, she'd become very adept at this sort of thing. At the mere touch of a fellow's lips, her mouth would fly open like a trap door leaving you with only one place on earth to go. If I had been inclined toward dentistry in those days, I might have cottoned to this kind of intimacy, but as a man of sport, I naturally found it pretty disconcerting. The basic dilemma is this: after your tongue has ferreted out all the nooks and crannies it wants to, what else can it do in there? You can't keep exploring another person's bicuspids forever. I always made a good show of it with a lot of writhing groans and much searching, searching of the tongue, and I enjoyed it all, but after a while, I was ready to give it a rest.

One lovely, romantic twilight evening at the state park, Marian and I strolled together through the woods and bitter weeds, amidst the dense, sweet smells of wild honeysuckle, pine needles, and magnolia blossoms.

At the edge of the water, we paused and noted the reflection of the crescent moon, which looked like a slice of honeydew melon on the inky surface of the dark and fathomless reservoir. At the "No Swimming—Polluted" sign, we lingered a while in each other's arms and agreed on the particular Platters hit we'd call *our song* and chatted about the world at large, the mysteries of the sea, and so forth. Soon our faces drew close, as an early summer breeze drifted across the water from the new housing project and caressed Marian's pageboy and made it glisten like homecoming glitter on the streets of Marshall. Finally, our lips met, whereupon Marian's jawbone promptly went slack and plopped down like the gate of a landing craft on the beaches of Normandy. Deciding this was as good a time as any to make a move, I held my tongue in its natural position and dropped open my mouth, too, instead.

So there we stood, two young lovers poised on the rim of the reservoir with open mouths pressed together like a couple of empty coffee cups in the gloaming. When I got to thinking we probably looked as though we were comparing fillings or introducing our tonsils to each other, I felt called upon to come up with something to relieve the situation.

It happened to be the wrong thing. "Say 'Ah,' please," I said, which mortified Marian so completely, she instantly clamped shut and bolted for the parking lot.

"Marian—come back!" I pleaded as I chased her through the private docking area. Catching up as she was about to leap over the chain that encircled the parking lot, I snatched her arm and thrust myself hard against her padding and begged her forgiveness even though it was only our third date. While I hugged, I assured her that her sensual ways had captivated me so, I didn't realize what I was doing. I swore to her my tongue was now as ready as an anteater's for any use she might want to make of it.

All these entreaties didn't mean a thing to her, however. Marian tearfully informed me that as of a few minutes ago, her entire life had been changed. From this hour to the date of her death, which by the way could now come this Thursday week, as far as she was concerned, she would never stoop to kiss another living soul including her relatives from St. Louis who brought those very nice Christmas presents every year. Having made this announcement, she scurried across the pavement to the car.

For the longest time, she sat in Dad's '55 Ford Fairlane 500, sheltering her mouth with her trembling hand saying nothing, while I sat knowing somehow I had stupidly stepped on her dignity. Finally, at the red light in Marshall, she turned to me with a profound sadness in her voice.

"Teddy," she said, "I want you to promise me something."

"Sure," I said. "Anything you want."

"You are never to mention this again, do you hear me? Never, ever! Not as long as you live! Do you swear you will never breathe a word?"

"I swear," I said. "Not a word."

A few years later, Marian lost her identity at city

hall. When all her friends took to burning their bras in protest of the things that bind a person, Marian resolved to do the same. In a fit of mob rule at a Ladies for Peace rally, she burst open her blouse, stripped away all her shapely foam, and flung it helter-skelter into the roaring bonfire in front of the city hall. As a crowd cheered wildly and a librarian covered her eyes in shame, Marian stood with her arms crossed and watched her synthetic specialness smolder on the flames in front of God, the mayor, and everybody.

Nancy, assuming that all bosom lore was feminine territory, was very distressed over the incident. "It's perfectly awful, what they're saying about her," she said to me. "They're going around saying she had a double mastectomy at city hall!"

I said nothing.

"Well, I think it's terrible!" she cried. "I don't see how you can let people say such things about an old girlfriend like that!"

A few days after that, I called Marian. But she wouldn't see me. She was probably afraid of what I'd think of her, now that she had let her breasts out of the bag. After not nearly enough trouble, I stopped calling and let it go.

I was a married man, after all, and I had other responsibilities, and—in other words, I ran away from it.

When the door of Marian's apartment finally opened, a slender woman appeared wearing a hairy gray sweater that looked as though it might have once roamed the

Alps, a pair of designer jeans from the children's department, and scuffed-up sneakers as old as France. I was surprised. This lady was once attractive; now her hair looked as if she had just been scared out of bed; her eyelids were as puffy as cow ticks, and her pale, spotty face was as dull as the belly of a toad. For all that, for some reason, she still looked good to me.

As soon as her eyes managed to focus on me, she screamed, "Oh, Teddy!" and flung everything she had left into my arms.

Marian's chest was now as flat as a spatula, of course, and even though hugging her angular frame was like making a pass at a bank building, I liked it, because I had never been able to get this close to her before with all the foam in the way.

After our mutual squeeze, she eased away to swipe some of the sobs off her face and confess she was so happy to see me, she was in a regular tizzy. When it occurred to her to let me in, I walked into a stuffy room lined from one shoe molding to the next with a thousand years of *Jackson Daily News*, *Clarion Ledger*, and *Times-Picayune*. It looked as if she'd been paper-training a pack of wolves.

"I see you like to keep up," I said, checking out a few of the headlines.

"I'm sorry it's such a mess," she said, then plunged into a frenzy to straighten up the kennel. While making her debut at housecleaning, she conked a bottle of gin off the coffee table, smashed an ash tray, and toppled an aluminum tumbler to the floor. At last, in frustration, she gave up and plopped down on the sofa. "Oh, what difference does it make!" she sighed and plucked a pink

Scottie out of a box. "You've already seen what it looks like."

I felt very sorry for Marian as she honked like a horny drake into her tissue. In her chore-girl clothes and wearing only the face she was born with, she looked as washed up as Bonnie and Clyde. I wanted to stay and comfort her, but I had business to take care of that she could help me with. Assuming the wicker heap to the right of the sofa was passing as some sort of chair, I took a chance on it. "I'm sorry about Temple," I said as I settled in.

While I cracked around in the sticks, Marian assaulted another Scottie. "I might've known you'd know about that," she said. "Is there *anybody* who hasn't heard about Richard and me?"

"Maybe a few Chinese from the mainland."

She tried to stop her tear ducts with a corner of the tissue, but it didn't work. "I know you won't believe this, Teddy," she said in a soft, damp voice, "but it wasn't just sex or attention. I really was in love with him."

She had me wrong, of course. Being familiar with her amatory techniques, I could readily believe it wasn't the sex. I liked Marian a lot, but I was sure she made love like a train tunnel. "I'm very glad to hear that," I said.

"I don't care what people are saying, I'm proud to have known him," she confided. "I happen to believe Richard Temple was a great man. Everything he did was dedicated to making the world a better place to live in. Oh, I know he liked other women, but when I was with him, that didn't matter. I felt important."

I waited a decent interval after she blared forth another one of her mating calls to get to the point and ask her where Bubba obtained his previously-owned Lincoln Mark VII's.

Marian stared at me while she silently reviewed our association and wondered if maybe she hadn't been giving me too much credit all these years. "What possible difference could it make to you where he got them?" she wanted to know.

I didn't want to say. "Could make a lot," I said.

She scraped her eyes with a crisp new Scottie, the way she might have scrubbed a sink if she had ever kept house. "If you really want to know, he gets them in New Orleans," she said. "From LaSalle Motors, on Tulane Avenue."

"Thanks. Mind if I use your phone?" I leaped out of my cage and located a pink Princess languishing beneath the Sunday paper, on an end table. In three minutes, I was in touch with Russo, who, as usual, was working at the office on his definitive book on the college bowl scene.

Catching him on a rise, I had to listen to a strained set of analogies in which spectators at a New Year's Day game were tiny black ants clinging to the edges of a sugar bowl, and the players were tiny red ants scurrying about on the bottom of it.

When Russo began to die in his metaphors, I broke in to ask him to run down to Research to find out about LaSalle Motors. While I waited by the Princess for his return call, I was diverted by a long, transcendent monologue on Marian's love for Richard. Although I wanted to scream for the apartment manager or that guy searching the heavens outside, I kept my mouth shut the whole time, the way I should have kept it that evening in the state park. I may have cared a lot for Marian, but I just didn't have time to spend the evening with a woman who had as tight a grip on herself as a delegate to the Democratic Convention.

When Russo called back, he boasted about his shrewd detective work which had turned up a real, A-Number-One schlang for me.

"Does this prick of mine have a name?" I copped his language in order to show him I appreciated his work. There wasn't much else I could do for a fellow like Russo.

I had done right, for he warmed up to me soon after that. "Tell me something, Ted," he quizzed me. "Do the three little words, 'Paul David Benadetto' mean anything to you?"

"Sounds like somebody's patron saint."

"You're way off. P.D. 'Benny' Benedetto happens to be the biggest head in the New Orleans mafia!"

That hit me like the bow of an ice-breaker. I stood with my mouth gaping as if I were warming up for a kiss with Marian.

"You don't sound pleased to hear it," Russo said.

"Are you sure about this?" I asked.

"Oh, yes, I"m sure. And if I were you, I'd tuck my tail between my legs and haul my ass back to civilization on the very next conveyance. These mob jocks play real rough."

"I've heard that."

"Don't you think you'd better tell Agnew what's going on down there?"

"I'll tell him later," I said. "Thanks, Russo. I'll be in touch."

While I was wrestling with this revolting news, Marian was losing herself in a vain effort to reshape her nose with a finger and a thumb wrapped in tissue paper. As pathetic as she was, I wanted to shake that skinny frame of hers over the newspapers until the truth fell out in gobs over the syndicated columns. However, I was determined to use a softer approach with her for once and ambled over to the sofa, where I casually asked her if she knew Bubba was involved with the mafia. She didn't have to answer; without a smear of makeup on her face, the guilt was exuding out of every one of those open pores. "How did he ever get mixed up with the mob?" I asked her.

She didn't figure she had to field that one either. "Why are you doing this, Teddy?" she countered. "Why don't you just let it be!"

"Temple was investigating the mafia, wasn't he?" I said. "That was the story he wanted to give me."

She shook her head. "I don't want to talk about it," she said. "Richard said I would never have to talk about it."

"Marian, the man is lying on a slab in the cooler. How much good will it do him to play dumb now?"

"I'm sorry. I just don't see why you have to go into it, that's all."

"I'm going into it because people we care about are involved."

She drew her arms in close. "You don't know that!" she cried. "He could've been killed by somebody from New York for all we know!"

"Or he could've been killed by Bubba Henderson."

"No, I don't believe that! Bubba would never do anything like that!"

"Why not? He's a crook, isn't he? He buys and sells stolen cars form the mafia—"

"It just couldn't have been him, Teddy. His name wasn't even in the notes!"

Marian's jaws snapped shut like hands applauding as soon as she realized what she had just said.

"What notes?" I asked her calmly.

She gazed at some of the papers on the floor and pretended to check the weather forecast for a while. "I never asked to see them," she said after a while. "But he insisted on it. He took them out of this hidden place in the wall of his study and made me look at them. Not that we ever actually met at his house," she added quickly. "I mean, we never met there intentionally. Lord, why does all this sound so sordid? It wasn't like that!"

On an impulse, I grabbed her wrist and yanked her to her feet. "Put on your coat," I told her. "You're going to show me those papers."

"Teddy, I can't go there! Why don't you let me tell you where they are? You can go there by yourself."

"I want you to show me." I kicked a stack of papers out of the way. "I want you to stop hanging around this place and do something that matters for a change."

On that, she whipped her hand free. "Are you saying the way I felt about him didn't matter!"

"I don't know, Marian. Maybe it did. To him."

"What is the matter with you! We were lovers, Teddy. I gave myself to him!"

"You gave your body to him. You've never given yourself to anybody, Marian, any more than I have. Neither one of us has ever cared enough to act responsibly. I've never realized it before, but that's why our relationship fizzled the way it did. We never did anything to hold it together."

"But it wasn't that way with Richard!"

"Prove it."

"Teddy, I can't!"

I looked straight at her. "Will you just help me, Marian?" I said. "Please?"

"I want to. . . ."

"Then do it!"

She took a deep breath and stiffened her upper lip. "All right," she said. "I will. I'll go to that awful place and I'll show you those notes. But only to prove to you how much Richard and I meant to each other."

"Thank you," I said. I felt grateful enough to her to kiss her, but I didn't even try. For some reason, kissing Marian Henderson at that moment seemed like the worst thing in the world I could do.

* * *

Cleveland Plain Dealer

BOOK DEPICTS RISE OF THE MAFIA
Second in a series

EDITOR'S NOTE: In the second excerpt from his upcoming book on the Richard Temple murder, *Life on the Line*, Theodore Miller examines the mafia's connection with sports gambling in America.

Sports betting plays a vital role in the rise of organized crime

Although the idea of organized crime has been with us for a long time, only recently have we realized just how pervasive it is becoming or how many Americans are actually contributing to it. Those 25 and 50-dollar bets you make on the Rams or the Fighting Irish on Monday morning very likely are sucked into the underground pipes of one of the most expensive economic drains on America that exists today.

In 1986, the President's Commission on Organized Crime estimated that the crime syndicates in this country take in more than $100 billion a year. This isn't free money by any means. Every U.S. citizen is the poorer because of the drain. Even by conservative guess, the economic output of this nation is decreased by $18.2 billion a year, and consumer prices increased by .3 percent. All this costs the United States 414,000 jobs and the individual worker almost $80 a year.

For all the alarming numbers, the trend continues unabated. The commission formed by President Reagan in 1983 recommended a number of drastic measures which could be taken to stem the flow, such as drug testing of government employees to curb mafia drug traffic. But since the mob is a shadowy spectre, too many groups could see only the repressive nature of the recommendations and resisted them as a violation of their rights.

California Representative Don Edwards, Chairman of the Sub-committee on Civil and Constitutional Rights, for instance, turned up his Democratic nose at the commission and said: "Testing like that is repugnant to our system."

The American Federation of Government Employees staunchly declared that such procedure would be a heinous violation of the Fourth Amendment.

Meanwhile, 26 million regular users of marijuana, cocaine, and heroin continue to buy their sustenance from the mafia and keep trying to muddle through their lives.

Bookies are easily drawn into the mob

While there are buckets of money to be made in sports betting, it isn't usually the lure of riches that pulls a bookie into the mob. Actually, most of these guys would be content to work their ten hours a day, six days a week, and go home to Mabel and the kids with a living. But a businessman with no social standing to act as a buffer is as easily preyed upon as a sitting duck on a reflecting pond.

The bookie's problem is that he must have a backer, an individual or organization that can weather the losses until the profits fall. But banks and savings and loans are notoriously reluctant to finance illegal operations. And very few legitimate businessmen are willing to risk their hard-gotten reputation on an association with an unsavory character.

Those who are willing to take a chance usually have neither the patience nor the resources to make the arrangement work. A Long Island backer explained to me in the solemn atmosphere of the Museum of Modern Art why he decided to cut the silver cord to his bookie, "Tom."

"Simple," he said. "I was losing my ass."

This 48-year-old real estate broker is overweight, with deeply-etched wrinkles running across his thick pink face. He admires the work of Picasso and Chagall, but "can't see wasting money on an impractical hobby like art."

As he stepped back to get a perspective on Matisse's "Red Studio," he told me he had lost nearly $40,000 the first year he was in. "I don't like to piss away money," he said. "So I told Tom I had to get out."

"What was his reaction?" asked him.

He turned his head to look at me. "The son of a bitch accused me of betraying him," he said. "He went on and on about his poor wife and two girls, and claimed he was done for. I felt so sorry for the guy, I gave him the name of this fellow, Lee Moletti, who was a backer for a couple of bookies I knew in Jersey. I told Tom everybody said Moletti was a good man, but he was connected in some way with the Genovese family."

"Did that intimidate him?"

He shrugged his shoulders. "It didn't bother him at all," he said. "I guess he really was desperate, because he didn't even flinch when I said that. He just stared out the window for a while, then asked me if I'd set up a meeting. I figured, why not? After all, I've told him what I know about the guy. I put them together in a room at the Plaza, and two days later, Tom was back at the phones."

"How did it work out?"

"It worked fine, until Moletti ran in some of the mob, and Tom was pushed out. There was nothing he could do about it, of course. Who does a lowly bookie complain to?"

"What happened to him?"

"Last I heard, Moletti had given him a lowly job in a casino in Atlantic City. He's probably making a couple of hundred a week and lucky to get it."

Sometimes supplanted bookies aren't so "lucky." Sometimes, when the mafia chews up a gambling business, the independent bookie is simply spit into the gutter.

In Cleveland in 1978, William C. Reynolds, a disbarred lawyer, divorced, alcoholic, on his last psychological leg, opened a bookie joint in the rear of an appliance store on Euclid Avenue. Although Reynolds knew the mafia controlled sport betting in Cleveland, he gambled that if he let them go their way, they would let him go his. He didn't want to encroach on anybody's turf; all he wanted was to strike back at the system that had rejected him.

The business plodded along for a year or so, and

Reynolds made a profit. All the while, members of the mafia were quietly placing bets with him and refusing to pay off. At the same time, other mafia folks were permitting the bookie to issue them IOUs for their winning bets. At the end of five years, the bettors all at once demanded immediate payment from the bookie or else. When Reynolds tried to call in the debts of the other mafia bettors, they were nowhere to be found.

It was at this point a slick Italian middle-aged man in a gray three piece Ceruti suit sauntered into the appliance store and offered to bail Reynolds out of his dilemma for a 50 percent share of the take.

After a lot of resisting, Reynolds ultimately gave in. Within six months, he had lost control of the bookie operation. Within ten, he had signed over the appliance store. Within a year, he was out on the streets. On the morning of December 28, 1985, he was found curled up under a bench in Wade Park drunk, unconscious, and suffering from pneumonia.

Two days later he died.

The mob began as a vigilante group for the oppressed

William C. Reynolds' story is not really all that unusual. Every working day, the mafia squeezes the life out of its competition without fear of reprisal. It can do this not only because it is elusive, but also because it's cloaked in mystery. No one knows for sure, for example, how the mafia began. Apparently, it started in Italy about 700 years ago as a vigilante group organized to help landowners fight the oppressive French Angevins. The name of the gang may have been taken from the first letters of their battle cry: *"Morte a Francia Italia anela!"* ("Death to the French is the cry of Italy!")

But since the origins of the group are shrouded in obscurity, there actually may never have been such a cry. What is known for sure is that, after centuries of faithfully supporting the oppressed, the mafia turned rotten in the 19th century, spread beyond its original boundaries, and made its first American appearance in New Orleans, Louisiana, in the late 1800s.

In 1890 a flamboyant, outspoken, good-looking chief of police by the name of Peter David Hennessey decided to threaten two Sicilian families, the Matrangas and the Provenzanos, who were alternately cutting throats and prices in their efforts to gain control of the Mississippi River docks.

"I will put an end to this reign of terror on the city docks," Hennessey told the Matrangas and the Provenzanos, "if I have to run every one of you dagoes out of town on a rail!"

Boldly ignoring all kinds of threats and bribes, Chief Hennessey proceeded to play the families against each other until the situation became intolerable to both. Then he called a press conference and announced to the public that he had personally uncovered a vicious, wicked secret society in New Orleans. "It is know as the mafia," he declared. "And I am going to eradicate it!"

A few days later, as Hennessey walked to work from his town house, a gang of men suddenly peeled out of an alley and spattered his body with thousands of buckshot from half a dozen double-barreled shotguns. By the time his assistant managed to reach him, Hennessey had only breath enough for one last word,

"Dagoes," before he died.

Shortly after the assassination, a grand jury convened and indicted 19 members of the New Orleans mafia. But the witnesses were bribed or threatened before the trial, and 16 of the accused were acquitted, three deferred. This was a clear cut, resounding victory for the mafia. While the 19 Sicilians stood in prison awaiting their release, mobsters in the city danced and sang in celebration on Royal and Bourbon Streets.

Law abiding citizens, meanwhile, were working up to a rage. Tempers were flaring hot in every non-Italian section of New Orleans. Finally, all tensions exploded at once, and a crowd of 5,000 whites, blacks, Creoles, Spaniards, and Frenchmen stormed the prison, cracked down the door, and dragged the screaming defendants out by the heels. Seven were mercilessly gunned down just outside the gates. Two had their necks stretched from lamp posts in the streets, while onlookers cheered and chanted choruses of "The Ballad of Peter David Hennessey." A few of the others turned up later as butchered bodies; some never reappeared at all.

These upstart Sicilian gangs had become so outrageous in the city that hardly anyone was sorry for what had happened. For the record, the mayor of New Orleans considered the lynching deplorable, but still "a necessity and justifiable."

A resolution supporting the massacre of the acquitted defendants was passed and signed by members of the most influential business firms of the day, including the prestigious Cotton Exchange and the Board of Trade.

The mafia has adapted itself to American life

The mafia has learned a lot about America since those early days in the Crescent City. The organization has managed to become part of the fabric of our lives by adapting itself to the inevitable trends and movements of history. In the first decade of the century, the mafia was fairly limited because its Black Hand tactics were directed mostly against fellow Sicilians and Italians, whose language and customs were familiar. These were the days of the Manhattan mafia led by Nicholas Morello vs. the Brooklyn Camarra led by Don Pelligrino Morano.

When the prohibition of liquor raised the stakes of criminal commerce, the territorial battles between Sicilian syndicates naturally became more numerous and grew much bloodier. Murder was rife during the Roaring '20s. Between 1920 and 1930 in New York and Chicago, more than 2,000 people were slaughtered by gangs. In these violent times, big-shot gamblers lived like kings. Al Capone of Chicago, for instance, had a personal income of more than $20 million a year and occupied a 50-room suite at a plush downtown hotel. The IRS in 1930 estimated that Capone's syndicate earned at least $95 million a year in profits from its bootlegging, prostitution, and gambling operations.

After the repeal of prohibition, a new wave of mafia leaders concluded it would be more profitable for all concerned to get organized. In the Depression, the warring families agreed to form a cartel, complete with a high tribunal which would decide on assassinations beneficial to the new organization. FBI Chief J. Edgar

Hoover constantly denied the existence of such a group, preferring the meaningless term Joe Valachi gave him— *Cosa Nostra*, or "Our Thing" (or more appropriately, "Our business"). But the dominant force in the powerful syndicate was actually the old mafia.

Most of the contract killings ordered by the high court were carried out by Sicilian and Jewish youngsters recruited from the Brownsville and Bath Beach districts of Brooklyn.

I talked to one of these contract hit men a month before he died of stomach cancer in a crowded ward in Queens General Hospital. As hard as I tried, I could see no trace of guilt or remorse in the old man's pale face as he admitted to having cold-bloodedly murdered "a hundred or more" people from 1930 to 1945.

"Hell, I was proud to be on the payroll," he said. "For a punk like me, a $100 a throw was real big money."

When I asked him how the contracts were arranged, he raised up in his bed. Remembering seemed to pump new life into his tired, withered body. "There'd be a meeting somewhere," he said, "and somebody'd decide on a target. Then my man would call me in. He'd give me a bus ticket, some expense money, and some info on the guy I was supposed to knock off.

"I'd blow into a place like Miami, for instance, and hole up in a pretty nice hotel for a couple of days. I'd take in the sights, fool with a couple of local whores, you know, in general have a good time. Then I'd do my business and go home. I didn't know till later there was somebody watching me all the time. I guess as long as you did the work, they were satisfied."

Did he have any regrets?

"Well, I guess I wouldn't do anything like that now," he said. "But back in those days, it was all right. That was the way life was. It was all part of learning how to get along. I tell you, son, I learned a lot about human nature by killing people."

After a while, the contract business began to change. "The new kids out of the old neighborhoods didn't have the loyalty," he explained with a faraway, misty look in his eye. "They couldn't be trusted to do the job. Not like we could," he added proudly.

To rectify the situation, mafia bosses turned to the home land for recruits and began smuggling Sicilian youths into the country by the hundreds. "Guys from our neck of the woods were passed over," he said. "Sicilian Americans were out."

While this return to the source did temporarily restore some vitality to the syndicates, it soon became clear that there could no longer be an all-Sicilian mob in such a diverse country as this one. By the early 1980s, the mafia was starting to recruit other ethnic groups to carry out many of its low-level operations.

The 1986 President's Commission discovered that the mafia's extensive use of such gangs as the Hells Angels in Licavoli-controlled Cleveland was rapidly changing the face of organized crime in America.

What made this diversification necessary was the nature of the mafia itself. As anyone who has seen *The Godfather* knows, these people are extremely family-conscious. Unfortunately for the unity of the mob, however, mafia bosses consistently make every effort to keep their own children out of the organization. Carlo

Gambino, for instance, set his sons up in legitimate businesses and threatened to break their legs if they broke the law.

Eventually, this tendency weakened the substructure of the mafia and made ethnic and social branching out mandatory. For this reason, the mafia today is far more cosmopolitan and is becoming far more pervasive than the mafia of former years. Black gangs, Chinese gangs, Koreans, Jews, Chicanos—all are being used to expand the base of operations of organized crime.

Once the mafia consisted of 24 crime families which operated exclusively out of these 23 cities: Atlantic City, Baltimore, Binghamton, Boston, Buffalo, Chicago, Cleveland, Denver, Detroit, Kansas City, Las Vegas, Los Angeles, Miami, Milwaukee, New Orleans, New York City, Niagara Falls, Philadelphia, Rochester, Rockford, St. Louis, San Francisco, and Syracuse. Now it has begun to spread into the rest of the country.

The mafia is taking root in America's grasslands

The movements of the mafia coincide with the flow of money and people throughout the country. When the population shifted into suburbia after World War II, for instance, so did the demand for gambling. As Americans became affluent and television promoted and publicized national baseball, football, and basketball games, sports betting became very popular and profitable. Before long, the mafia moved in.

Now, as the elements of the nation are drawn closer together through the national media, the mob is starting to reach beyond the urban and even suburban limits.

It is now beginning to infiltrate small-town and rural America.

* * *

From the moment of its conception, I could tell that this trip with Marian was not going to evolve into the Great American Adventure.

First, after our dramatic confrontation at the cliff dwelling, I had to hang around in a ruin of newspapers while Marian swiped some cosmetics on her face and made her selection of a cute cat-burglar outfit for the evening do. Then, on the way to Temple's house, I was regaled like a Canterbury pilgrim with a succession of nervous tales of life and lust.

This was not exactly high cotton I was wading through.

"Do you know," Marian told me, "the first night we spent together, he didn't even touch me? It was lovely. We just lay naked on the bed and stared at the ceiling and talked!"

"I've had nights like that," I said.

"What I mean is, he respected me!"

Sure, Marian. He respected you. Then twenty-four hours later, he screwed you. God, what timing. Here I am, dragging an old flame through stiff wind in order to help us take hold of ourselves, and all she can do is test my sexual I.Q. with a rash of Sunday supplement tales of modern adultery. When she threatened to draw me into a tête-à-tête on the pressing subject of female orgasms (Richard gave her her first), I considered chucking her out like the evening paper on somebody's driveway and carrying on with the job alone. Fortunately, Marian was sensitive enough to detect my discomfort.

"Am I boring you, Teddy?" she asked sarcastically.

"That's okay," I said.

"Well, this wasn't my idea, you know," she reminded me.

No need to do that. Hannibal had an easier job of it hauling his mastodons over the Alps than I had pulling this woman across the campus to the scene of the crime. For all my efforts at cajoling and encouraging, she resisted me as if I were forcing her to return to school or into premature labor. After we spent about a week on the grass, we finally drew close enough to spit at Temple's little white house, which in the gloomy light looked as stark and bleak as an MA thesis. As I reconnoitered the place, I felt my stomach tighten and wrench itself into knots. When we stepped up to the porch, my testicles hardened into ice cubes and tried to rise like balloons into the navel area. But I said nothing.

While I sprayed the flashlight around, Marian took the spare key from behind a loose brick in the column and opened the front door. Inside, she held her own pretty well, until I turned on the floor lamp and lit up the big blood stain on the carpet.

Then she gasped in horror. "My God," she cried and spun away. They didn't even clean it up!" It was the last thing I expected a housekeeper of her caliber to say. "Why is there so much blood?" she groaned.

While Marian was recoiling, I knelt down to the floor to examine the chalk image. It was mighty sloppy work. Holman's zealots had traced the outline of the corpse so spastically, it came out looking like a cartoon character in a coloring book. It wouldn't have surprised me to see it pop off the floor and lead us in a Walt Disney sing-along.

"He was shot five times." I gave a belated answer to her clinical question. But since she was too keen on her own thoughts to listen to me, I ran the coroner's scenario through my brain again to see if I could hit on anything new. Shortly after Temple came to the door, he was hit with a .45 slug in the face. Slouching back into the house, he took another shot in the stomach, then flopped on his back on the living room floor. There his body was pounded by three more bullets in the heart and groin.

All of that made sense—except the sixth shot. An .833 average at the free throw line might look fine on TV, but here it was a pretty feeble percentage. In fact, it seemed to me after five solid hits in the vitals, a miss of six feet was impossible.

Unless it had been intentional.

In the scholar's study at the back of the house, Marian moved stiffly across the room and pointed like the Ghost of Christmas Future at the niche where the files were hidden in a wall behind a row of Will and Ariel Durant's *The Story of Civilization*.

"Richard said that'd be the last place a thief would think of looking for something of value," she said.

Distracted only by the eerie silence and by my partner's tendency to meander around the room like a new kid at recess, I carefully pulled the stack of papers out of the niche like a baby from a womb and laid it on Temple's desk. It only took a minute of scrutiny to see I had my hands on some explosive material. The man hadn't missed a rock; there were two hundred pages of affidavits, interview transcripts, confessions, correspondence, and detailed profiles of football players. The fuse to this pile of dynamite was the school superintendent's radical proposal to eliminate all athletic programs from Marshall High School.

After I ran through the amazing document a couple of times, I looked up at Marian who was standing on the threshold of the study gazing wistfully down the hall at the living room. I could tell she was sick at heart thinking about her dead lover. Maybe it wasn't just attention she had been after. Maybe she had loved him. When I asked her about the memo, she turned around and started pacing back and forth in the dim light.

"Teddy, I'm not sure I can handle this," she said. You've got the papers. Can't we go?"

"I want to know about this proposal," I said.

After wringing her hands a while, she decided the quickest way out was to cooperate. "Richard found out that some of the football games were fixed," she said, running her fingers through her hair. "Anybody else would've shrugged it off, but he wasn't like that. He was like you; he could never let anything go. He had to go and find out the mafia was controlling the betting on the games."

"How did the board respond to the idea?"

A sad, sour look crossed her beleaguered face like a cloud over the massacred few. "They turned on him," she said. "They tried to get him fired. But Richard didn't care. He just dug in deeper." Marian started at the flash of a car light on the window. "Lord, I hate this!" she cried. "I keep feeling we're defiling a grave!"

"Who else knew about this?" I asked her.

"I don't know, Teddy," she said. "And I don't want to know. Why did I ever agree to do this? We don't have any right being in this house!"

A glance down at Temple's football profiles sent a cold shudder over me. "Marian, it's not just Bubba that's involved."

"Don't say any more about it!" she cried. "I don't want to hear it!"

"Marian—"

"I'm sorry, Teddy. I've done all I can. I just can't stand here and watch you rummage through those papers. I did love him, I swear I did. But what good will all this do!" After that outburst, she bolted for the door.

By the time I returned Will and Ariel to their rightful place in history and caught up with Marian, she was sitting in the Thunderbird blowing a new Scottie apart. When she saw Temple's files in my arms, she glared beneath the dome light, but she was too disheartened to say anything. All the way home, she stared silently ahead with her hand to her nose, reliving old times.

In front of her apartment, she snorted one last good one and looked over at me. "You think I'm a real gutless wonder, don't you?" she asked.

"I think you're like the rest of us; you're afraid of facing the truth."

"It's just that I can't deal with anything right now except the fact that he's gone. I don't know if I care enough, or if you do, or if anybody does. But, Teddy, one thing I am sure of: what you're doing now is going to end in something truly awful, and I just will not be a part of it. I'm sorry, but I just can't be what I'm not."

"I understand."

"Well, if you do, I wish you'd explain it to me sometime!" All awash with tears, she jerked open the door, slid out to the pavement, and sprinted toward her apartment with a tissue clogging up her nostrils. At the door, she plundered through her jeans for the keys, then tried to open up by shoving them through the lock. At last, she managed to break in and disappear, rolling the cover stone behind her.

Safe in the cave at last.

For a long time, I sat in the car watching the door waiting for Marian Henderson to come out. But it was ridiculous for me to waste the time, with the football game going on. I knew better than that.

Still, I waited until there was no longer a light in her window. Then I left.

* * *

Clarion Ledger/Jackson Daily News

SPORTSWRITER'S BOOK DETAILS CORRUPTION
IN MARSHALL
Third in a series

EDITOR'S NOTE: In the third excerpt from his coming book, *Life on the Line*, sportswriter/columnist Theodore Miller examines the role of the mafia in small-town America.

The mafia is on the move these days

Most of us associate organized crime with urban areas. The particular city we pay attention to depends on the prevailing mood of the country. Thirty years ago, it was Chicago and New York. Ten years ago, San Francisco and Honolulu; lately it's been Miami and Los Angeles.

We even grudgingly acknowledge the mafia's reach to the suburbs. A while back, a saturation of racketeering in Mount Vernon, New York, and Nassau and Suffolk Counties in New Jersey was exposed in the papers. In the '60s in Westchester County, federal investigators discovered that even the garbage collection system had been in the hands of the Genovese and Gambino families for a generation.

But we seldom think much about the slow, steady migration of organized crime into the small towns and rural parts of the country. Enticed by a non-urban population of over 45 million (more than the entire population of Spain), the mafia has discovered that the easy-going small Southern town is especially suited to the slow, relentless infiltration of the mob. The climate for corruption is particularly good there. Local police forces aren't prepared for sophisticated crime, and conscientious civilians are not very alert to the signs of the encroaching evil.

Marshall, Mississippi has been infiltrated by the mob

The mafia is starting to flourish in rural America because of its tendency to plant its roots in poverty. I know of no finer such soil any place than my home town of Marshall, Mississippi.

This quiet, picturesque little community of 2,000 is located in the center of one of the poorest counties of the most economically destitute state in the nation. When you drive into town on Highway 51 beneath a deep green canopy of magnolias, the old-fashioned brick streets and broken sidewalks seem to be posing for a photograph for a quaint picture postcard. But as you move along Main Street and look around, you see a curious mixture of wealth and poverty—of haves and have-nots. Fifty years ago, there was no such thing. Marshall was a booming cotton and lumber community crowded from one corner to another with sawmills, lumberyards, gins, and compresses—even textile mills and six-story hotels.

There is no uniformity like that today. The hotels, gins, and compresses are gone. The only vestige of the textile industry is a dirt-poor shanty area across the tracks they call Milltown. Where once were fields of cotton are now fallow acres, pasture land, or crops of corn and soybeans. Many railroad-related businesses dried up in the '50s when traffic took to the interstates leaving only rusted rails, broken flags, and abandoned cars behind.

Even now, Marshall could be called a victim of progress, hit, run over, and reduced to a statistic by the rush of time. Most of its residents, like those of a city slum, have a tainted image of themselves. Poor, frustrated, and bored, they want desperately to be important, to occupy some sort of niche in the parade of modern life. This great need has made them extremely vulnerable to anyone who knows how to play on the weakness.

Local businessmen give in to organized crime

The devastating way in which organized crime and low self-esteem make complementary bedfellows can be seen in the case of a certain car dealer in Marshall.

I have known this stocky, balding, 45-year-old man for more than thirty years. As a youth in Marshall, I watched him dream lofty dreams of changing the world. While the rest of us muddled through our days, he stood up for things. He championed the law. He defended order. He acted as an advocate for the poor, ignorant, and oppressed. But when he became a man, the harsh light of reality intruded upon his adolescent dreams.

Two failing semesters at the University of Mississippi wiped out his ambition to become a lawyer and took away his sense of place in the universe. He was tough enough to survive the blow and work his way into possession of a car dealership in Marshall, but even in that comfortable corner, he continued to lick the wounds inflicted by the world he had wanted too much to help.

While he transformed a languishing business into a profitable one through some shrewd deals with illegal used car suppliers in Louisiana, a phenomenon was occurring in town. The high school football team had put together such an astounding winning record, it had begun to gain prominence in the state. Newspapers picked the Marshall Lions as the best team in the South. When they stretched their unbeaten string to 85, they drew national attention.

In a way, it was natural for my old friend to try to raise his spirits by identifying with the successful team. After all, it must have felt pretty good to be associated with a winner for a change. To enhance his own self-image, he bet on the games and won. To make sure he held on to it, he began to lean on referees to favor the Lions.

In the meantime, his dealership had turned into a prime outlet for a mafia-controlled car theft ring operating out of New Orleans. Eventually, his work and his recreation came together, and he was representing the mafia in his underhanded negotiations with football officials.

In order to live with his lingering, faded dreams, he rationalized them. "Hell," he said to me, "if I didn't fudge a little every once in a while, I'd be taking up residence across the street with the niggers."

To all appearances, this is a pleasant, well-meaning,

good old boy. But it's not hard to see behind that smooth, pallid face cracks of anger, resentment, and bitterness. The man I knew as a boy must always preserve and maintain a positive image of self, no matter who has to suffer. Whatever threatens that, threatens his worth as a human being.

Many policemen in Marshall take favors from the mob

The need to hang on to a positive self-image is par for a poverty-stricken course like this one. Even for the police.

In Marshall, law enforcement is a family affair. The local police are friendly, congenial sorts. Their mission is to maintain the community, not control it. If they decide that an operation such as sports betting is a vice which the majority of the town desires, they do what they can to preserve it.

"Why come down hard on folks for having a good time?" said Chief of Police D.T. Bundley. "Aren't we better off chasing speeders or going after the guy who holds up a convenience store?"

I don't know. Maybe they are. And maybe all the sports betting in town would have continued to be harmless fun—if the high school football team hadn't been so good. But the facts are in 1984, almost as a novelty, a national betting line was established for the Marshall Lions, and with big money at stake, bookie operations throughout the county started falling one by one to the pressures of the mob.

Although Bundley denies it, the police were well aware of the infiltration of the mafia. One young officer explained to me that "Everybody was so revved up over all this national attention, they were scared to death something negative would come along and take it away."

This was why the chief sent word down to the ranks to "go easy on vice for a while."

Since a crime organization isn't likely to base its operations on the whims of a police chief, the mafia reached into the very heart of the local force. According to sources in the department, six Marshall policemen were given secret stipends ranging from $16,000 to $28,000 above their usual wages.

Although there is no record of Chief Bundley himself receiving any money in addition to his salary of $26,000 a year, corruption in the department was certainly widespread. Even policemen who weren't on the take had to go along. While they were never actually prevented from raiding a bookie joint or closing down a mafia restaurant, they soon discovered that pinches of the sort resulted in no bonuses, no pay raises, no promotions.

"To top it all," one young officer said, "we kept getting all these holiday hams and turkeys from guys like Mr. Scarlotti. They told us it was because we were doing such a great job. It made us think a lot of ourselves, but it was a lie. It was nothing but a bribe."

Small-time politicians line the pockets of the mafia

Certain local officials thought a lot of themselves, too, because for the first time in their lives, they were making big money.

David J. Moore, the mayor of Marshall, was elected to his office thanks to a campaign made up of contributions of $130,000 from Dr. Richard Wilkins, Dr. Joseph Hewitt, and Mr. Vincent Scarlotti. Wilkins is the brother-in-law of Hewitt, a compulsive gambler. Scarlotti is a man we'll look at in depth later.

Because of the mob, the mayor and his council are in the gravy these days. Here's an example of their graft. In 1981, David Moore, Buck Haymon, Ed Myerson, and Billy Watkins learned from Scarlotti that a gigantic country music theme park was going to be built on 250 acres of pasture land south of Marshall. Within six months the mayor and his boys had bought 218 of those acres which they later sold to Heart & Countryland, USA, Inc., for more than ten times the original price.

The total combined profit: over $300,000.

Although the mafia (which now operates Heart & Countryland, USA) may have made no money on the deal, it now had the top echelon of a little town in its gold-lined pocket.

In less than a year, Moore and company were waist-high in kick-backs, "finder's fees," and fixed seal bids for mafia-controlled contractors, builders, and developers. In the grand tradition of organized crime, local politicians busily enhanced their image of themselves by making pots of money while the mob took hold.

Even before Heart & Countryland, USA opened its gates in 1984, the leaders of Marshall were steadfastly loyal to the shadowy presence of the mafia.

A local dry cleaner is a controversial figure in Marshall

One of the mob, though, is very visible: Vincent Mario Scarlotti, the owner of City Cleaners and a fistful of other small businesses in Marshall. This 52-year-old husband and father, one of the most respected citizens in the state, is a mafia boss.

Scarlotti's background is sketchy. After immigrating from Palermo, Sicily, in 1950, he worked for six years in a dry cleaning establishment in Newark, New Jersey. The next four years, he was apparently unemployed, although his former acquaintances now contend he did occasional jobs for the Bonanno family in New York and for the Marcellos in New Orleans.

Soon after he appeared in Marshall in 1960, he opened City Cleaners. Five years later, he was investing heavily in real estate and independent insurance companies all over the country. In 1970, he started a chain of "Q" convenience stores throughout southern Mississippi and Louisiana.

Scarlotti is a renowned community benefactor. Brother Richard Taylor of the Cherry Street Baptist Church estimates that Scarlotti has donated over a million dollars to six different churches in town. "I, for one, am extremely grateful," he told me. "Without his support, our educational complex would be nothing but a dream."

So would the special diagnostic wing of Travis Memorial Hospital. In fact, let's give him his due: Vincent Scarlotti has regularly contributed to each of the following associations: American Heart Association of Mississippi, Marshall Boys' Club, Marshall Public

Library, Mental Health Association of Marshall County, Mississippi Kidney Association, Muscular Dystrophy Association, and the March of Dimes Defect Association.

For all this wonderful charity, the man is a crook.

In June, 1987, when I revealed to him on the phone that I had acquired evidence of his early dealings with the mafia, he denied nothing.

"Why don't we get together and talk about it?" he offered.

Vincent Scarlotti walks a tight rope

At his suggestion, we met at a Holiday Inn restaurant off Interstate 55 near Brookhaven, Mississippi. He was drinking coffee at a table with a linen napkin spread across his lap when I arrived ten minutes early. He sat erect and confident, a portly man with a cracked, spiny face, and hair the color of a storm cloud. In his tailored gray suit and $500 Italian shoes, Scarlotti comes off as an operator—a man accustomed to being entirely in command of a situation.

In fact, he'd already ordered my favorite meal for me. How he knew that I had a passion for medium rare ribeyes, baked potatoes with chives, and green salad with thousand island dressing, I'll never know. I couldn't help but cringe when he pointed at the Nutra Sweet.

"I made sure of that," he told me. "I know how much you like it in your tea."

As off guard as I was, I swiftly got down to business and showed him six affidavits I had gotten in New York, each a testimony swearing that Scarlotti had once worked for the mob. I asked him if he denied what the affidavits said. He answered without a flinch.

A: Who knows? Maybe I did. I understand the mafia owns many legitimate businesses in this country. I doubt if all the people that work in them are criminals.

Q: Not just "work," Mr. Scarlotti. Contract work. Murders.

A: You folks have been watching too many movies, Mr. Miller.

Q: Mafia executions aren't confined to the movies. I remember very well the murder of Carmine Galante in Brooklyn in 1979.

A: What does one killing prove?

Q: It proves the mafia puts out contracts for murder.

A: Well, if they do, let's hope they would be better handled than that.

Q: How would they be handled now?

A: I should think, with kids, wouldn't you? I don't mean the boys on the payroll; that would be too risky. I mean youth gangs. The best way would be with young people who stood to lose a lot if the murder wasn't committed. You know what I mean: CIA-type assassinations.

Q: Mr. Scarlotti, are you a member of the mafia?

A: If it's as pervasive as you think, who could truthfully say he wasn't?

Q: Tell me, how can you rationalize corrupting your own neighbors? You've lived in Marshall for over twenty years. The people in the town are your friends.

A: True, I do live down there, but my home will always be in Sicily. I will always consider myself an outsider in America. Since we live on foreign soil, we sometimes act like Americans act in other countries. By that I mean we act upon others, but we do not hurt our own.

Q: By "we" you mean the mafia.

A: I mean Italians. Sicilians.

Q: Mr. Scarlotti, all these affidavits say you were a member of the mafia in the 1950s. It's a matter of record that you were even tried for murder in Brooklyn in 1958.

A: Tried and acquitted.

Q: You were acquitted because a key witness for the prosecution happened to fall down an elevator shaft.

A: Is that what happened? I don't remember that. I guess the man was not only a liar, but an oaf as well, huh?

Vincent Scarlotti has become so entrenched in Marshall, not even a dose of the truth will make his fans reconsider his image. When I mentioned the murder trial to Brother Taylor, he merely shrugged his shoulders.

"Personally, I don't believe it," he said. "A man who attends and contributes to the church can't be all bad."

"But he can be a murderer."

"Now we don't know that, do we?"

"Brother Taylor, the man has his hands in gambling operations, drug traffic, prostitution. I have proof of it—"

"Not here, he doesn't. Not in Marshall. To my knowledge, there is none of that here."

Marshall Drug Store owner Sidney Black heaps praise on Scarlotti for the financial help he gave him during the uncertain Carter years. So does Edward Kelso, whose new liquor store in the old depot building was made possible by Scarlotti money.

"Damn fine fellow," he says. "Hell of a nice guy. I don't want to hear nothing bad about Vince Scarlotti."

Organized crime exists with the permission of the public

These days, the mafia has become an acceptable guest inside the corporate limits of Marshall. No, more than that it has become a welcome guest. Allowed to enter the public buildings, institutions, and homes of the town.

But then, what better place for the mob could there be than a run-down Southern hamlet whose people have not been able to manage even a mouldy piece of the American dream? Crime puts money in your pocket and, in this country, a wad of bills says you have value as a human being.

In Marshall, every religious sect from the Catholics to the Holy Rollers, has profited from the mob. Local charities have gotten dirty money; so have underprivileged children, deaf and dumb kids, academic institutions, hospitals and women's clinics. And, of course, public officials such as David Moore have grown corpulent and complacent on graft.

Thus do the *haves* remain happy while the inherent evils of the mafia—such as murder and extortion and drug traffic with children—are conveniently kept out of sight and therefore out of mind.

"All that crap is what happens in the cities," said a road supervisor in Pike County. "We've always had us a nice little place here."

Not just a welcome guest: an invited one. Organized crime exists only if it is wanted by the populace.

This is a cozy and convenient situation for the leaders of the community. But what happens when morality intrudes? What happens when a right-thinking person stands up and challenges the system? What happens when all this desperate stroking of the self-image reaches beyond the desks of city hall and the pews of the Baptist Church to the young people in the town?

And what happens when the invited guest decides to enroll in the school?

* * *

Even though the Lions were leading the Panthers 10 to 7 late in the fourth quarter, the hometown fans were so disgusted with their boys they were chewing on the red and white bunting and spitting up pink on the bleacher seats. Nearly three thousand people huddled together on wooden stands were squirming around like termites in a stump, growling and grousing and asking each other why God and the Marshall Lions were letting them down.

From where I was standing, members of the team looked the same as they had in the gym. On their favorite play, for instance, quarterback Davis rammed the ball into Lewis' gut, then pirouetted to the left, while Barbio and Smith tripped over the twenty yard line. Lewis squirted the ball out between his palms, and punted it with his nose directly into the arms of the opposition. It looked like perfect execution to me.

The throng of fans, however, considered it otherwise, and leaped to their feet and vehemently heaved everything that had ever had a lid on it out on the playing field. Dodging Coke bottles and Mason jars right and left, Derek's defensive unit chugged out on the gridiron like a herd of Holsteins coming home through a fog. Before they could find their bearings out there, Brookhaven was sending Red Rover through the front line into the linebacker's turf where he hurled himself aboard Derek's chest and triumphantly claimed the high ground for the visiting team.

Local fans were shocked and disgruntled by the play.

"What's the matter with you, Miller!" A bald-headed man furiously flung his baseball cap from the stands. "You're letting 'em run all over you! You bum!"

Derek looked so down-hearted from his position beneath the cleats of a Panther, I felt an urge to hustle out on the grass and help him to his big feet, but I restrained myself and watched him wobble upright and hold himself ready for more of the same. This time, the last thing he apparently ever expected to see in a football game came spiraling through the October air, striking him with a thump between the pectorals, then bouncing on the ground in front of him like a coconut on the sand. But the boy was on the alert. Spreading his hands like elephant ears, he scooped up the ball, tucked it into his armpit, and lumbered across the grass in the direction of the nearest tree behind the goal post on the north end. But a referee's frantic whistle brought him back to some of his senses, and he pulled to a halt.

"Where are you going, Miller!" the bald man taunted.

"You've gotta catch it on the fly, you jerk!"

On third down, a Marshall cornerback found himself intercepting the ball on a Brookhaven pass play which developed as subtly as a burning bush. Once he realized he now had what others wanted, he lit out for the same goal post Derek had had designs on earlier. Down the sidelines he raced like an Italian leaving the Bowery and spurted across the line for a score and a spike. Wild and delirious cheers erupted and partially eaten banners flew aloft as Derek scrambled to his feet and placed himself behind the quarterback to kick the P.A.T. Evidently, he figured the farther you kicked the ball, the more points you got, for he reared back and launched one end-over-end that missed the goal post by at least a furlong and landed in the void beyond the bleachers, probably in another county. The score remained Marshall 16, Brookhaven 7.

With a nine-point bulge under its belt, the crowd now relaxed and considered the brilliance of the team. What poise and finesse these youngsters had! The Marshall Lions could feel out the opposition like a groper at a Mardi Gras parade. If only *Sports Illustrated* could see them now!

The squad itself evidently considered this touchdown as something the rest of us ought to date the century by. Players hugged each other's pads and patted and squeezed one another's behinds and banged on the tops of helmets, to see what, if anything, was inside. It was while they were indulging in all this personal contact that I noticed a thin, pink Band-aid on Gregory Lewis' right index finger, and my heart sank into my stomach like a cow patty dropping in the tall grass. With a pounding heart, I snared a pair of binoculars off the neck of a retiree and raised them to my eyes. The terrible, cold instant I put together the image of that bandage with those of Davis' injured hand, Derek's bloody finger, and the rank smell of iodine reeking from Jackson Smith, I began to shake all over. I was in such a state, I hardly noticed the retiree snatching his glasses back.

"See all you wanted to see?" he grumbled.

Too stunned to answer, I turned away from the field holding my sick stomach and walking aimlessly around the stands. I had been leaning against the back of the concession booth a long time when I saw a great Watusi approaching me wearing a cracked leather jacket, tight blue jeans, and a pair of boots big enough for the Little League to hold a tournament in.

After looking me up and down for a full minute, Duke Curtis asked me if I were all right. "I'm fine." I tried to straighten up. "Must be something I ate."

"I've been looking all over for you," he said. "We've got to do something, Miller! They're saying now my boy's mixed up with two murders in Hinds County. They're going to take him up to Jackson tomorrow morning!"

What an empty sound that sentence made in my ear! "It doesn't matter where they take him," I told Curtis. "They'll have to let him go."

Curtis shifted his weight. "You must not know them like I do," he said. "When it comes to something like this, they don't have to do anything!"

"I'm telling you, your son is not guilty."

"Hell, I know he's not. But I'm saying, they've come

up with some new evidence against him, anyway!"

"What kind of evidence?"

"I don't know. Something to do with the gun that killed Temple. Bundley said I'd be hearing about it on TV."

"Sounds like he's fishing."

Duke launched a wad of spit that spattered the ground, foaming up at least a yard of gravel. "I want you to talk to them, man," he told me. "If they take Tommy off to Jackson, I may never see him again!"

The soulful, mournful look in his eyes reminded me of a racehorse I once saw that had just realized he'd been poisoned. This man was as big and powerful as a thunderstorm, yet all he could do now was look to me for help.

All of a sudden, cries of panic blew up from the bleachers as a Brookhaven player crashed into the secondary, and loped down the sidelines. "Kill him! Kill him!" the fans shouted hysterically. "Break his neck!" When the kid had been caught and properly mashed into the earth on the Marshall thirty, the complaints went out again. "What the hell's the matter with the Miller kid?" they moaned. "He's walking around with his head between his legs!"

But it was now time for the finale. With seven seconds to go, Brookhaven was setting up for a Hail Mary pass play. Spectators were holding their breaths and clinging to their loved ones as the players took their positions. While they understood it was too late for the Panthers to win, they knew a touchdown and an extra point would reduce the point spread to two.

And that meant every man, woman, and child who

had bet money on the Lions would lose.

"Get in there and hold them, you pussies!" the bald man screamed. "Damn you, Miller—get off your butt and play ball!"

While I was watching all this, Curtis was watching me. "Are you listening to me, man?" he said. "I'm asking for your help!"

I nodded my head. "It'll be all right," I said weakly. "For you and Tommy."

He wrinkled his brow. "Oh, yeah?" he said. "What does 'all right' mean?"

"It means I'm going to give Bundley those responsible for Richard Temple's murder," I said.

As he puzzled over that, a desperate Brookhaven flanker dived through the air to snatch a pass. The instant he snagged it, he was up-ended by a Lion, brutally spun like a propeller, and dropped with a thud on the goal line. A whistle blew shrilly, the referee cried "No score!" and thirty Brookhaven players spilled out on the field to protest. But by now the horn was honking like a tornado warning, and the field was being swamped with shrieking fans. In all this confusion, my son was kneeling in the grass clutching his helmet to his chest. When I saw him lower his head to the turf, I truly wished I were dead. Worse than that, I wished I could take his place.

"Tell Essie everything will work out," I said. I had to push hard to make my way through the mass of frenzied fans pouring out of the stands to congratulate the team.

Curtis tore through the tangled arms and legs like a Kenyan with a machete. "Where are you going!" He grabbed my arm and squeezed it hard.

"I've got an errand to run," I said.

"Now you listen to me, friend," he said, "I don't know what the shit you got yourself into here, but I can tell by that hound dog face of yours, you're headed into some bad trouble. And whatever it is, I want to be counted in."

A mass of screeching girls shoved hard against me on the way to the field. "It's my responsibility," I told Curtis.

But he stood as firm as a rock in the rapids. "Oh, no, it's not," he said. "It's my kid they've got in jail, not yours!"

We were now surrounded by thrilled and jubilant spectators, who flung body and soul against us, blew red and white plastic whistles in our ears and chanted "A hundred in a row!" over and over. Some even went so far as to suggest they were Number One.

Since I could no longer stand, I forged ahead against the rising tide. It was as if I had to collide with the whole world just to get out of that football stadium. But at least I wasn't alone. Not with a stubborn and honorable black man as tall as a redwood stalking close behind me.

On the way to the police station, the image of my behemoth son down on his knees, contemplating the football turf would not leave my mind.

It wasn't the way you'd expect such a pre-planned child of nature to act. Nancy had informed me while hooking her bra on our honeymoon that all this bumping around in the motel room was okay as far as it went, but what was really going to suit her was the Big M, motherhood. Having studied all about it in *The Joy of Sex* and *McCall's* and having duly noted the generous sizes of the hips on various madonna statues, Nan had concluded that she had just the kind of body that God had intended a mother to have.

Somehow, all this natural inclination turned out to mean a lot of trouble for her, though, including regular peeps and probes into the uterus area by qualified physicians, charts and diagrams of her menstrual cycle, and complicated cervix exercises in front of the situation comedies on TV. It also meant riding up to a Jackson clinic to learn how to grunt and heave properly, and how to strengthen certain critical muscles at home with a chair, a half-hour, and a Mississippi blind-made broom. She also signed up a host of her friends in the League of Women Voters as alternate natural childbirth coaches, in case I turned up with a heart murmur or came down with a toothache and couldn't make it to the delivery room. I told her I doubted if Yahweh had all this in mind back when the Neanderthals were knocking each other up in the Mousterian caves of Gibraltar, but Nancy never being one to allow history to rudely intrude on the present, stuck tenaciously to her masterplan and went right ahead and ovulated and conceived on schedule and soon delivered a child in a dimly lit room to a long-haired obstetrician's gasps of "Beautiful! Beautiful!" and to the commiserating sounds of a Bartok string quartet on a tape recorder.

Once Derek's shiny bald head had been gripped in the forceps like a damp clod of clay in the blades of a posthole digger and the boy had slid safely into life, Dr.

Farley-Smith proceeded to stamp his approval on Nancy's butterfat content and ordered the nurse to haul the little bugger into the room for some natural nourishment. To my wife's dismay, however, Derek immediately revealed a decided preference for the left (in this case, the smaller) of the two breasts being offered to him for breakfast. Naturally, this quickly upset his mother's cart since part of her plan had always been for her baby to nurse exclusively on the dexter side, thereby draining the larger bosom down to a size roughly comparable to the other.

"I thought at least while I suckled my own child," she moaned, "I would be normal!" But weeks of playing musical nipples with Derek went by and never would he bother to test the big one out. "What am I supposed to do?" she asked me. "He won't even touch it!"

"Maybe it's too intimidating," I suggested. "Try to see it from his point of view." I cupped my hands around her right breast. "Look at how huge this sucker is," I said. "I happen to love it, but it's bigger than Derek's head!"

"It is not!" she cried.

While Derek chewed contentedly on his favorite food, Nancy began to languish on the bed as full of chagrin as she was unused milk. "I'm starting to get more one-sided than ever!" she groaned and threw up her hands at the whole affair.

Could it be she never forgave her son for screwing up her dreams of achieving, for once, a perfect balance in her life?

To wipe such idle thoughts from my mind, I glanced

over at Curtis, who could have been on his way to the folding chairs and artificial grass the way the tall guy was peering into space with his knee caps around his ears.

I wondered if he were thinking about his son, too. Had there been an earth-tone version of the chubby eighteen-month-old in our house who staggered around the carpet like a sailor on leave and stuffed spiders and plaster of Paris giraffes between his gums as soon as your back was turned? Had his child of nature explored the inside of his diaper the way most kids dug around in cookie jars, as mine had?

This particular habit of Derek's was rather vexing, even to a natural mother like Nancy. "You're a man," she said to me. "Tell me why a perfectly decent little boy would keep doing that!"

"Maybe something itches," I said.

"And maybe pigs can fly!" she retorted and stormed out of the room.

Worried and confused about it, she eventually took her case to Mom. "He even does it in the mall!" she cried. "It's so embarrassing!"

"Well, of course it is!" Mom heartily agreed. "But that's the way the male of the species behaves! That's why it's so much nicer to have little girls!"

It certainly would have been safer during the changing of the diapers, which was hazardous, since Derek not only got a kick out of spouting Moby Dick-like streams of urine into the air, but doing it only when someone was around to appreciate the performance. He was a bundle of cuddles and coos, until the diaper was peeled away, and air struck flesh. Then his tiny hose would curl upward like a cold toe and out would spew a runnel of his recycled formula until my shirt would look like I'd been recently hugging the commode in The Daylight Lounge.

He had such an uncanny aim with the thing that we had to resort to strapping on safety goggles and paint masks in order to protect ourselves from the mettlesome pee. Once, Nancy chose to abandon the cover since the goggles were screwing up her bangs and bravely folded back Derek's diaper and cautiously patted his round, plump belly. Perhaps, she hoped, his fountain had run dry.

"There, now," she said and reached for the replacement. "That's a good boy, Derek. Please don't spray Momma. That's right. Just hold on for one more minute. Now, Derek—"

Her words were erased forever by a vicious shot in the neck, which came at her with such an alarming force, she had to look away while she tried to stem the flow with the heel of her hand. "Mom is right!" she said as the yellow water tricked through her fingers and Derek giggled to beat the band. "Next time, I am definitely going to have a little girl!"

On the AM radio in the car, an ex-jock by the name of Joe Dan Suggs was offering some insights on the Marshall victory. In an effort to forget about Derek, I listened to Joe Dan's paean to the inhuman courage which he had witnessed in the incredible play of the Lions. He figured for the guys to come through at the end after playing their guts out between the white lines all evening was the greatest testament he could think of to intestinal fortitude.

Thank God the Panthers hadn't brought their momentum shift with them, though. That would have spelled lights-out for the Lions for sure. All she'd written. Having seen a few of these things in his day, Joe Dan realized a momentum shift could eat up a game plan like one of those giant African snakes swallowing a cow. He didn't know anybody who was exempt from it either, not your blue chip players, the guys who give you 120 percent every day, or the natural athletes with the best upper-body strength in the conference.

"But in my final analysis, Jack," he said to the announcer, "I've gotta say to the folks out there: quality always comes through."

"That's true enough," Jack agreed in his Midwestern, disk-jockey voice, hoping to put an end to it right there.

But Suggs wanted to elaborate on his idea. "I've always maintained, quality does it all," he said. "Now, if this game's not an example of greatness, you just tell me what is. I'm not talking about just out there where it counts either. I know these kids. Every one of them is a quality person in his own right."

"They all played a good game," was as far as Jack would take it.

"Hey, you know what?" Joe Dan had another thought. "That player's name we tackled was Ed *Washington*! Now, how's that for patriotic, huh?"

When we reached the police station, I clutched Temple's papers next to my chest and lugged them into the building like a former medal-winner puffing in with the Olympic torch only—as it happens in stadiums sometimes—not many folks noticed my arrival. I was told by a blonde woman with a stiff face that Bundley was still out celebrating the win, and if I just had to see him tonight, why didn't I go ahead and sit down on the bench along with the black guy and wait? When Curtis and I had taken our seats, she turned up the radio for us.

"All right, folks," Suggs was saying, "I want to do something special before we go off the air this evening. I want you people out there to take a moment of silence in tribute to the school superintendent, Richard Temple, a man who we all know died recently. I just want to say this: here's a guy, would've wanted this game to go on exactly as it did go on and with the same results. Let me tell you something, folks. If the team hadn't played and won tonight, this man's ghost would never have forgiven us. That's the kind of classy guy he was, and the kind of classy game football is!"

After all this class-consciousness and an eternity of Muzak, which somebody with a voice like Announcer Jack's kept claiming was "easy listening," I was at the point of dumping my goods on the blonde with the stucco skin and fleeing when the chief of police finally entered the station, came to a stop, and glowered at us. "I told you before, Curtis, there's nothing else we could do," he growled.

"And I told you, I don't believe it," Duke said.

"Now, listen here, I'm not talking to anybody. And that includes reporters!"

Since I hadn't endured Joe Dan and Johnny Mathis for an hour to be sent on my merry way, I blithely followed Bundley into his office. Before he could settle into his seat, I had slung the papers on his desk like a saddle on a mare and was telling him about Vince Scarlotti, the owner of a local dry cleaning store. This fine Italian American was a pillar of the town and a member of a mafia family in New Orleans. According to Temple's research, Scarlotti and his men had a couple of dozen prominent Marshall citizens in their pockets including the illustrious mayor and eight officials of the police department.

All this time, Bundley did nothing except listen and occasionally push the pile of notes with his finger as if to see if it were still alive. No matter what I said, it was obvious from his expression that I wasn't telling him anything he didn't know already. Finally, when I was through, he said, "If you think you can tie the New Orleans mafia to this man's death, Miller, you're flat pissing on the wrong tree."

"Why is that?"

"Because we found the murder weapon hidden out at Hammer Creek. You ever heard of the mafia working that way?"

"Chief, if Tommy Curtis had even touched that gun, his fingerprints would have been all over it."

Bundley shot me a sneering, surprised look. "I don't know how you know they wasn't on there," he said, "but an absence of prints don't necessarily mean a thing. Anybody can wipe the prints off a murder weapon. Happens every night on TV. But one thing we did find was the boy's blood type on the gun."

"You mean on the trigger, don't you?"

"All right, the trigger."

"Along with several other blood types?"

He cocked his head suspiciously. "Who told you that?" he said.

"I guessed."

"Yeah, well, we're working on that part of it right now. I don't claim we have all the answers here, but I'm not dismissing the possibility that this could tie that boy up with two other murders in which the victims had Type O and Type B blood."

I waited a minute, then hit him with my idea that the existence of the various blood types on the trigger meant not that there were other victims, but more than one killer. "That's why the trigger was smeared and the rest of the gun wasn't," I told him. The killers made a pact. Each man pricked his finger and swore a blood oath to murder Richard Temple. Then each took the gun and pulled the trigger."

"You mean a ritual execution."

"That's right. As in 'mafia.'"

Bundley massaged his pliable face for a while, then raised his wide butt off his seat as if it were being scraped from a grill. After pacing the floor for a while with his palm pressed like a spatula against his belly, he turned to me. For the first time it was obvious that he had already concluded the same thing. He rubbed his neck as he checked the papers on the desk again. "So. I reckon you're hell-bent on making all this public, huh?" he said.

"Yes," I said and a chill swept through me like an Oklahoma wind.

"Miller, you're a real pain in the butt, you know it?" he said. "You got my ass on the edge of a razor here. There's no way I can go out and arrest anybody in this town for murder and claim they were acting on orders from the mob. I don't have much of a daily life here, but

I'm still kind of fond of it."

"You don't have to move a step," I told him. "All you have to do is wait here and let me dump it into your lap. That's why I came to you first. I wanted to know what you'd do if I gave you these notes and turned in one of the murderers."

After considering the idea for a long time, he rose to his feet. "I reckon," he said, "if this murderer of yours confessed to the crime, I'd have to carry out my sworn duties and put the son of a bitch away. Wouldn't have any choice of that. Not even Scarlotti could quarrel with that, could he? Not if somebody else brought him in."

"No, he couldn't," I said. "And somebody will," I promised.

In the car a few minutes later, I sat shivering on the driver's side watching a street lamp through the windshield pulsate in the darkness like a beacon in the fog. It sent a chill deep into my blood to consider what I was about to do. But I didn't believe I had any choice. As I pushed the key into the ignition, Duke wheeled around at me finally out of patience.

"When are you going to tell me what is going on here?" he said. "Were you telling Bundley the truth in there? Do you really know who did it?"

"Yes," I said. "I had to know what he would do before I could say."

"Shit, Miller."

I looked over at him. "My daughter says the team always has a party after the game. Do you have any idea where it would be?"

"Who cares, man? We don't want to go down there."

My tongue felt as thick as an arm in my mouth. "I've got to go pick up one of the killers," I said. "Before the news of Temple's notes leaks out. Now, do you know where it is?"

He paused a moment, then shrugged his shoulders. "Kids tell me, it's back in the swamp south of town," he said.

I started the engine, shifted the gears, and headed south. "Do the kids tell you who owns this place?" I asked him.

"Yeah, they say it belongs to that Ford dealer," he said. "What's his name—Anderson?"

"Henderson," I corrected and stepped on the accelerator. "J. B. Henderson."

* * *

Los Angeles Times

Book Exposes Mafia Connection In Mississippi School
Fourth in a series

EDITOR'S NOTE: In the fourth excerpt from Theodore Miller's *Life on the Line*, the author finds evidence of organized crime in the public school system.

Public schools in Marshall have been severely bruised by integration

Picture Marshall High School as an innocent child—molested, battered, the subject of abuse and neglect. For all its intrinsic social value, forced integration has been eroding Mississippi schools for over twenty years. During this time, teachers have been threatened, classes have been boycotted, buildings have been abandoned, people have been maimed and killed, and not much has been taught. In Pike County, where 45% of the population is black, the social distinction between the races is as clear as the black print on this white page. Negroes and Caucasians stand by each other on identical squares of a board, but the games they are playing just aren't the same. Doubt and diffidence continue to haunt these schools over 35 years after the integration of Central High School in Little Rock.

The most pernicious abuse of Marshall High has been its starvation. Stubborn resistance to civil rights has pushed hundreds of competent teachers out of the system and into the 96 private segregated "academies" that scatter the state. Thousands of the best students are sent there, too, by affluent white parents willing to pay up to $2,000 a year to keep their offspring from having to associate with blacks.

The approach is different in neighboring states, but the effect is the same. In New Orleans, for example, over 35,000 students are enrolled in parochial schools. Of the 85,000 that attend public school, 85% are black. Since public schools are often composed mostly of blacks and poor whites, Southern leaders choose to neglect the growing needs of the system and refuse to nourish it.

"The best people in the state resist the public school system," a Congressional Representative told me. "They'd rather be shot in the groin than to turn over their hard-earned money to a bunch of blacks."

What they prefer is for the federal government to shoulder the responsibility. "After all," he said, "they're the ones that created this mess." Today, the U.S. Department of Education reports that Mississippi is the most dependent of all the states on federal money: three times the national average. At the same time, it annually spends only about $2,080 per pupil on public education—making it 49th in the U.S.

The result of this defiance and apathy is pretty predictable. The salaries of Mississippi teachers rate 50th among the states. The average ACT score of a Mississippi student is 15.5, which is 3.1 below the national figure. Of the 28 states using the ACT, this one comes in dead last.

No wonder the student dropout rate, even in an impoverished area where work for teenagers is practically non-existent, is 6th in the nation.

This was the dismal home environment for Marshall High for many years. The school lay in a corner of indifference with a broken back—until the football team became famous.

Organized crime subverts the athletes

The subversion of the high school coincided with the defiling of the town. As municipal spirits surged up a ladder of consecutive football victories, so did the betting stakes at the local bookie joints. But Marshall's leaders, men like Moore, Hewitt, and Wilkins, were so thrilled to be stuffing their wallets with mafia money, they didn't object to the control of gambling by organized crime. Neither did the police. Even when they realized the job was influencing the outcome of games, they turned their heads away. They were feeling too good about themselves to object.

Before long, athletes were being treated like kings. Or, as a black former basketball player in Marshall put it, "like a herd of mean, spoiled stallions."

Richard "Duke" Curtis, an intense, violent man with a body like a redwood tree, says succinctly, "When they get horny, the coach gets them a gal. When they get hurt, he gives them dope. When they want to move around, he gets them wheels."

Curtis told me that in order to keep the gold mine going, "somebody" provided money, drugs, and women to the boys while Coach Wilson Reed and the good alumni stood back and nodded their approval. Even former Marshall players now in college were paid to convince the current crop that the only chance they had to succeed in life was to make it in sports.

The school helps out the mob

In order to keep this flood of good spirit rising, school officials pushed deficient student athletes through the grades and put diplomas in their hands, never caring that they were shoving them out of the nest ignorant and unprepared.

Gregory Lewis, for example, a high school All-American, managed only a 500 on his Scholastic Aptitude Test. Wendy Nardi of the Educational Testing Service in Princeton, New Jersey, explains that in order to score a mere 700 on the test, a student need answer only 25% of the questions correctly.

To score 400, all he has to do is sign his name.

Considering his distressing performance on the SAT (along with his score of 13 on the ACT), Gregory Lewis' final grades for his junior year at Marshall High sound positively ridiculous:

1. English	B+
2. Algebra	B
3. American History	B
4. Agriculture	A
5. Latin	A

Of course, the colleges that recruit the healthy young bodies have been encouraging this duplicity for a long time now. At the Jan Kemp trial in 1986, Vince Dooley, University of Georgia head coach and athletic director, owned up to some of the double-dealing currently in athletics while testifying in court:

"If we raised the standards for admission to the student body level, it would disarm our football program and our athletic program, and we would not be able to compete at any level—and chances are I would not be the football coach."

Attitudes are beginning to change, as students realize they have become victims of a free ride. Mark Hall, for instance, recently sued the University of Minnesota to have his academic ineligibility overturned. His contention was that he was denied due process when University coaches recruited him despite his poor high school grades.

Mark won his case.

The NCAA is also tightening academic requirements among its member institutions with the controversial Proposition 48. Unfortunately, trends that don't make money come hard in the world of athletics. For a long time to come, coaches will continue to think of high school as a training ground for players, and school administrators will continue to shirk their responsibility to uphold standards.

When Marshall High officials chose to dilute the school, they were actually cooperating with the mafia. To keep the team and the spirit high, rules were skirted, grades were changed, Mickey Mouse courses were created. How easy it must have been for a few greedy souls to manipulate such a mangled, helpless school as this.

And how easily the Lions rolled along, offering glory to some, while bestowing riches upon others—until a man named Richard Temple came out of another world to become Superintendent of the Pike County School District.

This man would lay his life on the line for his ideals. And he would lose it.

Richard Temple was an open-minded, dedicated man

No one ever said Richard Temple was an ordinary man. His personality was magnetic. There was an air of excitement about him. He was dedicated and compassionate. His opinions were clear, strong, and liberal, and he held on to them with heartfelt conviction and zeal.

He was also tall, slender, and good-looking. And seductive.

"I figure he got his job by charming the pants off somebody," Edward Kelso told me. "He was always doing stuff like that."

No doubt his attractiveness did lead to problems. It was no secret that this husband/father was a philanderer. He had affairs with at least a half dozen women in town. One of them was black—a definite no-no in Marshall.

But it wasn't his indiscretions that did him in. Marshall is like any other community in that respect. It can tolerate seduction, adultery, and miscegenation, for those are the dark pitfalls all creatures of desire are subject to.

What it ultimately couldn't handle was his determination to make Marshall High into an academically excellent school. However nice the notion sounded, it proved to be too much to bear. It not only made folks uneasy about their own lack of excellence, it violently rattled their fragile images of themselves.

Temple was a qualified administrator

A native of Boston, Richard Temple attended the University of Connecticut, received an M.Ed. at the University of Chicago in 1974, and promptly did a nine month stint in the public school system in Washington, D.C. From 1975-1980, he taught general science at the predominantly black Ribault High School in Jacksonville and helped institute the Florida high school functional literacy test. In the five years he was at Ribault, he helped raise students' average SAT scores by 30 points.

After three years as an assistant principal at East Jefferson High School in Metairie, Louisiana, Temple became Superintendent of the Pike County Schools in 1983.

He had impeccable credentials for the job. After breezing through prep school, college, and graduate study with a spotless academic record, he gained distinction as an instructor (winning two Teacher of the Year awards in Louisiana) and as a scholar. Besides publishing an armload of articles in periodicals such as *Journal of Teacher Education, The Journal of Special Education,* and *Review of Research in Education,* he spent his summers either taking post-graduate courses at various Midwestern universities or working at the Center for Social Organization of Schools at Johns Hopkins University in Baltimore.

Temple was driven by a single, exalted goal. He wanted to transform Mississippi education—starting with Marshall High. A letter he sent to Wayne D. Greenburg, Florida State Board of Education, shows how passionately he believed in that goal:

Dear Wayne,

Thank you very much for the offer, but I'm afraid I must decline. It's taken me all this time to get a crack in the door here, to let in a single shaft of light. Now that I see it, I don't think I could face myself in the morning if I were to walk away.

I'm sure you understand. My God, these students so desperately need what I have to offer! They are wonderful kids, Wayne, but they are only now starting to flicker in the darkness. It wrenches my gut to see their potential being wasted every day, but I really believe there is reason to hope for better things now.

If there's even the slightest chance I can pull this off—if I can yank that door open just one more inch—I've got to stay here and do it!

Temple's ideas met with resistance at the school

Richard Temple's grave determination to save his students from a life circumscribed by ignorance met with an opposition that sometimes must have seemed impregnable. Most of the faculty, led by Sarah Moore, the mayor's wife, resisted him at every turn, voted 22-4 against his idea of requiring athletes to pass a functional literacy test.

"They just all felt threatened by the proposal," explained Essie Curtis, a black teacher at Marshall High. "They thought he was blaming them for all the problems of the school."

Parents unanimously rejected the idea of such a test. "They claimed it was too one-sided," Curtis told me. "It would be unfair to all the kids who weren't bookworms. If you can imagine the irony of it," she added, "they said it was discriminatory!"

In the face of such antagonism, many men would have retreated or at least modified their approach. Not this one. Richard Temple had a specific task in his mind, and all the sniveling parents and teachers in the world weren't going to keep him from pursuing it. Instead of re-thinking his position, he redoubled his efforts. With the energy of a scholar, he began to investigate ways of circumventing this repugnance.

As soon as he started digging around in the field, he turned up a few skeletons, a few live rats. Beneath all those accusations of foul play and discrimination were other, more desperate motivations. To his astonishment, Temple learned that the tentacles of organized crime had not only reached into Marshall, but into the school as well. Football players under his jurisdiction were being catered to, given money, entertained with drugs and prostitutes. Conference officials were taken on trips, paid to make certain calls in crucial games situations. Even the local school board, composed of Moore and Hewitt, among others, were squatting on coffers which were being regularly filled by the mafia.

So many people had wrapped their egos and their wallets around the fortunes of the team, they simply couldn't afford to let anyone challenge the status quo.

Temple was sitting on this information the only time I ever saw him. One autumn morning in Marshall, I met him as he was picking up his paper. In his casual green sweater and scuffed Adidas tennis shoes, he looked like a Presidential candidate on a retreat. As soon as he recognized me, he complimented my work on the Pittsburgh drug trials. I couldn't help but wonder why a high school superintendent would be so familiar with the efforts of a New York sportswriter.

He was quick to sense the shell I was throwing up around myself. "I'm not flattering you, man," he told me. "I've got a hell of a story for you."

Having no idea he had been rooting around in the mafia, I dismissed the story as nothing.

I was wrong about that.

On that very evening, he was murdered because of it.

Five players were nurtured by the mob.

I never got the "hell of a story" Temple offered me. Not all of it, at least. But I did turn up the personality profiles he wrote on every Marshall football player and their connections with Vincent Scarlotti and the rest of the mob. Some athletes were never paid a dime, some were only vaguely aware of the presence of organized crime. Others, in particular, the stars of the team, were in very deep indeed.

Since Temple's records are as thorough as his scholarship, I have distilled his analyses of the five seniors who were carefully nurtured by the mob.

1. Gregory Lewis [Black. 6'1", 198 lbs. Running back. High school All-American (AP). Illegitimate son of Armada Lewis]

Said to be the best running back ever to come out of the state, Lewis has compiled a list of impressive statistics (in his junior year, he averaged 12 points and 200 yards rushing a game). Gregory's six brothers and sisters think of him as the head of the family; sometimes they even call him "Poppa." The Lewises live in an unpainted tenant farmer shack in the country. Although Armada is a sickly woman who has never had any regular work (she occasionally takes in laundry), there is plenty of evidence of money around. In the house are an expensive TV set, stereo, refrigerator and freezer, and three rooms of Ethan Allan furniture.

Temple documents seven instances of money paid to Lewis and two meetings with the mayor. "Three times," he wrote, "Lewis was seen coming out of Scarlotti's City Cleaners—which is ironic, since his mother does laundry."

His assessment: "Gregory Lewis has become severely dependent upon his status as a star football player. He has become just as dependent upon the unsavory characters that have infiltrated this team and have helped him maintain that status. Football has become like the cocaine he sometimes uses: a reassuring, but damaging drug."

2. Johnny "Step" Davis. [Black. 6'3", 190 lbs. Quarterback. Known as a superb drop-back passer, better than average runner. Son of Tom and Elvira Davis]

Although Johnny Davis isn't as poor as most blacks in the county (his father is a carpenter, his mother does custodial work at the lingerie plant), he has a pretty hard time of it. Frail and shy in elementary school, he was taunted and teased by his peers. When the other kids learned they could make him do anything they wanted, they nicknamed him "Step-and-Fetch-It." In the football program, however, Step Davis developed his body and excelled as a player.

Assessment: "Davis so closely identifies with his role of a football player, he refuses to consider himself as anything else. His parents have been unable to get him to study anything but his game. Although his IQ tests indicate that he has average intelligence, Johnny Davis is a functional illiterate. There is no doubt that he has been promoted through the grades only because he is a player. Football, a game controlled by criminal forces has shaped not only his body, but his mind as well."

3. Jackson Smith. [Black. 5'10", 260 lbs. Center. Quick, powerful offensive lineman. All-State 2 years. Son of Daniel and Mavis Smith]

Assessment: "Jackson Smith is a good-natured boy with a pleasant, self-effacing personality. But he is a slavish follower; wherever Lewis and Davis go, he goes, too. He has been devoted to Gregory Lewis all his life. He even calls him 'Poppa' at times."

4. Wilson Barbio. [White. 5'9", 210 lbs. Fullback. Described by sportswriters as a rough, head-on, Jim Taylor-type runner. Son of Paul and Edna Barbio]

Will Barbio came to Marshall from New York City in 1981 to live with his sister, Mrs. Thomas Mabry of Milltown. The product of a broken home (his father is serving time for armed robbery, his mother is a prostitute who ran off with a client who hated kids), Barbio arrived in Mississippi with a chip on his shoulder.

Instantly disliked by the others, this Yankee tough did nothing to endear himself to anybody. His first year at Marshall High he got into seven fights and was suspended from school twice—once for carrying a loaded .45 automatic pistol in his coat.

Not long after Barbio made the football team, his peer image began to change. The more yardage he racked up, the less objectionable he seemed. By the time he was averaging 100 yards a game, he was a hero.

Assessment: "After being a social pariah for two years, Will Barbio is now a BMOC. For the first time in his life, he is a desirable human being—all because of football. Barbio is smiling now, but he is still a hard, unyielding person. I suspect whatever he deems necessary to maintain his position (even if it means cooperating with gangsters and racketeers), he will do."

5. Derek Miller. [White. 6'4", 250 lbs. Linebacker. Big, mobile, and aggressive. All-State 3 years. Son of Theodore and Nancy Miller]

It sent a chill up my spine to read Temple's file on my own son. His analysis was shrewd, thorough, and correct. He saw Derek as a young man driven by a despondent need to impress (and therefore be loved by) his famous absentee father. "Derek," he wrote," is not very articulate; he tends to bottle up his emotions."

[For some reason, the communication barrier between us seemed inevitable. We were so different. I was never at a loss for words; he never seemed to be able to find any. We were like a pair of stupid rams, old and young, butting our heads together. Painful. Pointless. Silly. It was no way to reach each other, but we could come up with no other.]

Temple's assessment: "In order to gain the approval of his father, Derek Miller has become very proficient in football. He has worked extremely hard to perfect his athletic skills. While his father investigates cocaine traffic in the major leagues or the use of steroids in horseracing, Derek gets better—and more dissatisfied with himself."

Temple's plan to expose the mob

For a man who loved his students as Richard Temple did, it must have been tough to expose the connection of the mafia with the high school football team. He had to know that whatever else would happen, the athletic careers of these five seniors would end, for no college would ever allow such tainted players to wear their pads and colors.

But armed with the explosive facts he had uncovered about the team and the school, he had no choice but to make that decision. As Superintendent of Schools, he was all set to reveal the truth and follow it with an announcement that every athletic program at Marshall High School would be eliminated.

This was the "hell of a story" I paid no attention to. This was the story that leaked from the school board and from there to the mafia.

This was the story that got him killed.

* * *

When I parked the car in front of Bubba's swamp house, I found myself checking the Lincolns and Cadillacs for chunks of bumper dirt.

Strange that I should think of Derek's favorite toddler food. Although he had never been much of a purist about his meals, he had staunchly preferred his dirt as it came to him from nature, which is to say, straight off the chrome. He was particularly fond of Louisiana grime, which apparently had a certain Old World flavor to it, for the moment a Louisiana vehicle appeared in the driveway, Derek would burst out from under the cedar tree and waggle to the bumper to scrape off a snack or two.

Of course, when visiting happened to be a bit sluggish or the season was dry, he was forced to settle for what he could scare up in the neighborhood. In time, he became a hit with the little girls, for while other boys might attend their tea parties under the carport and even grudgingly praise their mud pies and brownies, only my son would actually eat the things. Lucy Hazlitt once confessed that Derek was the only guest she knew who truly appreciated all the work that went into a quality dessert.

There wasn't as much agreement on Derek's habit among his relatives, however. Uncle Harley said that the boy had swallowed so much dirt already, he might just as well go ahead and run for the Senate and be done with it. At least he'd have the jump on his opponents. Aunt Reba, as knowledgeable as she was about such things as dirt, was mum on this subject, as she was on nearly all others. Dad was convinced his grandson's soil-consumption was natural behavior for a kid his size and weight. "If he can pass it, let him eat it!" was his motto.

Mom, on the other hand, being more sophisticated,

was of a different mind. Child of nature or not, anybody who had such a fixation on filth was a bad bet for the reputation of the family, and she was going to break him of this habit once and for all. During most of this phase of my son's maturation, Mom policed our place after school and on weekends in order to hose down every dirty car that showed up in our driveway.

"That's one dinner Derek won't be having!" she would gleefully exclaim as she blasted a bumper with water and watched all the delicacies slide into the gutter in tiny streams.

Whatever effect all this had on Derek, it turned out to be one hell of an experience for our visitors. Uncle Alfred, for example, was flabbergasted when, after a long, hot drive up from New Orleans, he wheeled into the driveway to see a slobbering kid in dirty diapers waddling like a frightened Druid out of the trees, then an enormous woman with a New Collegiate Dictionary clutched to her huge bosom storming out of the house yelling, "Derek—don't you dare!" in a booming voice. Uncle Alfred stomped his brakes to the floor just as Mom dived into the shrubbery in search of the garden hose. When she finally located it, she raised it over her head like a viper, popped out the kinks in the air, and proceeded to douse the car with all the force she had at her command. Assuming all this frenzy was due to his Pontiac GT being on fire, Uncle Alfred hastily pulled Aunt Alice, the two squalling kids, and the barking German Shepherd out of the automobile and through the spray in order to save them from the lethal flames.

Later, while all was being explained, Uncle Alfred chewed thoughtfully on some of Nancy's syrup-dipped fruitcake and drank a few cups of that coffee-and-chicory he always took along on trips. The rest of the day he spent referring to my "poor mother" and alluding to some of the excellent work that was being done these days in the various state-supported mental hospitals in the area.

"I got to be a lunatic," Duke Curtis was muttering to himself. "I'm in the middle of a swamp, hunting a bunch of killers for no reason, and you're standing around grinning at the cars!"

At the sound of his disgusted voice, I suddenly felt the damp wind rustling around us and heard the loud, rasping music rattling the windows of the house at the end of the walkway over the swamp. I shuddered as I thought again of five high school students conspiring to murder their superintendent.

"Why don't you stay here," I said.

But Curtis moaned and shook his head. "You must be dumber than I am, Miller," he said. "If those kids did do it, send the police in after them. They're not your concern."

"One of them is."

He started to speak, then stopped while his eyebrows bent like bows and his yellow eyes swelled to the size of eggs. "You mean your own son?" he said.

"That's right. That's my boy."

"Shit, man!"

"I agree."

"What kind of kid would do such a thing as that?"

"A kid whose father avoids taking responsibility for

him," I said.

"Listen, are you sure about this? I mean, do you *know* he was one of them?"

"Yeah, I know," I said. "I'll be back in a few minutes."

As I walked over the creaky planks toward the house, I noticed the place was resting on cinderblocks over the water. It reminded me of the treehouse I'd built for Derek many years ago. In the middle of an ice storm, we had huddled together like a pair of damp socks in a dresser drawer until he told me that treehouses must be for the birds, and he preferred something more human, like a bed.

After stalling on the porch for a moment to peck idly at the glass wind chimes and remember the old times, I pulled the front door open and stepped inside. The hot, stuffy living room smelled like the Hudson River on a Sunday morning. A tall, thin girl in a blue jump suit wrinkled her mortician makeup at me, then vamped it over to a clutch of similar ladies who were sucking on marijuana cigarettes that made Uncle Harley's makings look like Lucky Strikes, snorting cocaine with some lunch room straws, and betting on whose period would be starting up next. Meanwhile, the guys were hanging on the sectional furniture while they joked and drank Lite beer and tried to compare the score of the game with the numbers on their jerseys. I guessed from the not-at-home look on their faces, they weren't having much luck doing it.

Panning the room through the reeky smoke, I recognized Lewis, Davis, Barbio, Smith, and the yellow-faced Douglas lounging at the bar with three unidentified adults. At last, in an isolated corner of the house, I saw a heap of flesh that looked like a mountain gorilla wounded by poachers. The boy was wrenched into a crouch with his arms and legs pulled in close like giant fingers curled into a fist.

Elbowing my way through the party, I went over to him. "Derek?" I said. When he raised his head, I could have cried. He was cuddling a stupid can of beer the same way he'd held his dead kitten once. I had brought him to this. I had to get him out of it.

"I don't feel very good, Dad," he said. "I'm sick."

"Get up, Derek!" I yelled and snatched the beer and flung it as hard as I could against the wall. All this unexpected fury shocked the party into silence. As I pulled Derek up by his wrist, the music ceased, and a wall of people began to form around us. Soon a thin, New Jersey accent was whining out of the crowd.

"What do you think you're doing, Miller?" it said.

I let out a sigh of disgust. "Do you really care what I think I'm doing, Barbio?" I said.

His olive face flushed red. "You better listen to me," he said. "I'm asking you where you're going with Derek!"

"I'm going out."

"Oh, yeah? Where is 'out'?"

I gritted my teeth. "I'm taking my son to the police," I said.

"Oh, no, you're not!"

"Come on, Derek," I said to my son. "Let's go."

But Barbio held his hand in front of my face like a traffic cop. "I can't let you do that, Miller," he said.

"Do you really believe I need your permission,

Barbio?"

"You're not listening to me, man. What I'm saying is, we're a team around here. We stick together!"

Something in me snapped so hard, I reached out and grabbed his wrists. Ripping the Band-aid off his finger as abruptly as I could, I shoved his hand into his face. "And what I'm saying is, you also kill together, you little punk! You and Lewis and Davis and Smith—"

"Let me go, you bastard!" Barbio struggled loose, plunged his hand into his pocket, and came out with an old-fashioned pearl-handled jackknife. "I told you he knew," he said to the others. "I told you!"

"Shut up, Will!" Lewis said. "Put that thing away!"

Barbio sneered and angled the blade toward my throat. "That son of a bitch Temple had it coming and everyone knows it!" he said. "He just wouldn't let us alone! He was on our backs all the time! Always trying to get us on probation, always trying to make somebody quit the team. He was going to do away with football!"

"So it was high time a handful of teenagers went out and butchered him. Good thinking, Barbio."

"You don't understand, man! He was bad! He was going to ruin all our futures. Look at us. Look at how poor it is around here. Football is the only way we can be anything. Without football, we're nothing!"

"Who worked that one out for you, Will? Your friend Douglas? Vince Scarlotti? You muscleheads! Temple was threatening to expose their gambling operation, so they decided to wipe him out. All they needed were a few dummies to do the work for them. That's the way they stack the deck, Barbio! They worked you up so much, you were willing to go out and execute a human being! They suckered you into committing a murder!"

"Shut up!" Barbio snarled. Only now he was beginning to realize the enormity of what he'd done. But he still couldn't admit it was wrong. "You don't understand!" he cried. "What did he expect us to do without football! Without sports, this whole lousy state would dry up, and you know it. Anyway, look at the way he was screwing around all the time. Right, guys? Hell, we did every man in this town a favor!"

"Get out of the way, punk!" I said.

Barbio's squat body seemed to spread out as he aimed the point of the knife at my neck. "Mr Ames!" he hollered toward the bar. When he got no response, he wiped the blade on his jersey and called out again.

"Mr. Ames is gone, Will," Lewis said. "They're all gone."

Barbio was desperately trying to think, to hold in his panic, but he was squirming like a kid with a full bladder. "Nobody else is leaving, I can tell you that," he declared. "Don't you move an inch, until we figure this one out," he said to me. "I swear to God, I'll rip you open from your belly to your balls!"

Since I was committed to taking my son out of Bubba's house, no matter what, I figured I had nothing to lose by ignoring him. Taking a deep and secret breath, I pulled Derek past this boy and his knife and led him out of the house. In the chill of my spine, I could sense something stalking behind us about to pounce. Never was I so glad to see anything as I was that black giant Curtis standing with his head in the trees and a lug wrench in his hand like a colossus over the swamp.

Not a muscle or vein moved when he spoke to the crowd coming after us. Not even an eyelid. "This man is taking his boy home," he told them. "Anyone who objects will be asking to have his wagon fixed with this tire iron!" As Derek and I slid around him and headed for the car, Curtis chased the party back inside with a growl and a brandish of his weapon.

"Better get out of here, Miller," Duke said when he crammed his knotted body into the back seat of the car. "There's no telling what kids on booze and drugs will do."

No sooner had I gotten Derek and myself into the car than a round, waxy face appeared at my window, followed by a stout finger tapping one, two, three on the glass. When I lowered it, Bubba peeked in at Duke, at Derek, then at me.

"Evening, Ted," he said in a tight voice. It was so hard it vibrated in the wind like a saw hit with a rock.

"Bubba," I said.

"I just saw what happened from the kitchen," he said. "You sure screwed up my party, didn't you, ole buddy?"

"It was getting dull," I said.

"Looks like you're determined to screw up a lot of other things, too," he said. "Including your friends. I thought we agreed you'd stay out of my business."

Duke tapped me on the shoulder. "They're coming back out," he said.

I looked back up at Bubba. "What do you want?" I asked him. I decided I owed him a minute anyway.

"I just want to know what you're planning to do,

Teddy," he said. "Marian called a while ago about the papers you two dug up over at Temple's house. I don't know, I figured we could look them over together and talk about it."

"Too late, Bubba," I said. "I've already turned them over to Bundley."

His face fell. "I see," he said. "So now the hotshot reporter's going to have everybody all head-up over the presence of organized crime in the community."

"I don't have time to go through this now, Bubba."

"Can't anybody get through to you how it is around here now, Teddy? Look, all right, so the mafia is in Marshall, Mississippi. So what? What's the big deal? It's not like they're thugs with the Tommy-guns you see in the movies. These are damned clever businessmen who do a lot of good for the community. And you don't have to join them in order to do business with them either."

"But you do have to approve of their methods."

He shifted his eyes from me to Derek and back. "I'm not denying things sometimes wind up beyond the law. But why should that bother me? What's the law ever done for me? The law wanted no part of me, Teddy."

"Do you know what you're saying? Goddamn it, man, you used to stand for something! Now you're telling me you approve of cold-blooded murder!"

"I never said I approved of it. I didn't even know anything about it until it happened. I swear to God."

"I've got to go." I cranked up the engine.

"Teddy." Bubba's heavy hand on my shoulder made me cringe. "It's all this damn poverty, you know," he said. "If there wasn't so many rednecks and good ole boys and corrupt politicians—"

"There'd be more room for Bubba, right?"

His face hardened. "All right, let's get serious, okay? I'm telling you, if you turn this boy in, all hell is going to break loose around here. First thing you know, there'll be a grand jury investigation, then who knows what'll happen? They might railroad me into prison. I may have skirted the law a little, Ted, but you don't really believe I deserve that, do you?"

"Goodbye, J. B.," I said and slammed the selector lever into Drive. As I dug out of the driveway, I saw that the party had rejoined the host. Although it was too dark to make out any of the dreary faces among the cars in the swamp, I could tell by their general demeanor they were no longer having fun.

In that quiet rented car on the way back to town, the big shape propped against the window looked like a swollen version of the same kid I once drove across town to Linda Bowen's house for his first date. He was a nervous little fellow then, in his elastic necktie and an oversized polyester suit he'd picked for himself from the rack at Penney's. On the way there, he reverted to his earlier days and scratched at his trousers below the belt like a bird trying to get back into the cage.

I let him go at it because I realized a first date was serious business for a kid, and if hanging on to the genitals helped, so be it. In front of Linda's gabled house on Maple Street, he straightened up and shook my hand and muttered a sad "Goodbye, Dad," as if he were off to the crusades with no food or water, and turned to face the music.

"I'll be here if you make it back," I told him.

By now, he had stretched his tie so much, the elastic hung like a noose around his neck. "Well, I reckon I'll go on, then," he said and trudged like a doomed man slowly up the long walk. I found myself whispering the Twenty-Third Psalm as he walked through the shadows to the door.

The instant my poor terrified son rang the bell, Linda's big brother Henry, who was lurking inside the hall in search of mischief, flung open the door and bellowed like a hungry cow into his face: "What you want, boy!"

This gruff outburst took Derek by such surprise that he squawked like a blue jay, spun around in terror, and crashed down to the sidewalk banging his right knee on a sharp rise in the concrete. A minute later, he picked himself up and returned to the car with his head held low and the knee of his new suit pants ripped away, exposing his broken and bleeding body.

"I take it, we're early," I said.

"Dad," he announced, "I don't ever want to go up to anybody's house again!"

I kept a straight face. "Let's take a look," I said and knelt down to examine the leg. "It's pretty bad all right," I allowed. "But I think we may be able to save it."

He jerked his knee away. "All I want to do is go home," he said.

"You can't go without your date," I told him.

"I don't care about that."

I looked at him very seriously now. "Linda's waiting for you to take her to the movies, son," I said.

"I don't care! I never wanted to go out with any girl,

anyway! I don't know why I even asked her!"

"Yes, but you did ask her," I said. "And now it's your responsibility to pick her up."

"I don't want to!"

"Do it, anyway."

"I can't."

"Why can't you?"

"Because I'm scared!"

God, that hurt. A blast of deer shot in the spleen wouldn't have felt any worse than those three little words in my ear. But I would rather have died than to show it. "Who isn't?" I said. "Linda's probably a lot more frightened than you are."

That was a notion he hadn't considered. "I don't see why," he said, "She's nothing but a girl."

"Yes, but you see, girls don't have as many ways of being approved of as boys do," I said. "So things like dates are very important to them. Just imagine how Linda's going to feel, all dressed up and smelling like Dial soap, sitting in her room all alone tonight, thinking she did something wrong."

"It wasn't her, Dad. I just changed my mind. I don't want to go."

"But if you don't go, Linda will always believe it was her fault. She'll remember this night as long as she lives."

He thought about that a long time. "I don't want her to feel bad," he said manfully.

I was proud of my son after that for seeing life from a different perspective for a moment, and I couldn't help but be amused at the way he became suddenly concerned about his appearance. "But what about this?" He pointed at the knee. "I can't go on a date looking like this."

"She won't mind."

After weighing that with everything else, he nodded his head and gazed up the walk at the foreboding door. "Would you come with me?" he asked.

"She's not my date."

"I guess not," he agreed and began to march slowly up the walk to take his medicine. Twenty minutes later, after I'd been reduced by anticipation to counting the freckles on my forearms, Derek emerged from the house with a fresh-faced slip of a girl walking proudly beside him in a crisp, blue dress. As they came closer, I detected a blush and a grin on his sheepish face, then the reason for both: the trouser leg in question had been clumsily, but proudly stitched together with dark gray thread, with all the patience, skill, and loving care a thirteen-year-old girl could muster.

"What is this, man?" Duke Curtis quickly unfurled his long body out of the car in front of the police station. "What are we doing here? You're not going to turn the kid in!"

I slammed the door behind him. "He's turning himself in," I said.

"Are you crazy! You're going to blow the only chance you've got to get him out of this mess?"

"This is the only way he can get himself out of it."

"Listen to me, man. Take your boy and go. Leave this state. Take him up to New York or somewhere and hide him out. I swear to you, I'll never say a word to anybody about it!"

"Running away wouldn't help," I said. "I know. I've done it."

"Damn!" Curtis banged his big fist on the roof of the Thunderbird. "This really makes me feel like shit, you know it?" he said. "I never meant for anybody to have to trade his son for mine!"

Leaving him mumbling helplessly to himself, I went around the car, opened Derek's door, and looked in. "Are you ready to go?" I asked him.

With eyes like a St. Bernard puppy caught peeing on the rug, he peered up at me. "I didn't shoot him, Dad," he said. "Honest, I didn't. I couldn't do such a thing!"

I took his elbow and helped him out, surprised at just how easy it was to move the team's star linebacker where you wanted him.

"I thought we were just going to scare him!" he said. "All of us made this vow and all. It was like we were playing a game, or something. It didn't seem real! Barbio just pointed the gun at him and pulled the trigger. It was so crazy! He just shot him, Dad, the way they do on TV. One minute Mr. Temple was standing there asking us what we wanted, the next Barbio was blowing his face apart all over the place. It was so hard to believe it was happening. There was all this blood everywhere. Then Greg and Davis and Smith took the gun and shot him again!"

I took a deep breath. "What did you do?" I asked.

His eyes fell to the ground. "They gave me the gun and hollered, 'Shoot him! Shoot him!' But I couldn't do it."

"So you fired the last shot into the floor."

He nodded his head. "I keep seeing it happen over and over," he said. "I keep seeing Mr. Temple saying, 'What do you boys want?' and Barbio shooting him. Over and over. His body keeps coming apart, and Greg and the others keep shooting him. It's so I can't do anything anymore, Dad. I can't even go to the bathroom."

"Did you try to stop them?" I asked him.

"How could I? It happened so fast!"

"Didn't you even ask them to stop?"

"I didn't . . . think they would." His thin, low voice trailed away like a train whistle receding in a tunnel. "God, I'm sorry, Dad," he said. "I'm so sorry!"

I rested my hand on his thick shoulder for a moment, but I think he was too hurt and confused now to notice. He was afraid to think what would happen to him when he walked into the police station to give himself up. No wonder I'd been thinking about his little date with Linda. It was coming down to the same thing. After all these years, the very same thing. He was scared.

In just the way he had years before on Maple Street, Derek swallowed hard and offered his hand to me. It was cold and damp as I squeezed and shook it. "I guess I'd better go on, then," he said. Off to the crusades again.

"Yep," I said.

"Do you have any idea what they'll do to me?" he asked me.

"No, I don't," I answered.

After glancing at Duke, who was leaning over the roof of the car, he smiled sadly at me, let go of my hand, and turned toward the station. I felt the bitter, cold bite of helplessness gnaw at my stomach as I watched my son walk away. How small he looked as he opened the door and disappeared inside. He looked so small that I wanted to run up the walk and grab him and run away.

"I reckon this is what comes from eating bumper dirt," I said. As absurd as that must have sounded to Duke Curtis, I felt a compulsion to say it anyway, to keep what I was witnessing at a distance.

As I stood with my eyes locked on the lighted steps of the police station, Duke eased his tall, slender body around the car. "You know sending him in there is going to make you dog meat in this town," he said. "Folks will say you never cared about your boy. They'll say you just blew into town, dumped him into jail, and left."

All I cared about now was what they were doing to Derek inside. But I refused to go see. He had to do it alone. "I wish I could've made him understand," I said. "It's as much my fault as his. But he had to go in there himself."

Duke shrugged his shoulders. "If he's as smart as his old man, he'll figure it out," he said.

"I wonder."

Duke cleared his throat and shot a load of spit over the slick hood of the Thunderbird. "I never did thank you for your help," he said.

"Forget it."

He nodded, stared at the police station with me. "Shit, man," he said. "No way I could've turned in my kid like that."

"I've got to go home," I said. "I've done enough for one night."

* * *

Washington Post

BOOK CALLS FOR RE-INVESTIGATION OF SCHOOL SUPERINTENDENT'S MURDER
Fifth of a series

EDITOR'S NOTE: In the fifth excerpt from *Life on the Line*, Theodore Miller gives an account of the murder of Richard Temple which includes information until now unknown to the public and calls for a grand jury investigation of the case.

Richard Temple was murdered by a conspiracy of five

While the truth and nothing but the truth of the murder of the Superintendent of the Pike County Public Schools may have surfaced during the trial of Wilson Barbio, Gregory Lewis, Johnny Davis, Jackson Smith, and Derek Miller, the whole truth was kept under cover. The following chronology of the crime is based on facts presented in court. Additional information gathered from research and interviews is noted in parentheses.

Thursday, 11:45 p.m. Barbio, Lewis, Davis, Smith, and Miller met on a practice field south of the Marshall football stadium. Barbio, the self-appointed leader of the group, showed the others a .45 caliber revolver which he had gotten "on the street," and declared that they were meeting this evening to put an end to an enemy's life. (Each boy swore an oath to take part in the murder of Richard Temple and proclaimed three times, *"Niatri representam La Cosa Nostra. Sta famigghia e La Cosa Nostra"*—"We represent the Cosa Nostra. The family is our business." The five conspirators pricked their fingers with Barbio's jacknife and pressed them together as a symbol of their dedication to the murder. A mafia ritual similar to this one is described in an article in *Time*, August 22, 1969.)

Friday, 12:08 a.m. When Richard Temple answered a knock on the screen door of his house on the campus of Marshall High School, he groggily asked, "What do you boys want at this time of night?" (Immediately, with a cry of *"La Cosa Nostra!"*) Barbio fired the revolver through the screen door into the school superintendent's face. Somehow, with a bullet lodged in his nasal cavity, Temple managed to stagger back into the house to the foyer, where Barbio shot him again, this time at point-blank range. The force of the bullet ripped open his chest and knocked him to the floor of the living room.

12:10 a.m. (Gazing at the lifeless body, the boys clasped their hands together and swore the oath again.) Then Gregory Lewis took the pistol, aimed it at Temple's heart, and pulled the trigger. Davis and Smith followed with shots to the stomach and groin. Then came a hitch. The fifth conspirator refused to do his part. With urgent commands to "Shoot him! Shoot him!" ringing in his ears, Derek Miller shut his eyes and unloaded the final shot into the floor.

12:15 a.m. The five boys left the house by the back door

and regrouped at the practice field. ("We all sat on the ground, breathing hard," Derek said. "Even though it was cold, we were all sweating. We just kept staring at that gun, saying nothing, feeling real sick at the stomach. Finally, Barbio got up and buried the gun near the creek. With the gun out of sight, we all felt relieved. What we'd done didn't seem so real anymore. After that, we got up and left. I don't think we ever said anything to each other, the whole time we were there.")

12:25 a.m. The conspirators returned to their homes.

7:01 a.m. Temple's mangled body was discovered by a Marshall High School maid, Edna Wills. Within minutes, the Marshall Police Department arrived at the house, examined the body, and contacted the victim's wife, who was visiting her daughter in Durham, North Carolina.

7:32 a.m. Tommy Lee Curtis, 16, a former yard boy for Temple, was arrested on the premises and unofficially charged with the murder.

7:35 a.m. Passing by the house on a morning jog, I stopped to see what the commotion was about. At the scene of the crime, I was told by Chief of Police D. T. Bundley that he believed he had already found the murderer.

9:30 a.m. Although classes were suspended for the day, Coach Reed called his players to the gymnasium for "skull practice." There the football team spent the day, lying around on mattresses, playing cards, and practicing their plays on the basketball court.

12:30 a.m. (At the Haymon Ford Co. on Elm Street, I discovered that the owner, J. B. Henderson, was retailing stolen cars.)

4:20 p.m. After talking to Coach Wilson Reed, I ran into the five conspirators in the Marshall gym. They were nervous, excitable, and rude. (While I was there, I learned that Johnny Davis' hand had been "injured," and that my son's finger had been cut. Unaware of the connection between his pricked finger and the ritual, I joked with him about it.)

5:32 p.m. The murder weapon mysteriously turned up at Bundley's office. At the trial, the chief of police "couldn't say" whether it had been turned up by hunters or kids playing near Hammer Creek. "All I know is, somebody on the phone informed us where to look," he said. (Actually, it was my son who told them where to look. "I called," Derek said to me, "because I couldn't stand it anymore. I had to tell somebody something. But it was a woman I talked to, and I just didn't have the guts to tell her I was involved.")

6:31 p.m. (I learned from a colleague at the *New York Times* that J. B. Henderson's used cars were being furnished by a car-theft ring operated by the New Orleans mafia.)

7:28 p.m. (With the help of a friend, I located Richard

Temple's research notes in his study. This important material cites facts, gives names, and provides convincing evidence of the presence of organized crime in Marshall. It also clearly states that Temple was threatening to expose illegal sports betting operations and game-fixing in the town. This crucial information was ruled "irrelevant" at the trial, and therefore was never admitted as evidence in this case.)

7:30 p.m. The conspirators participated in the Marshall-Brookhaven High School football game.

8:00-9:30 p.m. After making photocopies of Temple's notes, I went to the football game with an idea how the crime was committed. When I noticed three other Marshall players with "injured" right hands, I knew there must be a mafia-instigated ritual crime.)

11:00 p.m. (After waiting for an hour at the police station for Bundley, I turned over to him a copy of Temple's notes.)

11:25 p.m. At a weekend house owned by J. B. Henderson, I picked up my son and delivered him to the police station where he turned himself in.

11:45 p.m. Derek Miller formally confessed to his part in the murder of Richard Temple.

Saturday, 12:20 a.m. Wilson Barbio was arrested at the home of his sister.

12:35 a.m. Johnny Davis was arrested at the home of his

parents.

1:45 a.m. Gregory Lewis and Jackson Smith were arrested at a service station in Hammond, Louisiana.

2:17 a.m. Tommy Lee Curtis was released by the Marshall Police Department and taken home by his father.

3:48 a.m. The five boys were charged with, then later indicted for the murder. Eight months later, four of them were convicted as principals in the first degree. The fifth, Derek Miller, was convicted as a principal in the second degree.

All references to the mafia were deleted from court transcripts

There is no mention of the mafia, the mob, or the Cosa Nostra in the official transcripts of the trial of Barbio, Lewis, Davis, Smith, and Miller. There are only seven allusions to organized crime.

And every single reference to Richard Temple's notes has been expunged from the record.

On the stand during the second day of the trial, I was asked by Walter Simmons, the defense attorney, why I had gone to the police station after the football game. I answered simply, "I went to give Bundley Temple's notes on the mafia."

Instantly, the district attorney, John David White, objected vehemently, and the judge concurred. "Strike the witness' answer from the record," he ordered the court reporter. "The jury will disregard the reference to 'Temple's notes on the mafia.'"

SIMMONS: Your Honor—

JUDGE; Mr. Simmons, we have already agreed that information is irrelevant.

SIMMONS: I know we have, Your Honor—

JUDGE: Then move on to something else.

SIMMONS: Yes, sir.

Later in my testimony, I was asked how I knew my son would be at J. B. Henderson's house.

MILLER: I knew Henderson was connected to the mob.

WHITE: Objection.

JUDGE: Sustained. The jury will disregard the witness' reference to the "mob." Mr. Miller, I've warned you not to use that term in this courtroom.

MILLER: Sorry. I meant to say "the mafia."

WHITE: Your Honor—

JUDGE: I'll ask you again to confine yourself to the facts.

MILLER: All right. The fact is, Bubba Henderson was buying and selling stolen cars from the mafia.

WHITE: Objection.

JUDGE: If you use that word again, Mr. Miller, I will have to hold you in contempt.

MILLER: I think I'm being held there now.

JUDGE: I have told you, this court does not recognize any organization by those names.

MILLER: What name would you recognize them by?

JUDGE: Mr. Miller—

MILLER: Judge, we can call these guys Freddie and the Dreamers, if that's what you want, but we can't just ignore them.

WHITE: Your Honor, in view of the recalcitrance of this witness, I would like to ask that the testimony beginning with "I knew Bubba Henderson . . ." be deleted from the record.

JUDGE: Do you have any objection to that, Mr. Simmons?

SIMMONS: I suppose not, Your Honor.

JUDGE: Then why don't we do that? The witness' comments since "I knew Bubba Henderson" will be removed from the record, and the jury will disregard Mr. Miller's words after that point. . . .

Simmons later told Derek that he had decided to drop the mafia angle altogether. "It's doing us more harm than good," he said. "The judge and the DA just aren't having any part of it."

Newspaper coverage changed dramatically during the trial

Most of the early newspaper accounts of the trial contained general references to the "connections of the mafia with Marshall" (*Times-Picayune*) and to "organized crime in Marshall" (*Jackson Daily News*). The *Clarion Ledger* acknowledged the "rumored underworld affiliations of Douglas Ames and J. B. Henderson." One reporter in that paper even mentioned citizens Vince Scarlotti and David Moore as individuals who had "allegedly been in contact with the mafia in the past."

But the mob was squeezed out of the proceedings, its

relevance to the case evaporated, and allusions to organized crime in Marshall disappeared. In the middle of the trial, the editor of the *Jackson Daily News* boldly asked, "What has happened to the mafia connection in Marshall?" but the only response he got to his query was silence.

By the fifth day of the trial, not even spectators at the courthouse seemed to know that such a thing existed.

The context of the crime was not established at the trial

The motive for the murder was adroitly extracted from Temple's notorious notes, which were ruled officially irrelevant to the case. The five boys allegedly killed their school superintendent because he was threatening to eliminate the football program at Marshall High. The DA cited a letter from Temple to the school board to show that the man was trying to destroy everything that was worthwhile from the lives of these young men.

This threat, he argued, was the sole reason they were compelled to commit murder. One witness after another testified that yes, Barbio, Lewis, and the others were indeed convinced that a loss of football would be unbearable.

"Let's face it," Mary Tolar, a history teacher, told the jury. "Gregory Lewis is a poor black kid in a Southern town. Take his dream of being a football player away from him, and who knows what he's capable of?"

"Jackson Davis admitted it to me, himself," school counselor Lettie Todd testified. "When I advised him to drop football and concentrate on his schoolwork, he said, 'I'd rather be dead than to do that!'"

"Five frightened and desperate young men," the district attorney summed up to the jury. "Five young men whose very identities as human beings were wound up, rightly or wrongly, in the game of football. When Richard Temple threatened those identities, they fought back. But not as you and I would fight back. Not in an acceptable social manner. No. I submit to you that these five frightened and desperate young men plotted and carried out a cold-blooded murder. . . . "

The result of the emphasis upon this single motive to the exclusion of all adult influence was that the five conspirators were convicted—and not a coach, parent, teacher, fan, or any other grown person was held in any way responsible.

And thus was a community let off the hook.

The community's self-image should have been brought to trial

I wish it had been possible for Marshall's self-image to have been brought to the stand to testify.

Of course, it would have been hard to drag such a poor, weak creature out into the open. And it would have been tough as the dickens for folks to recognize it, once it was there.

But maybe with such a lowly, cowering thing before us, we might have been able to see why five basically decent adolescents chose to commit the most violent and anti-social act a human being can commit.

I have a feeling we would come to realize just how weak this image is. How it draws on ignorance to harden its prickly shell and protect itself. How it harbors a soothing prejudice and wards off everything different from itself in order to justify its place in the scheme of things. How it clings to abject poverty to sustain a culture which ignorance and prejudice must have in order to survive.

Marshall's self-image could have shown us how we are bound to barter away truth and justice for any little scrap of money or recognition that will announce to the world out there that we do, in fact, exist.

Marshall, Mississippi, continues to thrive on vice

Some things have changed in my home town since the trial of Barbio, Lewis, Davis, Smith, and Miller.

Today, the high school football teams do not attract national attention. They seldom rise to the top of their own little conference in fact. No longer is there a pole to rally the citizens around on Friday nights.

Sports betting, however, has expanded its base under the auspices of organized crime, to five efficient and sophisticated gambling operations which turn over millions of dollars every year. Gaming has spread to electronic and pinball machines and bingo from one end of the county to the other.

Drug traffic is on an inevitable rise. By tacitly approving of the influx of money from the mob, the community has opened itself as a distribution center for massive amounts of cocaine and marijuana brought in from New Orleans.

Marshall is now even beginning to provide a fairly regular pipeline to mob-controlled "dating services" in various cities of the South.

Meanwhile, Barbio and his buddies sit in separate cells and wait for the Mississippi Supreme Court to review their case.

The process will likely take several years.

With the convicted felons safely out of the picture, school administrators have carefully blotted their faces from the graduation photograph which hangs in the hallway of Marshall High.

And things go on.

A grand jury investigation is needed

By all rights, a grand jury investigation should have preceded this trial. But for all the rumors and promises, none was ever appointed.

"Somehow or other," Simmons told me, "the thing got blocked at every turn. It just never came off."

But it isn't too late. With the appeal to the Supreme Court still waiting in the corridor, Marshall now has a chance to step up and take an oath and put itself on the stand. It has an opportunity to pour a measure of moral strength into that frail little image of self by owning up to its responsibility to its native sons.

Such a step can never be taken without a great deal of fear and trembling, of course. You risk pain and humiliation, even annihilation, when you go looking for the whole truth.

But maybe this is a chance that ought to be taken. The influencing circumstances that surround the murder of a school superintendent by five high school boys cry out in pain for another, more objective look.

This is a time when people who care about the way

we're becoming these days should demand to be heard.

It's a time for a community once and for all to rise up and lay its own life on the line.

* * *

When I woke up on Saturday morning and saw the steely eyes of my ex-wife peering at me over the end of the couch, I knew I had lost her forever. I would never be able to explain to her why I did what I did. She'd probably always believe that I blamed her, not myself, for the way our kids turned out.

"Just tell me this, Teddy," she said severely. "Are you doing this to spite me? Do you really hate me that much?"

Swinging my heels over the edge of the sofa sent a pain through my spine. My back felt as if somebody had been using it for a bobsled all night. "I don't hate you, Nancy," I said. It would've sounded insane to add, "I love you," so I didn't.

"Then how can you be so cruel?" she cried. "Dear God in Heaven!"

I held my eyes open long enough to focus on her red and gray plaid scarf and bright red coat. "Where are you going?" I asked. "A fire?"

"I'm going to see a lawyer," she snapped. "I'm going to try to help my son." On the way out of the duplex, she paused for a parting shot. "And if you're still in this house when I get back," she said, "I will have you arrested!"

"For what?"

"For breaking and entering, for rape, I don't care. I

just want you out of here. And out of our lives!"

After she'd crashed through the door out into the hostile cold, I pulled my remaining virtues together, got dressed, and packed my bag. When Jennifer finally came downstairs, she ignored me like a homework assignment and passed on into the kitchen. By the time I joined her, she was digging around in a box of trail mix like a Yellowstone bear between intermittent slugs of Hawaiian Punch from the can.

I thought she looked unusually alert this morning with her hair stretched above her head as if she'd been pulled out of a well by her locks. Her face was perfectly startling, though, streaked with very bold lines and blocks of red and brown stain. She looked like a model for Cubist art.

"Good morning," I said to her.

She turned away from the counter toward me. "I can't believe you did it, Daddy!" she said. "I really can't!"

"I guess you had to have been there."

"I don't understand! How could anybody do such a thing? How could anybody arrest his own son for murder!"

I sat down at the table and considered her outfit for a while. It wasn't like eating at the Four Seasons with a fashion plate. My daughter looked like a magnet that had attracted all the wrong clothes. "I turned Derek in because he was an accomplice, Jennifer," I explained. "I don't believe he actually shot anyone, but he was involved."

All this seemed to reach beyond her, so she shook it off like a sign from the catcher. Her preplanned response suited her better. "You know what makes me sick?" she said.

"A square meal."

She bristled. "What makes me sick is, I was the one that told you about that hundred dollar bill. If I hadn't taken that money from my brother's room, he wouldn't be in jail today. Why can't I ever keep my big mouth shut?"

I said nothing. I kept wanting to reach out and hold her hand over the box of trail mix, but there was a lot more than dried fruit and hard nuts and a gaudy punch can in our way. I'd lost too much time and too much psychological space to make it all up in one elegant meal.

"I feel so rotten about this, I don't know what to do," she told me. "And the fuck of it is, Mother was right all along!"

"The 'fuck' of it?" I said.

"Yes! You just didn't care about us!" she cried. "You just didn't care at all!"

It was my day, I suppose. Amy was leaving my parents' house just when I arrived there. As I walked up to her in the driveway, I could read between the lines in her face that she had prepared a speech for me, too. I decided to let her deliver it and get it over with.

"Well, does this make you feel smart, Teddy?" she said. "Do you think it's clever to arrest your own son?"

"That's one feeling I missed, Amy,"

She waved a handkerchief through the air as if she were guiding one of our boys down to a carrier in the

Pacific, then blew into it. "I just want you to know," she said, "that if the Lord had seen fit to give me children, instead of you, I would be in there defending them with my very life, not sending them to jail. I swear to God, I would have done anything for my children!"

"I hope they would have appreciated that."

That brought a shake of the head from my sister. She said dejectedly, "What I can't understand is why I used to respect you so much. I don't know if I will ever get over what you did to your son, Ted. I hate to say it, but right now, my own brother looks to me like some kind of . . . germ!"

With this searing simile, which she'd probably worked up with her current lover, Amy squeezed into her Toyota, backed it out of the driveway, and screeched down the street as if she had somewhere important to go.

I'd already gotten three lofty exit lines, and it wasn't even ten o'clock yet.

In the house, the cat had apparently gone for the winter, and all was quiet, except for the inevitable drone of Dad's TV set in the den. While he pretended to be completely engrossed in an Irish Spring commercial, I pretended everything was swimming along normally. "I'll be on Judy Moon's news show Monday," I reminded him.

"I know, Ted," he said. "I'll watch it."

"Where's Mom?" I asked him.

"Your mother's upstairs," he told me. "For some reason, she's feeling real low this morning." I heard him add as I was leaving, "I guess we're all feeling pretty low."

Mom was moping around in the annex study, stuffing books and notes into cardboard cartons on her desk as if she'd just been fired in a company-wide purge. As soon as she noticed me at the door, she made a show of cramming a shock of yellow legal pads into a Coronets box. "I don't know what good it does, anymore," she said. "Why should I bother with all this study of man and his family? There's no such thing anymore. A family instinctively protects its own. It does not turn on them!"

I wanted to explain to her that I was trying to protect my son, that I was trying to do right by him for once in my life, but she was in no mood to hear a defense. So I asked her instead how her novel was coming along.

She laughed scornfully. "What novel?" she said. "That's nothing but a joke. I'm not a novelist. I'm not even an anthropologist. I'm nothing but a second-rate junior college teacher nearing retirement with nothing whatever to offer my culture."

"What about your findings on the mongoloid strain?"

"I'm giving all my work to the public library," she said. "I don't see why I should keep doing all this research when none of it makes any sense anymore."

"That's never stopped a scholar before."

She shot me a cold look. "Is all this funny to you, Theodore?" she asked.

"Not very, no."

"Then stop joking about it!"

"Yes, ma'am."

"I want you to know before you go on that TV show, you're still my son and I will always love you. But what you have done to Derek is a terrible, ghastly thing, and I'm not going to stand here and pretend I'll ever approve of it."

"I don't 'approve of it' either, Mom. But I couldn't just let it go. I'm responsible for my son!"

"Well," she said, and returned to her packing, "all I know is, I'm sick and tired of everything right now."

"I'm sorry to hear that, Mom."

She frowned, then shook her head. "I don't think I will ever understand you," she said. "You're such a brilliant man, Theodore, but I guess you just don't think the way the rest of us do. I don't know if it's because you've lived in New York too long or what. But sometimes I wonder if you'd ever fit in down here again."

"Maybe I wouldn't," I said. Feeling myself starting to wilt under all this great moral support, I kissed my mother on the cheek, assured her for the record that I would be staying in touch, and left the room.

"Goodbye, Theodore," she said as I walked down the hall. "Take care of yourself."

The freezing, unintentional irony of my mother's last words made all the others I had heard this day sound like rousing cheers for the conquering hero.

By Monday afternoon, word of the arrest of Barbio, Lewis, Davis, Smith, and Miller had spread through the county like a new way of expressing the sex act among the young. As I reported to the TV station for the interview, I had to swim through a feeding ground for frenzied reporters who circled and snapped at me as I ran up the walk. Inside the cinderblock building, I was grabbed by a grim-faced girl with very few words and a chin the shape of an anvil and shoved like a coal cart down a darkened hall into a studio the size of a potato bin. My reflection in the control room glass was as calm as the surface of a sewage lagoon, but underneath I was stirring and fretting, trying to prepare myself for another great disappointment. I reminded myself that Judy Moon was a member of the same species as the sharks outside, and that today, I was bait.

I could hardly say my name when she finally glided into the studio, shook my hand, and introduced herself. What could I say? After all these years, the act of touching the soft skin of her palm was like touching the light from a star. After politely wrestling her small hand out of my enormous grip, Judy led me over to the set and instructed me in a smooth Southern voice to relax. But with a heart throbbing like an abscessed tooth, I could hardly act as if she were just anybody. There was such an angelic quality about her, and there was such a troubling apprehension in me. Judy Moon could be nothing but an illusion after all. That angelic quality could be nothing but the glow of a moment I had been dreaming about for years or the glint of studio light upon the blonde in her hair.

When the red bulb went on, Judy spoke to the camera as if she were talking to a friend in the living room of her home. "Our guest today," she said to the lens, "is Theodore Miller, the well-known writer for *The New York Times*. We'll be talking to Ted in just a minute. Right now, stay tuned to Seven as the news continues."

Five seconds later, the lights clunked off, the Tegrin commercial popped on, and Judy turned to me. "You look as if you've done this before," she said.

"So do you."

"Well, I have been at it for a long time," she said.

"I know. I've watched you every step of the way."

After giving the comment some curious reflection, she talked over a sequence change with the director in the control room, then made a smooth transition back to the camera when the lights snapped on again. Well, this is it, I told myself. Now I get to face reality. "Judy Moon Impales Luckless Journalist on Live TV." "Anchorwoman spears sportswriter by asking him how it felt to have his own son arrested for murder."

I waited for the blow, but seconds passed, and her face did not become hard. As I shifted in my seat, and the room closed in around us, I wondered if it were possible for an idol to be human too. I could sense the technicians behind the cameras moving curiously toward us, prying, prying as the interview began.

On the air, Judy said to me, "Ted, there is something I have always wondered about sportswriters."

"That's what my wife used to say."

"What I mean is, do you consider yourself a sports person-turned writer or a writer who uses sports as a subject?"

It was a good question. Relaxing a bit, I crossed my legs in the vinyl chair and answered her with a couple of anecdotes about my early efforts to become a writer. Once I had sent a story off to a correspondence course which was advertised in the back pages of a men's magazine I had found under the rack in a pool room in McComb. Evidently, there was a clump of famous writers out there who were so desperate to find other writers to compete with, they would get together in an office in Newark and develop some more through the mails. The ads usually posed a clutch of saintly-looking folks in a library in front of a lot of Mark Twain with a bubble over their heads which said, "Can you write?" After my work was scrutinized at Newark, it was returned to me stapled like a fence, along with my ten dollars registration fee, and an answer to their question: "No, You Can't."

I told Judy Moon I was probably the only native-born American ever to be turned down by that course.

At the same time all this jovial self-deprecation was keeping me off the hook, I could feel the air seeping out of my balloon. I kept hammering away at it, though, and told her about the plot of the story I had sent to all those Famous Writers. It was an allegorical science-fiction tale which I'd written with a Flair during civics class. The hero was a caveman of the future, called Ted-E, his sidekick was his legal advisor, Bub-Ah, and their Archenemies were folks with big shoes and glasses called T-Churs who said words like "recess" and lived in grimy cloak rooms in a dismal place known as Mars-Hell.

But everything I said sounded dumb and forced, somehow. The more I talked, the harder and drier my words became. With images of my son and his pee tricks and his pebble sandwiches flitting through my mind, all my fumbling around in the past just didn't seem very funny any more.

But Judy Moon was there when I needed her, hanging on every word. "In your writing now," she said, " you are very good at extracting a clear meaning from a critical situation. For instance, a baseball player with a terminal illness, a tennis player fighting a drug habit—even difficult situations you experience yourself."

She had guided me so easily into the subject I was so anxious to avoid, I couldn't resist it. "Such as the one I had three days ago," I said nodding. "When I encouraged my son to turn himself in to the police."

"That was an ordeal for you," she said flatly.

"Not too much fun, no."

"And I expect a grand jury investigation of organized crime in Marshall would turn into an ordeal for a lot of other Mississippians."

"I expect it would."

"I wonder what personal meaning do you hope to extract from this?"

"I don't know. A lesson, maybe. To stay in my room."

She paused with her eyes still focussed unblinkingly on mine—so long that the guys in the control room, who require chatter the way the rest of us need air, began to squirm and make motions with their fingers behind the glass. Then she said to me, "I don't usually do this sort of thing, but I have a suggestion for you."

"Does it have anything to do with tar and feathers?"

"No, it has to do with writing. Something which I think you are extremely good at."

"Thank you. I'd rather write than eat. Especially lately."

"What I want to suggest, Ted, is for you to write a book on this subject—to put what is going on in Marshall into a meaningful perspective. I believe what you have to offer on this tragic situation would be unique and beneficial to us all."

"Do you think 'you all' would be interested?"

"Yes, I do," she said confidently. "People don't turn on the news every night just to hear what's happening. They're compelled to listen because they want to *understand* what's happening. Unfortunately, all a newsperson can do is report the things that affect our lives. It's left to someone like you to make us understand what they mean."

"It's a nice idea," I granted.

"Then consider it."

"I will. If I come up with something, I'll let you know."

"I'll hold you to that," she said and faced the camera. "We'll be back with more from Theodore Miller, after this."

After the interview was over, I hung around in the coils of wire in everybody's way to watch this splendid woman make her flawless delivery of the news of the day. What a strange, lovely paradox she was: a person who exuded elegance and charm at the same time she dispensed one capsule after another containing all the ills and horrors of modern life. As I noted how she skillfully combined grace with truth, I realized that for a very long time, I hadn't known much of either one. As I ground up my life to be somebody, I had developed a posture, a way of dealing with life, that let the truth pass right through my soul. I had taken my past and the people I loved and tucked them into neat little categories and funny stories and had called the resulting collection of anecdotes reality.

But there wasn't much truth in it.

There wasn't much grace in the way I looked at things, either, for while I was running around trying to find my name, I was allowing my kids to grow up with the part of me that I had given them left to shrivel up and die. I had let them become what they were not supposed to be at all.

Weak and loud and squirming for help.

Not their fault. Not Nancy's. Mine.

No wonder I have always loved Judy Moon. Somehow, deep where each of us has a light, I suppose I instinctively knew what she meant to me. But time, ambition, and selfishness had dimmed the glow for so long, I couldn't tell it from the darkness around it.

After nervously pressing my knees together while a man in a striped necktie weighed and tagged my luggage as if it were a pig at a fair, I hustled down the airport tunnel like a clown on stilts to the men's room. After I had gotten some much-needed basic relief and felt obliged to rejoin the human race, I stepped out of the stall and met the curious eyes of a black man about my age who was watching me in the mirror over the lavatory. He was wearing a smirk on his face as he sprinkled Comet over the porcelain like salt on a steak.

With an easy, fluid motion, he scraped the Comet off the lav with a dry paper towel, wadded it into a basketball, and fired it into the waste can by the urinals. "Good thing for you we was open," he said with a chuckle.

"That had occurred to me, too," I said.

"You'd have had it pretty rough about a week ago,"

he said. "Week ago, I had every one of them toilets closed for repairs. Sewer backed up."

"What a thought."

He grinned at me. "Yeah, you looked like it was real important, all right."

"Sort of a pressing need."

He laughed. "I see a lot of that around here," he said. "Folks get in a mighty big hurry in an airport."

I followed his ritual of dumping and whisking cleaner on another lavatory for a while, then asked, " You wouldn't be a father, would you?"

The question tickled him. "Man, that's about all I am," he said. "That's how come I'm working two shifts a day. I got young-uns running out my ears."

After a moment, I took Derek's hundred-dollar bill out of my wallet and handed it to him. "Why don't you give your ears a break and take your young-uns out to supper?" I said.

Very cautiously, he took the money, then held it like a delicate flower in his huge hands almost afraid to touch it. He gave me a look of absolute astonishment. "Man, this ain't for real, is it?" he said.

"As far as I know, it is."

"What I mean is, you giving this to me? A hundred dollars?"

"Why not?"

"How come?"

"I don't know. Maybe for being here when I needed you."

"Hell fire," was all he could say after that.

Leaving him to puzzle over his windfall, I stepped out of the men's room into the crowd that was moving frantically through the tunnel as if it were chasing a celebrity. I paused a while to peer into every face that passed by, hoping to spot a family resemblance in all those noses, cheeks, and chins. At the gatehouse, I checked for Uncle Harley. I would have given my column in the *Times* to see him perched there on one of those fiberglass taco shells rolling a cigarette, but he was nowhere to be seen.

None of my family was there.

At least the flight attendant with the Kroger Cheese Shop makeup recognized me. "It's good to see you again, sir," she said with a grin so sly, it practically broke her makeup. Figuring she was expecting more trouble from me, I gave her shoulder pads a pat to reassure her that this time, I was merely along for the ride. Following a line of Atlanta pilgrims into the belly of the plane, I found my window seat and gazed out the porthole the way Dad watches his Trinitron.

After a while, the jet engines moaned, the plane rose up, and the lights of Jackson looked like tiny, brilliant jewels sprinkled from one edge of the earth to the other in a case of black velvet cloth. As I watched the horizons of the city shrink, I considered how much all those jewels down there reminded me of my own little stories of Marshall. After collecting and polishing the tales of Homer and the Coon Dick and Freddie and Hattie's Dilemma for many years, I was now leaving them behind. With a knot in my throat, I kept my eyes fixed on the lights until they twinkled like sequins in the lining of the clouds, and finally blinked one last time, and disappeared.

Somewhere over Alabama, my stewardess stooped

over a no-nonsense IBM man and carefully deposited a dinner tray on my pull-out table like a bride with a load of pre-mixed pancakes the morning after. The dinner wasn't all that alluring. The slug of roast beef was as tender and juicy as a cypress knee, and I suspected something with a long name had been raised in the salad. But after a while, the food actually tasted all right and felt pretty good as it slid down the tubes into my empty stomach. When I was through with it, my hostess joyfully plucked up the tray and rolled her cart away.

Then, except for the IBM executive who was having a sales meeting in his sleep, I was alone.

Like a traveller in the bowels of space, I stared into my blank porthole and wondered what would happen to my son. What would be the result of the grand jury investigation of organized crime in Marshall? What would be left of the town after the mafia money was forced out? In the wreckage, there would be a murder trial of five misguided high school kids. Would they be convicted? Would Derek go to prison for his part in the crime? I hated to think of my precious little boy closed up like a fist in a vile, hard prison. But I knew Derek was tough, he would survive. And maybe, as Duke Curtis said, one of these days he might even understand. Whether that happened or not, though, it was certain he would one day return to the love and graces of the rest of the family. I could even imagine Uncle Harley waiting for him in his pickup at the prison gates, sucking noisily on a smouldering, homemade smoke and calling his great-nephew "him" and "that boy."

I could imagine it; but I don't believe I will ever be

there to witness it.

In the heart of Dixie, I boarded a different jet and climbed over a husky, bronze tennis player to claim my window seat. At the new porthole, I gazed out into the same old night. Then a strange thing happened to me. It caught me completely by surprise. At some time during the long and sleepless evening, I sat with my hands folded in my lap like a reverent lady at a revival and suddenly became so damned sad, I actually started to cry.

There I was, in a public place, next to a tennis player in an Adidas shirt, absolutely letting it flow. I don't mean a sobbing or a sniffing, either. This was a full, throat-clogging cry that soaked my face and neck and collar and made the athlete figure me for a natural idiot who was on his way back East to claim an inheritance.

At last, the tears dried up, and I was able to straighten up in my seat and fill my lungs with some brand new air. When my favorite flight attendant announced our descent into Kennedy, I looked down through the glass at a dazzling array of bejeweled lights. From one horizon to the other and beyond, the glitter spread before me farther than my eye could see. As we dropped lower in the sky, all the lights grew bigger and brighter and more wonderful, and I didn't feel quite so bad anymore.

In fact, I felt better than I had in a very long time.